Dreams Collide

The Collide Series

Book Two

Kristina Beck

ISBN-13:978-3-947985-01-2

To Rich, Bob, Ron, Deanna, and Betsy

Chapter 1

Tina

I yank my ironed outfit out of the closet, almost snapping the plastic hanger in half. So much for being calm and organized this morning. As I dart toward the bathroom door, my roommate walks out of the kitchen right into my path.

"Watch out, Alexa! I slept late, and I have a meeting at a restaurant in the city, somewhere in Hell's Kitchen. With my first client, no less. I don't know if I'll make it on time."

She swerves out of the way, almost dropping the coffee cup in her hand. "Slow down, crazy girl." She pats down her dress to check if any coffee spilled on it. "I'd offer to drive you, but I don't need to leave for another hour. Are you taking the one-twenty-eight bus?"

I rip my socks and flannel pajama pants off. I'm probably the only woman in America who wears winter pajamas and socks to bed in the middle of August. Alexa keeps this apartment like an ice box. "I still can't believe you drive into the city for some of your appointments. What a pain in the ass. Anyway, yes. I need to hurry to get the next one in twenty-five minutes." I'm out of breath and half naked when I slam the bathroom door.

In record time, I stand in front of Alexa with my shoes in hand. "Hey, does this outfit look good for a first meeting? I don't want to look too stiff or too casual."

She sets her coffee cup on the kitchen table as she looks me up and down. "Actually, you look kinda sexy," she says with a devilish smile.

I hop around trying to put my black peep-toe heels on. I'm glad I got a pedicure a couple of days ago with lilac nail polish. "A black pencil skirt with a purple sleeveless shirt doesn't necessarily scream sexy," I reply between heavy breaths.

She lifts her left eyebrow and smirks. "But with those high heels, you're a professional with sex appeal."

I twist my head side to side. "How about this fishtail braid? I had to improvise since I didn't have time to wash this head of hair of mine." I run to the kitchen to grab my black Coach handbag and then my computer bag near the door. "Does it look greasy?"

She looks to the ceiling. "Oh, would you stop worrying. You look gorgeous." She opens the door. "Just go and kick some ass. You can tell me all about it when we go to the gym tonight."

"And you're going to tell me why you got home so late last night," I say over my shoulder as I rush out the door.

"Boring business dinner and drinks. Nothing to tell. Now zip it— you'll miss the bus. Good luck."

I make it to the stop just as the bus arrives. It's packed, but I find an empty seat next to an old lady. I need to step over her since she apparently has no desire to move. This skirt doesn't make it easy. I slump into my spot and take a deep breath, then purse my lips. She smells musty, like her wet clothes sat in a ball for days. That's a major pet peeve of mine. I lean closer to the window and cover my nose with my hand. Please let there be no major traffic this morning.

I pull my phone out of my bag and open the email my boss, Thomas, sent me yesterday, with the address of the restaurant. I looked up the place on the internet, but the website was down.

I just started my job at Modern Web in Jersey City, New Jersey. During college, I became obsessed with advanced website and application design. My previous job gave me limited opportunities to share and implement my ideas, but I stayed there longer than I wanted to because the company paid for my graduate school. One day I looked in the mirror and said to myself, "You're thirty-one years old. It's time for a change."

When I was offered this job, I had a moment of clarity. Neither Dad nor my sister, Lisa, needed me anymore. I'd upheld my vow to take care of them after Mom's accident. It was time to take care of myself. Moving to Hoboken, New Jersey, a couple months ago was the best decision ever. I should've done it years ago, but guilt always pulled me back.

Alexa moved to Hoboken about a year ago for her job. She had a spare bedroom and thought it would be fun to be roommates. We've become close since Lisa married Alexa's brother, James. Alexa is practically another sister to me.

She drags me around everywhere. Every time we go out, she sees someone she knows. With her outgoing personality and good looks, it's no wonder she has so many friends and a list of interested guys.

She's a successful sales representative for a big pharmaceutical company. Her territory is within the tristate area. Because of her, I know Hoboken and the city pretty well by now. Well, at least where the cool bars and good shopping sections are.

I glance at my watch and see the time fly by. The bus is moving as slowly as a three-toed sloth. Why doesn't each seat come with a gas pedal? The air conditioner needs a shot of caffeine itself. But maybe I'm sweating from my nerves. I lift my arm discreetly to make sure I used deodorant. I exhale in relief.

With this new job, I'm a project manager. Basically, I get to run the show this time, implement my ideas, and manage my own team. The company guarantees to have a client's new website up and running within six weeks, regardless of how complex it is. When Thomas mentioned this project, I was ecstatic. I imagined it as a five-star restaurant with fancy food and a cool atmosphere. Hell's Kitchen is the place to be these days. I wondered if I'd be able to sample the food. Maybe the chef was famous. Maybe the chef was cute.

Then Thomas said it's a German restaurant with a traditional beer garden. Supposedly, it's been open for six months now and is pretty successful. But that didn't prevent the high-pitched noise of air streaming out of a balloon over my head. The image of Chevy Chase dancing in lederhosen in *European Vacation* sprang to mind. I know I have no right to be disappointed. This is my first real project, and I should be excited.

I push the blue button and shimmy out of my seat, struggling with my bags. The old lady is still not willing to move. I hope she's not dead. The bus stops short, and I slam against the pole, almost falling backward onto her lap. Nope, she's not dead—she spasmed, and a whiff of alcohol and mustiness found its way up my nose. Gross.

The doors open, and I filter out with the others. I step to the side to orient myself. The sun's glaring, so I search in my bottomless handbag for my sunglasses. This bag was a present to myself when I got this job. I fell in love with it at a Coach outlet but didn't notice it had no partitions inside. I need to buy one of those little lights to put in it so I can see where everything is.

I toss my handbag over my shoulder and put my sunglasses on. According to the address in the email, I'm on the wrong end of the block. Double shit! Walking fast in these damn shoes is near impossible. I weave through people, and some stare at me like I'm a crackhead. What the hell? City people are freaks.

Delicious aromas of freshly baked bread tease my nose as I speed-walk past a French café. The scent masks the constant city smells of stale urine and exhaust. Since I didn't have the chance to eat breakfast or drink coffee, I'm ravenous and on my last nerve. What would happen if I snatched a croissant off someone's plate? Breakfast is my favorite meal, but I'm hungry anytime. I love to eat. My fast metabolism allows me to consume what I want, when I want. Most females hate that about me, even though I do yoga and Pilates regularly. Alexa convinced me to sign up for a one-month trial at a gym down the street from our apartment. I'm up for anything new these days.

The noise of trucks rumbling, horns honking, and police sirens shrieking distract me. Hoboken isn't this loud. My watch says I have one minute. I need number 503. The restaurant should be across the street. I search for a sign with the name *Hofbräuhaus.* How the hell is that even pronounced? My eyes zoom in on the distinctive large blue sign.

I approach a red traffic light with a crowd of people, most of them playing with their phones or drinking Starbucks. I shuffle from one foot to the other. The traffic light beeps, and the walking man appears. As I nudge slower people out of my way, my forehead begins to sweat.

Two women pass me. One whispers to the other, and then they look at me and burst out laughing. I don't get it. What's the damn problem this morning? I touch my hair and forehead, thinking maybe a bird shit on me. There's nothing. Whatever. I don't have time to worry about this.

I straighten my skirt, pull my braid over my shoulder, and check my necklace is straight. I exhale slowly, hoping my pulse will decrease and the beads of sweat will evaporate.

I pull open the entrance door that has a strange large *A* on it. *What does the A stand for? A for appetite?* Well, mine is quite large right now. I shrug my shoulders as I walk into a massive room with high ceilings, archways, and traditional golden wood décor throughout. Carved wooden beams stand from ceiling to floor throughout the room. The tables represent a variety of shapes and can seat up to ten. They're covered with checkered cream-and-red tablecloths. Matching curtains drape the windows. Large, old crystal chandeliers hang from the ceiling. Barstools with red leather seats line the long bar. The restaurant is much larger than it looks from the outside.

The aroma of sautéed onions wafts from the kitchen, making my mouth water. Can I eat something during this meeting? Would that be rude?

I'm startled by a man clearing his throat behind me. "Can I help you?" His voice is deep but smooth with a hint of a foreign accent.

I love foreign accents.

I turn around and find a tall, bulky man with a buzz cut. My first thought is a teddy bear. He's dressed in black jeans and a snug white T-shirt that accentuates his broad shoulders and firm biceps. I assume the black, red, and gold flag on the T-shirt is a German flag, but what the hell do I know? Maybe I should've researched Germany last night instead of vegging on the couch, watching *Places Unknown*, my favorite travel show.

I plaster a friendly smile on my face. "Good morning. I'm Tina Schmitt, with Modern Web. I have an appointment with Gerry—I mean Mr. Maier." I scan the email again. "I hope I pronounced his last name correctly."

He looks at me long and hard with his eyebrows pushed together. He cocks his head to the side. "What are you doing?" he snickers.

I look around. "What do you mean? I just told you I have an appointment. Is there a problem?" *What is up with people this morning?*

He points to my face. I place my hand on my face and feel around. I still have my sunglasses on. What's the big deal? I take them off and gasp as I see what I'm holding.

Someone kill me now. How could I not have noticed?

One of the lenses is missing.

That explains the strange looks and laughter. This is beyond humiliating. I want to crawl under a table and never come back out.

I shove my sunglasses into my bag. It's so hard to look at him right now.

Blood sizzles up my neck to my cheeks. *Just suck it up and pretend it's no big deal. Shrug it off and be professional.* I roll my shoulders back. "Well, that was a great first impression." I'm sure he'll tell Mr. Maier this. "Let's start over. I'm Tina Schmitt. Can you please tell me where I can find Mr. Maier?"

His eyes widen for some reason, but he doesn't respond right away. I wish I could wipe the crooked smirk off his gorgeous face as he looks me up and down. I'm embarrassed enough. It doesn't help that he's sexy as all hell. Very sexy. Why does he have to be so damn sexy? To top it off, he has a scar above his right eyebrow, which makes him look rugged. It doesn't matter. He's probably one of the dishwashers or a busboy. I'll never see him again.

He rubs his chin. "I'm Gerry Maier."

Son. Of. A. Bitch.

My chin hits the ground. I believe one of the servers will need to help me put it back into place. Of course it's him. Why can't he be an old, fat man with a wart on his nose and a bushy unibrow?

He reaches out his hand, and I embrace it with mine. It's two times the size of mine. Warm and rough. We hold our shake a little longer than normal as we stare each other down. *Awkward...but thrilling.* Velvety tingles travel up my arm, making me think of soft bubbles of champagne bursting in my mouth. I pull away first, even though I like my hand in his. *Where's this coming from?*

I shuffle my computer bag to my right hand. "Well, that was the best ice breaker I've ever heard of. I think I'll try that with my next client." I chuckle.

He nods with his eyes still piercing mine.

"I'm sorry I'm a minute late. My alarm didn't go off this morning. I rushed into the city and wasn't paying attention to my sunglasses. I'm usually very punctual." *Shut up, Tina!*

"You didn't notice something was wrong when looking through the lens?"

Wiseass. He puts his hand over his perfect smiling mouth to prevent himself from laughing. I should slap him upside the head. Even though I'd rather curl up on his lap like a cat and cuddle. *Lack of food is surely screwing with my brain.*

I cock my hip. "As a matter of fact, I was too focused on finding my way here and didn't notice a difference. Cut me some slack."

He holds his hands up. "Sorry, but you have to admit it's funny. I've never seen a more beautiful pirate. Ahoy, matey."

He did not just say that.

Once again, my mouth drops open. I'm not sure if I'm shocked by him saying I'm beautiful or *ahoy, matey*. I should be annoyed by both, but I can't control myself. I burst out laughing. He joins in, and after a few seconds, I calm down and carefully dab at the light tears in my eyes. Now I probably look like a raccoon.

I walk to a table behind me where a server polishes the salt and pepper shakers like his life depends on it. I'm sure he's heard everything. "Would you mind if I left my computer bag on this chair?" The server nods and continues rubbing the shaker like it's a magic lamp.

I turn in Gerry's direction. "I need to freshen up after this little escapade. Then we can officially start our meeting."

"I can take your bag. I have a table set up for us out in the beer garden. It's still quiet since we don't open for another hour. I hope it's okay to be outside. It's a nice morning and not too hot yet."

"Sure, that sounds great. Maybe not in the direct sunlight though, given the state of my sunglasses."

He flashes me that sexy smile again. My heart speeds up. I think I'm going to like this project.

I hold out my bag but almost drop it when his hand touches mine. It feels too intimate but strangely normal. He's just a hot guy touching me again. Though if he were an old man with a wart on his nose, I'd likely feel violated.

His lips turn up as if he can read my mind. He points toward the back of the room. "The bathroom is at the end of the bar and to the right."

I look briefly.

"When you're finished, the beer garden is out through the double glass doors behind me." He glances toward the bright sunlight streaming through sparkling glass doors.

I nod and walk away, feeling his burning gaze follow my every move.

Is it bad that I like it?

"It's very bad!" I say out loud without thinking about it. The bartender stares at me with raised eyebrows while vigorously buffing a wineglass. What is with the excessive polishing here? I scurry to the bathroom like a dog with its tail between its legs.

Don't screw this up.

This job is important to me. Ever since my mom died in a car accident when I was sixteen, I've covered her role. I've hardly focused on my own needs or goals. Lisa was also in the accident but survived. Nothing was the same after that day. I took care of my devastated dad and grieving fifteen-year-old sister, who had lingering physical and psychological issues. I matured several years overnight. I never had the chance to grieve along with them. My penance for what I'd done.

After a few years, my dad came to terms with my mom's death and married Beth, my stepmom. Lisa had a harder time, since she was haunted by her permanent injuries. She had her ups and downs for a while, until a couple of years ago, when she met James. She doesn't rely on me the way she used to.

Now, with my dad and sister settled, my priorities have shifted. I took this position to challenge myself and find parts of the old me that might still be in there. It's my time.

This bathroom is spotless. It shines like the sun reflecting off a lake. Too bad my sunglasses are broken. Something tells me Gerry Maier is anal when it comes to cleanliness. Oh...I'm not complaining. I'm always afraid to see how dirty a restaurant's bathroom is.

I turn on the faucet and pump an excessive amount of soap into my hand. Once they are under the water, they turn into a bubble maker as I talk to myself.

It's not only my career. I want to enjoy life and be more impulsive. Before Mom died, I was the adventurous child of the family. My bedroom walls were covered with pictures of foreign countries I wanted to visit, and I dreamed of going to a university in Southern California. I wanted to explore, travel, and let loose. I didn't want to marry my high school sweetheart and live in the same town I was born in. It's fine for other people, but not for me.

Can I ever become that adventurous girl again? Living with Alexa has been a great start. I socialize more now than I did in college and graduate school. It would be fun to find someone who'll push me even further out of the norm. I can't expect Alexa to entertain me forever. Either way, I'm not going to sit around and wait.

I dry my hands and pull away from my thoughts. Remember, this is a business meeting, not two strangers meeting at a bar. *It's not personal. It's business!* When I walk out of the bathroom, I'll be professional. No more joking around or touching. I imagine myself pivoting on my feet and punching the air like Rocky to pump myself up.

You've got this! It's your time to shine.

Chapter 2

Gerry

Nein, nein, nein. I shake my head. It can't be her. But once she took off those sunglasses, I knew her face in an instant. She's the one I kissed that unforgettable night...the blindfolded kiss.

Little did she know, I watched her during my cousin's frat party that evening before I was asked to play the game. She wore the same color of purple as she's wearing now. Eggplant. Leave it to me to compare the color to food. Ever since then, I've had a secret purple fetish. Every time I see it, my heart tightens.

Though I never spoke to her, I memorized every curve of her face and how she felt against me. There's been no other woman comparable.

She's even more breathtaking now. Her skin is just as creamy, and her glossy, plump lips still beckon me to kiss them. I clearly remember the tiny, sexy beauty mark above the top left corner of her upper lip. Is she just a hallucination brought on by lack of sleep?

I never introduced myself to her or finished the game because I had to fly back to Europe the next day. My future career depended on it.

Even though I left her, that night wasn't a total failure. While being blindfolded, my other senses had increased. How she tasted, smelled, felt against my body, was amplified hundredfold. That experience sparked an idea which led me to become one of the youngest and most successful chefs in Germany and France. Until a year ago.

My eyes gaze at her curvy backside as she glides along the bar. I know it's inappropriate, but she's too hard to resist. This is not the type of business meeting I planned. I rub my face with my hand and head over to the beer garden.

The table sits under an old chestnut tree. I place her bag on one of the benches. This tree reminds me of home. It's a bit of a mess now since it's autumn and the massive chestnuts are falling, but the golden leaves make up for it. With the way I run my restaurant, the chestnuts and leaves are cleaned up regularly throughout the day. I don't need any lawsuits. The fallen chestnuts are then used as table decorations.

This restaurant was originally German, but it was old and run down. The beer garden was dilapidated, with old, plastic white tables and chairs. It looked cheap. Most good beer gardens in Germany have shiny wooden tables and benches. I couldn't resist the opportunity to turn this place into something new but still traditional.

A scraping sound on the path behind me catches my attention. Just as I turn, Tina stumbles.

"Oh!" she exclaims. "Today is not my day. Now it seems I don't know how to walk on cobblestone." She wobbles as she takes her time walking forward.

I quickly walk toward her. "Here. Let me help you." I take her hand again before she can respond. She stops moving but doesn't protest. Instead, she bends over and takes off her shoes with her free hand. That's three times I've touched her today. Every time our skin touches…confirms it's her. My body's naturally drawn to hers.

I try hard to act normal. *This is a business meeting.* Mixing business with pleasure is strictly against my rules, but working closely with her could be a game changer.

When we reach the table, she pulls her hand from mine. "That's much better. Sorry about all this. I must appear so unprofessional to you," she remarks as she stoops to slide her shoes back on.

"Our meeting is definitely unusual." I motion for her to sit down.

She smiles. "It's so nice out here." She removes a folder and pen from her computer bag.

A server approaches with a basket of fresh-baked soft pretzels and places it on the table.

"Thanks, Peter."

"Would either of you like a drink?" he says as his eyes dart from me to Tina.

"Yes. I'd like seltzer water with a lemon, please." She folds her hands on the table.

"Why don't you try one of the German beers we have on tap? I think you need it after the problem with your sunglasses. Come on—be daring."

Her eyes spring open.

"It's only ten thirty in the morning. I don't drink alcohol this early, especially during a business meeting."

I sense a tone of disapproval. *Ouch.*

"Well, Germans drink beer at any time of the day. When you walk down a street and pass a café, you'll see older men drinking beer or wine with their buddies and playing chess."

"We're far from old buddies and aren't in Germany, Gerry." She places her hand on my arm. "I'm sorry. Is it all right if I call you Gerry, or would you prefer Mr. Maier?"

I look down at her hand. She pulls it away and mouths *Sorry*. I wish she'd keep it there.

"Shouldn't I be the one asking you that, Miss or Mrs. Schmitt?"

Her shoulders relax. "At this point, you can call me whatever you want. Just not *matey*. But I think we're past the formality of Mr. or Miss."

She said *miss*. Not married but still, hands off.

"About our drinks. How about this—there's a great beer called *Weißbeer*, wheat beer in English. We have it alcohol-free too. It's actually healthy without the alcohol. It's great on a warm day. Try it, *bitte*. Sorry. I mean *please*."

She points her finger at me while smiling. "Do you promise it's alcohol-free?"

I glance at Peter. "Please promise Tina you'll give her the alcohol-free version."

He laughs as he holds his hand up. "I promise."

She perks up. "All righty then. I love to try new things. Why not now?"

I hold up two fingers. "Peter, make it two please. This is a business meeting, after all." I wink at her.

"No problem. I'll be back in a few minutes. The pretzels are fresh out of the oven. Enjoy." He turns and walks away.

I place the basket in front of her with a little dish of herb butter. "Please take one. I promise they're delicious."

"They look tempting. I haven't eaten this morning, and I don't need to be more embarrassed with my stomach barking. It smelled so good when I arrived here looking like a pirate." She laughs at herself.

"I like to serve our customers good traditional German food." *Not the modern shit I used to cook.* "You can't visit any part of Germany without having a soft pretzel, or *Laugenbrezel* in German."

She takes one and rips off a piece. "My manager, Thomas, raved about German pretzels yesterday."

I point at the butter. "Try it with this butter. We make it here too."

She spreads on a generous amount and takes a bite. Her eyes close. I hope in delight. Her large doe eyes open and lock on mine. Just now I see her eye color more clearly. I remember them being brown but I've never seen her eyes this close before. They're a rich brown with a hint of red. Like cinnamon sticks. Lovely and hypnotizing.

She interrupts my fascination. "Oh. So yummy. By far better than any city pretzel. I might have to question bagels too. These are probably great with spicy mustard. I can understand what my manager was talking about. Maybe I'll buy a few and take them back to the office for him." She pulls off another piece.

"You don't need to pay for them. I'll give you a bag to take back to the office. Well, *if* this meeting goes well."

She squints at me but can't respond, because her mouth is full.

Peter places our drinks on the table and then leaves.

She covers her mouth with her hand. "This isn't a glass. It's a mug. Thank God it's nonalcoholic." She wipes the corner of her mouth then lifts the mug to her lips.

I put my hand up. "Not so fast."

She stops in surprise.

"Another thing to learn. Before you take the first sip, tap the bottom of your mug with mine while keeping eye contact. Then you say, *prost*."

She taps mine and says, "*Prost*."

I wag my finger at her. "You forgot to look at me when you tapped my glass. Play by the rules," I tease. "It's seven years of bad luck in the bedroom if you don't make eye contact." *That was so out of line!*

Her face flushes, and she pulls the purple gemmed flower pendant on her silver necklace from side to side. "Well, I sure don't want that." She chuckles.

We try it again while our eyes lock longer than they should.

"Now drink." I watch her mouth and then her throat movements as the beer washes down. I look away and swallow in response. I take a couple large swigs of mine.

She nods with a smile I already love. "Mmm. That's refreshing, tasty, and thick. I'm assuming *prost* means cheers."

"Yes, but remember to keep eye contact when you say it. It's something Americans don't often do. It'd be a waste to not look into your pretty eyes."

"I never really thought about it. Thanks for the lesson," she says casually.

She takes another long drink and looks around the beer garden. "This is a great place to have a drink on a warm night. I love the white lights strung from this tree to each corner of the garden. It must look lovely at night. There's a generous amount of space for a lot of customers. I'm assuming it's not open during the winter."

She turns back to the table, and I swallow back my laugh.

She plays with her hair and straightens her back. "What's the matter now? Why are you smirking?"

I lean over the table and gently wipe the beer foam from her upper lip with my thumb.

She stiffens in response.

"You have a beer mustache."

She instantly wipes her upper lip as I lick the foam off my thumb. Her eyes follow every movement and freeze on my lips. She quickly looks away and plays with her necklace again. A nervous tic?

"What else can I do to embarrass myself? I started this job a couple of months ago. My manager wouldn't be so thrilled with me right now. To top things off, we haven't even discussed your ideas for your new website. He didn't give me any information yesterday. I think I'll need a dozen pretzels before I leave. And maybe another beer, but with alcohol this time," she mumbles.

"Please don't be embarrassed or stressed about this meeting." *I know what true embarrassment feels like.* "I wish all business meetings were this entertaining. We need to get to know each other before we work together." I put my hand on hers. "Don't you agree?" *Stop touching her, Gerry.*

She looks at my hand and crinkles her forehead. I pull away and stand up quickly, almost knocking over the bench. "I forgot to bring my folder outside. Let me go get it so I can show you my notes."

Her face softens. "Thank you. Let's get to it."

<h1 style="text-align:center">Chapter 3</h1>

Tina

I smack Alexa's arm and almost fall off the back of the treadmill. "Stop laughing at me!" I demand between giggles as I stabilize myself.

"That's the funniest story I've ever heard. My little pirate. I wish I could've seen it. Did you have a parrot on your shoulder? Or in our location, a pigeon." She dabs her eyes with her hand towel.

I push a strand of hair away from my face. "It was so mortifying, but at least I can laugh at myself."

She leans over to me. "Check out the guy on the stepper with the huge lamb chops and the sweatband on his head. Does he think he's sexy?"

I try not to laugh. "Be nice. We're here to work out, even if we're barely breaking a sweat or out of breath."

"We're moving, and that's all that matters. Okay. All seriousness now. You said Gerry's hot. Give me the scoop on him," she says as her eyes trail one of the trainers behind us in the mirror.

Our eyes finally meet, so I at least know she's focusing on me now. "First of all, he has a buzz cut, and his hair is receding from his forehead. The little bit I saw looked like dark brown. It might not sound sexy, but it made him look bitable." I take a sip of water.

Her face lights up, and she blurts, "Like Mr. Clean? Isn't he big and bald like a pirate?"

I choke on my water and lose my balance. I grip the handlebars and leap to the sides of the treadmill, just avoiding rolling off the back. Alexa braces herself on her machine too.

The trainer behind us walks up to me. "Are you okay, miss? Should I show you how the treadmill works?"

Funny. He's not looking at me. His eyes are frozen on Alexa.

"No, thanks. I'm okay," I say loudly so he acknowledges me. She dazzles men with her silky, long blond hair and bright-green eyes. Little do they know she's a genius hidden behind her beauty.

He glances at me as if I'm an afterthought. "Maybe I can show you how to use some of the other machines after you're finished with the treadmill?" His eyes shoot back to Alexa. "Or new ways to stretch after your workout."

Are you kidding me?

Going to the gym sucks. Not just because it's a meat market, but the sweaty smell. I turn away and resume walking. This is such a waste of my time.

"Maybe," she says as she trails her fingertip along her jawline.

He winks and struts away.

"Hey, what's your name?" she calls after him.

He turns around. "Tony."

She grins, then faces the mirror.

"You're crazy. We aren't stretching with him. Well, I'm not anyway," I mumble.

"He's kinda cute."

"Yeah...if you're into muscle heads. He can't even put his arms down."

Maybe I said that too loud, because he turns around and stares at us in the mirror. Alexa waves at him.

"Come on. Let's increase the speed." I push the button several times.

Alexa equalizes her speed with mine. "Let's get back to Mr. Clean." She swings her arms back and forth.

"Can I please talk without you dragging Mr. Clean into this conversation?" I point my thumb at myself. "I was the one who looked like a stupid pirate." I chuckle again. "How am I going to face him the next time I see him? I'll think of Mr. Clean when he stands in front of me."

"He better not have a conehead."

I howl in laughter. An older woman a few treadmills over gives me a dirty look, then steps off and walks away.

"You're going to get us in trouble. I'm going to pee in my pants if you don't stop. I haven't laughed so much in one day. Finally, I'm out of breath." I stop talking for a second to catch a breather. "He doesn't have a conehead. The shape of his head is perfect. He has peach fuzz. I was dying to touch it."

"I'm sure you were, among other things," she says.

I crinkle my face at her. "Anyway, did I say he had scruff? He was dressed casual and was so laid back. He's at least six inches taller than me, with very broad shoulders. I tried not to look at his body, but I gave in. He's bulky, like a big bear or bodyguard."

"Like The Rock?" she exclaims.

"No. Again, he isn't bald! What's with you and bald guys? I think you have a secret fetish."

She sticks her nose in the air with an impish smile.

I purse my lips to the side. Interesting. Maybe she does.

She flutters her long eyelashes. "What color are his eyes?"

"At first I didn't notice. Once we were outside and it was brighter out—a golden brown. Like fool's gold. It only added to his sex appeal. I've no idea how old he is. I guess between thirty and thirty-five.

"Anyway, are foreigners always so touchy-feely? We touched hands several times, as if it were completely normal. I shouldn't have liked it, but I did. I had a beer mustache, and he wiped it off my lip with his thumb."

Her eyes bug out.

"And then sucked it off his thumb."

Her mouth turns into an *O*.

"It made me tingle in all the right places. If you know what I mean?" I wiggle my eyebrows.

"No way!" she shrieks as she accidentally pulls the emergency cord with her hand and slams into the machine.

I stop mine and grab her arm. "Are you all right?" I say with a mix of concern and giggles.

She fixes her hair and looks around to check no one saw her. "I'm fine, fine, fine. Are there video cameras in here? I don't need something like that going viral."

We look around and don't notice anything. I'm sure there are but I'm not going to mention it.

"Enough with these worthless machines. Let's get off and find something safer. Where's Tony the Tiger?" She swivels her head to search for him.

I nudge her forward. "Forget him. Let's just go to the smoothie bar. I don't know why I agreed to do this trial with you. We don't get a workout at all. I'm more out of breath when I walk from the kitchen to the living room with a bowl of ice cream in my hand."

"Sounds good. I want to hear the rest of your story before one of us breaks a leg."

I order a mango smoothie, and she gets a strawberry one. We find two seats away from everyone.

"So continue with Mr. Clean?" Alexa says as she tosses her towel over the back of the chair.

I take my first sip and sigh. "It's wrong every way you look at it. I'm not allowed to like him. We work together. Even though it's wrong, I can't help the excitement in my belly."

Her demeanor changes as she swirls her straw in her smoothie. "It's a recipe for disaster. Mixing work with pleasure can be tricky. I've seen some crazy shit happen between sales reps and doctors."

I deflate in my chair. "That's what I thought from the moment I met him. I know this is business, and that's how it needs to stay. It's just not fair that my first client is a guy I'm attracted to. But it's not only how he looks or how I react to him. From the second we met, conversation flowed easily. There's a comfort level I've never experienced before with a guy. It's as if we've met before.

"I told myself several times to act professional, but I failed miserably." I sigh loudly and bang my palm against my head. "I need to stop thinking about him. I can't screw up this job. Our next meeting's scheduled for Monday, but it's at my office this time."

"Good. You'll be surrounded by colleagues and your manager. You won't be able to stare at his ass." She winks at me.

"I'm going to forget you just said that."

"Suit yourself. You know you're gonna do it." She bobs her head and grins.

"Maybe I should wear a potato sack and no makeup."

"Whatever. You hardly wear any makeup to begin with. You don't need it with your flawless skin and that sexy beauty mark. With or without makeup, you look gorgeous."

Her face becomes serious. "Not to upset you, but maybe he didn't feel the attraction the way you did. If that's the case, it'll be much easier for you to keep it business." She sips her smoothie.

What if that's true? Maybe he didn't think twice about me when I left the restaurant. But wouldn't that be better?

I clear my throat. "Let's talk about something else. What's up with you? Have you spoken to Lisa or James? I've been meaning to call Lisa. She left me a message yesterday saying she needs to ask me something."

Alexa perks up in her seat and swivels her hand. "Oh. Oh. Thank you for mentioning Lisa. I spoke to her this afternoon. She and James are going to a food-tasting event in the city and want to know if we'd like to go. It's next Tuesday."

That grabs my attention. "Food tasting. Right up my alley. What kind?"

"You know how Matt's wedding is in October? His fiancée Kayla's cousin is supposedly a star chef in Europe. He'll be catering their wedding."

I pull my head back. "Lisa and James are going?"

She nods.

"I'm surprised, since they live in New Jersey and it's a pain to travel to the city during the week."

"Well, James is Matt's best man. He should be there. Lisa said she needs to get out of the house.

"Anyway. The main dish has been narrowed down to two. We'll be blindfolded when we eat. Whichever dish we like better will be chosen for the main course at the reception."

I freeze just as I go to sip from my straw. "Blindfolded! What the hell for?"

She chokes on her smoothie. "What's with your screeching voice? Calm down." She looks over her shoulder to see if anyone heard us.

"I don't know the full details. It's something he's known for but doesn't do often in the States. It has to do with enhancing your other senses, which will make the food taste better or something like that. Whatever. It sounds like fun and cool since he's famous. Famous in Europe, not here in the States." Her face lights up. "Maybe he's the European version of Michael Voltaggio. Do you know who I'm talking about? The hot one with all the tats who won *Top Chef*."

I don't respond, because all I can think about is my blindfolded kiss years ago. The best kiss I've ever had.

"Do you want to go? It's free. I know how you love to eat, and you aren't afraid to try something new. It's also fun to check out a new restaurant," she says while adjusting her sports bra.

She looks up when I don't respond. "You're thinking about Mr. Clean's ass again, aren't you?" She angles her face with narrowed eyes.

I wish.

"So, what's up? This blindfold thing seems to have you unhinged. You're playing with your necklace again."

I let it go. "If I tell you something, do you *promise* you won't tell a soul? I never even told Lisa this."

She giggles. "This must be really juicy if you never told her. I love secrets. God knows, we all have them. Your secret is safe with me. Pinky swear?"

We interlock our pinkies.

She taps the table with her hand. "Spill it."

"I was blindfolded once before..."

Her interest clearly piqued more, she inches her chair closer and leans near me. If she tilts any farther, she might as well sit on my lap.

"A couple of days before my college graduation, I went to a frat party at Jackson College."

"Not too far from where you went to school at New Jersey Tech, right?"

I nod. "You remember my two college friends, Larissa and Cori? The ones I told you who want to stay with us for a long weekend next month?"

"Yes..."

"They wanted me to let loose, so they asked me to play a drinking game."

"Blindfolds and alcohol." She leers. "That could be dangerous."

"Yep, with blindfolds. I had to kiss three complete strangers. We all had to wear them and weren't allowed to see or speak to each other beforehand."

"Why were the guys blindfolded too?"

"We were all blinded because the initial physical appearance would interfere with our chemistry. If they saw me and didn't find me attractive, it would affect the way they would kiss me. My friends chose the guys randomly from the party. After I kissed them, when the guys weren't in the room, I'd have to say who was the best kisser. When the guys came back, Larissa and Cori would switch their order. Then we'd stand in front of each other and take off the blindfolds at the same time. Then I'd have to guess which guy was the one I'd said was the best kisser. If I chose wrong, I had to chug a beer."

"Wow, that was gutsy of you and maybe even reckless. I didn't know you had it in you." She nudges my knee.

I rest my chin in my hand and sigh. "At the time I didn't, but before my mom died, I was a different person. You wouldn't know it now, but I was the fearless rule breaker of the family. Always the first to try new things. Trouble was my middle name. Once she died, that version of me disappeared." *I didn't deserve to be her anymore.*

She grabs my hand and gives it a squeeze, knowing Mom's death is still hard on my family even after all these years. But she doesn't know my mental scars. Not one living soul does.

I drape my towel around my neck. "So when they told me about this game, the old me was begging to play. To break out of my innocent shell. I flip-flopped, and the old me won."

Her face is priceless. She looks like a dog waiting for a bone.

"I guess you're enjoying this story, and I haven't even gotten to the kisses yet."

"I played quite a few drinking games during college, but nothing like this. So get to the kisses. I want to hear some good stuff."

"Larissa stayed in the room with me while each guy came in. The other two guys waited outside the door with Cori." I rub my forehead with the towel and lay it on the table.

"I love these kinds of stories." Alexa titters.

I cross my legs, willing myself not to yank my necklace off. "Now here comes the juicy part." I lean a little closer to her. "I could sense the first guy, Number One, standing in front of me. His body heat radiated off him before we even touched." I close my eyes. "His citrus scent swirled around me, putting me in a trance. His large, warm hands moved up my arms, but every painstakingly slow movement he made seared my skin. In a very pleasant, unfamiliar way." Goose bumps form on my skin. After all this time, my pulse still kicks up a notch when I think about it. Probably more than when I was on that damn treadmill.

"His breathing increased. Mine did too. His right hand traced up my shoulder to my neck and then found my cheek. The anticipation killed me. I *never, ever* thought I'd encounter that kind of pull. His other hand cupped my other cheek. His thumbs caressed my face like feathers. My heart beat faster than someone running the Boston marathon." My hands rest on my cheeks. I'm breaking a sweat.

"You can remember it in such detail?" Alexa says in surprise.

I open my eyes and huff. "Come on. We've been living together for a while now. You know how I am. Stop interrupting. I'm enjoying this." *At least this part of the story anyway.*

She presses her lips together with her fingers.

I straighten my back and close my eyes again. "My shaking hands glided up his arms. As they moved over his elbows, I traced the solid muscles with my fingertips." I replicate the movement with my hands. "At that moment, I was happy I said yes. My hands rose further up, memorizing every solid curve of his biceps. I found his wide shoulders." I lift my hands up as if resting on his shoulders again. "By the placement of my hands and how high my arms were, he was much taller than me.

"He inched closer as his body heat and scent consumed me." I swallow deeply. "Our lips barely grazed. It was annoyingly suspenseful in a delicious way. The miniscule taste of him intoxicated me. He tasted a little bit like my favorite candy."

"Peanut M&Ms?" Her voice rises an octave. "That's just freaking gross."

I open my eyes. "That's Lisa's favorite candy, smartass. He tasted like black licorice."

She crinkles her nose. "That's even more disgusting. You're so weird with food. Move on before I lose interest or my smoothie."

I ignore her comments and get back in my zone. "I opened my mouth and touched his lips with my tongue to sample him again. He responded in a slow, teasing manner. I couldn't hold off, because he tasted so yummy. I yanked his shoulders forward hoping to meld my lips with his." I'm all riled up.

"Would you ladies like anything else?" My eyes spring open as I shrink in my chair. How embarrassing if she saw me acting this out.

"No!" Alexa responds sharply.

"No, thank you," I say with a smile. The server scowls at Alexa and walks away.

"Continue," she demands.

Where was I? "His tongue taunted mine. My hands moved to the back of his neck to intensify the kiss. His hands moved down my back and pulled me closer. I relaxed into his firm embrace. We kissed as if it was our first and so desperately our last. If he'd tried to kiss my neck, I would've let him." I touch my neck, wishing his lips were there right now.

I slump in my chair. "And then Larissa interrupted us. The moment was gone. He left the room." I'm silent because now I need to tell her the embarrassing part.

"The second and third kisses were mere pecks. At first, we couldn't find each other's lips, and I banged my head on Number Two's chin. It was like playing pin the tail on the donkey. Needless to say, absolutely no chemistry and completely awkward. The kisses were over before they even started. No kiss could beat Number One."

"So come on. Stop it with the suspense. What happened? Did you guess correctly?"

I bite my lip and look down. "We didn't finish the game. He took off before the game was over."

She smacks the table hard, drawing attention from the people sitting near us. "No way! Did he tell your friend why he left?"

"He supposedly came out of the room with his head down. He quickly walked away from Cori while mumbling something like he had to catch a flight. What a lame excuse. The only information Cori got from him was before the game started. He was from Europe, visiting his cousin who was the president of the fraternity at the time. But the real interesting part was Cori said I'd pointed him out to her before the game was even brought up.

"I remember looking around the living room and noticing him right away. He was tall with wavy dark-brown hair. I could tell he was different. He dressed more mature. His pants weren't hanging low, and he wasn't wearing a hoodie or flip-flops. He looked older than the typical college guy. Our eyes locked, and he flashed me a crooked smile that gave me goose bumps. But maybe it was a cocky scowl, for all I know. Or is it Gerry who has the crooked smile? Things are getting jumbled now." I pause for a minute. "Cori and Larissa asked who I was looking at. I carefully motioned to him so it didn't look obvious I was talking about him. They looked at him briefly but didn't seem impressed. I peeked over my shoulder and locked eyes with him once more. I turned away because Cori started talking to me about the blindfold game. When I looked back a few minutes later, he was gone. I never saw him again."

My ears feel like they're on fire. "The whole thing was so embarrassing. Even more than my sunglasses fiasco this morning. But I have *never* forgotten that kiss or his lips."

"It's pretty obvious. Do you act out your encounter in front of your mirror in your bedroom?"

I squint my eyes and sneer. "When I eat licorice, I always think of him. He haunts me. Maybe the entire mind-blowing experience was only because of the blindfolds."

"Maybe. But that didn't sound like it."

I drink the last of my smoothie. "It does enhance your senses. Maybe that's why I was in a trance. All my senses collided at once."

"It sounds more like your lips collided."

"After all these years, I still remember how he smelled, how he tasted, and the heat that radiated off his body. I have yet to experience that kind of attraction to someone again." *Until today.*

Alexa fans herself. "You keep getting me all worked up. No wonder people use blindfolds in the bedroom."

I chuckle. "Get your mind out of the gutter, young lady."

She sticks out her lower lip.

"It doesn't matter. Since he took off, he probably thought it was terrible. I felt trashy and like a complete fool. We left the party right after."

"I wish I knew what that kind of attraction felt like. Sadly, it's never happened to me." She deflates in her seat.

"Yeah, right. I don't believe that for one second. You have so many guys beating down our door. None of them have done it for you?" I ask in shock. "What about Tony the Tiger over there?" I gesture to where he's standing by the front desk. Probably waiting for Alexa.

"Once in a while there's a good tingle and I get something out of it, but never something I want for more than a couple of dates. Why do you think I'm never in a serious relationship or you've hardly met any of them?" She folds her hand towel and places it on the table. "The guys I meet are too easy, damn weird, or have no brains."

I raise one eyebrow. "Weird? Weird in what way?"

"A knee fetish."

I blink my eyes several times. "What? What the hell is a knee fetish? You mean these?" I point to my knees.

She takes a deep breath. "Long story short. A proctologist in one of the clinics I have sales appointments at...has a knee fetish. He always goes out of his way to talk to me. He's at least fifty years old, by the way.

"One day I went to fill a plastic cup at the water cooler. He walked up to me and proceeded to comment on how pretty my knees were. Who the hell looks at people's knees? He literally bent down and inspected mine. I was so relieved when a nurse called my name for my appointment. I walked away from him like a bat out of hell. After that, I purposely wear pants every time I go to that clinic. I saw him one more time in passing, and his eyes went directly to my knees, and he actually pouted." She shivers. "Fucking psycho."

"Men have boob or ass fetishes, but knees..." I don't press for more disturbing details. "Be careful one of your doctors or boyfriends doesn't become a stalker."

She waves her hand. "Don't be ridiculous. He was the only weirdo so far."

"Fine. Whatever you say."

I squeeze her wrist. "Again, please don't tell a soul about this game. I'd be so upset."

"Why? You were in college. That's the type of shit everyone does in college. At least you didn't take a ton of drugs or sleep with every guy around. Or go streaking. Don't be so hard on yourself. You need to look back at those years and know you did something crazy."

"I know you're right, but haven't you ever looked back at something you've done and cringed, wishing you had never done it?"

"I guess so. But I think you need to forget about it."

"Of course, I thought of him a couple of times today because Gerry's from Europe." I wave my hands around out of frustration. "I don't want to talk about this anymore, or my head will explode."

She grabs her towel and stands up. "Let's go home. You've had a hard day." Just as she says this, Tony the Tiger saunters up to us.

I have no desire to witness their flirting. "I'm going to the lockers to get my things."

"I'll meet you in front in a minute," she says with a sly smile.

After fifteen minutes, Alexa finally strolls to the front door, swinging her duffle bag.

"Real nice to make me wait."

"We have a double date this weekend. Or blind date for you."

I shake my head. "No way. Absolutely not."

"Come on." She nudges me. "It could be fun. Something different."

I hesitate. "Fine." I huff. "My new mission...to do something different."

I think.

Chapter 4

Gerry

Five more minutes until I see Tina again. I can't stop thinking about her. Nothing could've prepared me for when she stood in front of me the other day. We've since exchanged a couple of emails, but they were only about the website. I know it's the way it should be, but what I want is something different.

This whole situation is insane. It was just a stupid college game. I kissed her once years ago, never officially met her before our meeting last week, but I feel like I've known her for years. I'm usually a patient man, but now that we've connected again, it'll be nearly impossible to keep my distance from her.

"Hello. How can I help you?" greets the bubbly gray-haired receptionist behind the white shiny desk.

"Hi. I'm Gerry Maier. I have a two-thirty appointment with Tina Schmitt from Modern Web. Can you please tell me where she's located?"

The receptionist puts her hand up when the phone rings. "Please let me answer this call." She covers the receiver and whispers, "I'll notify her you're here. Please take a seat on one of the chairs near the window." She points her chin to direct me.

I nod and wander to the window that provides an amazing view of the New York City skyline. I place the bag of fresh pretzels and my computer bag on an empty chair. The sky is crystal blue with a ribbon of clouds drifting past. The city and the Hudson River glisten. It reflects a sense of peace from this side of the river in Jersey City. The Statue of Liberty stands proud in the clear distance.

I'm still amazed I've been living in the US for a year now. I made one bad choice, and it changed my life and career in an instant. While things snowballed back home, I flew here to stay at my aunt's house in New Jersey. My goal had been to take a vacation and hide, not move here.

Moving to the city over six months ago has given me the peace I've been searching for, though it's one of the busiest and loudest cities in the world. I can blend in with the crowd and make my own schedule.

I don't miss the hectic life I had in Germany. My agent had me overbooked for months straight. One day in Berlin for an interview, the next day in Munich to film a commercial, and then somewhere else to be a food critic in a famous restaurant. On top of that, running my own restaurant in Hamburg and catering special affairs. It was never ending, and it sucked the life out of me.

I view the skyline one more time and relax slightly. I need to behave and act properly toward her. Especially in front of her manager or coworkers. No touching or flirting under any circumstances. *Behave!*

"Hi, Gerry."

I hear her delicate voice, and my heart erupts. I turn around and see her glowing face.

"I hope you found the office building without any problems." Her hand rests on her collarbone and necklace.

My eyes scan her body. White pants, a black V-neck, short-sleeve shirt, and silver flats. Simply perfect. But she could wear a potato sack, and I'd still think she's sexy as hell. She's shorter this time without her heels. Her long, shiny, wavy hair flows down her shoulders just like it did all those years ago.

"Hi, Tina. It's nice to see you again. I had no problem finding this building." My lips yearn to kiss her cheek. I fumble and hand her the bag of pretzels instead. "I brought some pretzels for your department.

You mentioned how much your manager likes them, and you forgot to take some with you last time."

Her smile enlarges. "Thanks. If they don't want them, then they're all mine." She holds the bag close to her chest.

I motion for her to go. "Shall we?"

"Oh, yes. Please follow me. We're on the third floor. The elevator is right over here."

We approach the silver door. "How was your weekend?"

She faces me as we wait for the door to open. "It was interesting. My roommate, Alexa, convinced me to go on a double date with her. Well, a blind date for me. She met a trainer at the gym we go to. The blind date was the trainer's best friend."

I think I'm borderline obsessed. It pisses me off to think about her being with other guys. "How did it go? Was it love at first sight?" My smile couldn't be any more fake.

"It was a disaster. Our dates discussed how much protein they eat every day to gain a certain amount of muscle. I just wanted to go in a corner somewhere and play Candy Crush on my phone. Alexa wasn't impressed either. I pretended to feel sick so we could get out of there. We went to a couple of other bars after, which was fun."

I put my hand to my chest and pretend to stumble back. "I'm hurt. You didn't come back to Hofbräuhaus. The food is great, and so are the drinks."

"I'm sorry," she says, flustered. "We stayed in Hoboken, near our apartment."

I chuckle. "I'm only kidding. It's no problem. But you should stop by one night. I practically live there. I can promise you'll receive special service." I wiggle my eyebrows. *Already failing.* "Or I can interrupt your next date if it goes bad."

The door opens, and we step inside. "This is insanely small. Is this someone's personal elevator, or do only thin people work here?"

She giggles softly behind me. "Well, not everyone's a giant like you. You're the size of a linebacker."

I tilt my head to the side. "Is that a compliment or an insult?"

She shuffles the bag in her hands and almost drops it. "Sorry. That's no way near an insult."

Good answer.

We stand as far away as possible from each other, which isn't easy. If I'm too close to her, I know I won't keep my hands off her. My attraction increases every second she's near me. At least the pretzels are between us.

We both stand there and don't move to push the button even though the door has closed. We're more interested in staring at each other. This is going to be more difficult than I'd thought.

I move a centimeter. "What floor again?"

She jerks. "Oh. I'm sorry. Third floor." We both reach to push the button, and our fingers collide.

She snaps her arm back like she touched something hot, almost dropping the bag again. They're probably smashed by this point.

"Should I carry the bag for you?" I laugh to myself and push the right button.

She doesn't respond.

"Our hands act like magnets. They can't avoid the pull," I say to help break the tension.

She focuses on the floor while playing with her necklace. Definitely a nervous tic. I probably shouldn't have said that. I've been here for only a couple of minutes and have already broken my promise more than once.

Saved by the bell. The elevator door opens painfully slow, and she leads me to an open modern office space with several black, high-walled cubicles. To the right is a wall of windows. "What a great view to have every day when you come to work."

"That's definitely one of the perks," she says over her shoulder.

It's dead silent on this floor. We walk past several cubicles that have one to two large computer monitors on the desks. Her coworkers are so engrossed with their computers that they don't acknowledge anyone around them. No one's socializing. I know it's an office, but there's usually some evidence of life.

"Is it always this quiet? It would drive me nuts," I mumble to her.

"Yes. It's worse than my last job. However, my manager and a couple of others are fun to work with. They'll be my salvation from the silence."

"It's never quiet at the restaurant. I have to be social. It's part of the business. I'm used to noise."

We stop at one cubicle. "And this is where I work."

Her organized space is the only one that looks lived in. A large calendar with a picture of a tropical beach at sunset hangs on one wall. A dark-purple sweater hangs from a hook on the nearest wall. A mini fan stands between two monitors. She has a few pictures on her desk, as well as a small crystal vase with two large purple roses in it. Jealousy pools through me.

I point to the roses. "Are those from your blind date to entice you to play Candy Crush with him?" *Please say no.*

She sighs, but I notice her cheeks turn pink again. "No. Thankfully. But Alexa seemed to have impressed her date, because a dozen multicolored roses were delivered to our apartment on Saturday. I thought they were beautiful, so she told me to take as many as I want. I took the purple ones because purple's my favorite color. It adds a little life to this boring black cubicle."

I'd send her flowers every day if I could. She seems lonely in a way. She doesn't say anything directly, but I can hear it in her droopy tone.

She hugs the bag again. "Let me introduce you to my manager, Thomas. He'd love to meet you."

"That would be great. Can I leave my things in here?"

"Of course." She points to the spare chair next to her desk. I move forward as she tries to walk out of the cube. We bang back and forth into each other, then freeze in place as we're sandwiched together within the walls of the entrance. The only thing between us is the bag of pretzels. Definitely crushed. Her hands press against my lower stomach. They better not move any lower. Neither one of us tries to move. My heart pounds as hard as her breathing.

She says softly, "We'll only be a few minutes with him, and then we'll go into a meeting room to work. My cubicle's too small."

"I've noticed."

From the corner of my eye, I see someone approaching. I shift my body to separate us.

Tina exits the cube. "Hey, Peggy. How are you? Did you have a good weekend?"

The woman's eyes dart from me to Tina and back several times. She whispers something. Tina giggles in response.

She motions to me. "Peggy, I'd like to introduce you to Gerry Maier. You'll be working on his website for his restaurant."

We shake hands. "Hi. It's nice to meet you. I look forward to working with you," she says with a wide smile.

"Nice to meet you too, Peggy."

Tina interrupts. "Sorry, Peggy. I don't want to be rude, but I need to introduce him to Thomas. I'll update you after Gerry leaves."

"Sure thing. Have fun." She strolls off with a grin on her face.

Tina leans in and whispers, "She's one of the fun ones."

She leads me to her manager's office and knocks on the door.

"Come in," a man responds.

She peeks her head in. "Our client, Gerry Maier, is here. I thought you'd like to meet him. Especially since he brought some pretzels for the office."

"German pretzels. Awesome. I'm starving."

She opens the door wider to let me in. "Gerry Maier, this is my manager, Thomas Grant."

He approaches me with a welcoming smile. "Nice to meet you." He shakes my hand. "Please sit down."

Tina gives him the bag.

He opens it and looks in. "Let me try one of these pretzels to see if they taste like the ones I had in Munich." He pulls one out, and it's flattened like someone sat on it. *Scheiße.*

His face lights up when he tastes a piece. "These are awesome." With his mouth still full of pretzel and crumbs in his beard, he asks,

"Where are you from? I'm assuming you're German. I can hear an accent."

Tina angles herself in my direction. She looks curious too.

"My father's German and French. My mother is from New Jersey. I lived in Germany most of my life, with some time in France too."

"I vacationed once in Germany. A group of us went to Octoberfest in Munich. That was one hell of an experience. I never knew people could consume so much beer and pretzels. And the sausages…" He pats his belly and laughs. "I couldn't drink beer for weeks after that trip."

He breaks apart another pretzel and offers a piece to Tina.

She waves her hand. "No thanks. I'm more interested in what Gerry has to say."

"So how many languages can you speak?" she asks.

"I'm fluent in German, French, and English. I was lucky to grow up in a household with so many languages. At home, I spoke American English with my mother, French and German with my dad, and I learned all three languages in school. We lived, and my parents still do, in a small town about twenty minutes away from France and about forty-five minutes from Switzerland. It's also right on the border of the Black Forest. It's a beautiful area surrounded by vineyards."

"Where cuckoo clocks come from," Thomas chimes in.

I nod. "Exactly."

"It sounds terrific," Tina says. "I can only speak a little bit of high school Spanish. How about you, Thomas?"

He tries to respond, but crumbs shoot out of his mouth. He wipes off his shirt.

Ekelhaft.

"Same with me. You can say whatever you want, and I wouldn't have a clue."

She leans in my direction with attentive eyes. "Let's hear the difference between French and German. German always sounds so harsh."

"What would you like me to say?"

She looks around the office. "Something simple like, *the pencil is yellow*."

"In German you would say, *du bist wunderschön*."

She teeters her head back and forth. "Not so bad, but I'm sure it sounds prettier in French."

"In French it's, *tu es belle*."

She giggles. "Definitely prettier. French can make a pencil sound so romantic."

If she only knew.

There's a knock on the door. "Hey, Boss, sorry to interrupt. Here are the urgent documents you needed from me." Peggy hands them to Thomas. "Au revoir," she says when she walks out.

Tina glances to me again. "I'm so impressed with your language skills. You were lucky to learn them at such an early age. I'm jealous. Maybe you can teach me some words while we work together."

"As long as you meet the project timelines," Thomas sneaks in before he takes another huge bite.

"Maybe I'll learn a thing or two from you. I'm clueless when it comes to computers. I use them for basic things but not when it comes to creating my own website. During our first meeting, you used words like *widget*—or was it *fidget*?—*SEO*, *plug-ins*. That's a language too. My brain and hands are more creative with other things."

Her eyebrows rise, and a little smirk appears. I wonder what she's thinking. Hopefully, what I'm thinking.

It's not about cooking or websites.

Chapter 5

I'm sure he's creative with his hands. Maybe he can show me what he can do with them. He looks as tasty as those crushed pretzels when he's dressed in business casual. He has a crisp, white button-down shirt with the sleeves rolled up to his elbows and black business pants that fit impeccably in the front. I haven't seen the back yet. His scruff is still there and is the same length as the hair on his head. I wish I could feel it against my cheek. I'll avoid at all costs to look at his....

"Hello, Tina? Yoo-hoo." I faintly hear Thomas's voice.

I snap my head up and squirm in my chair. "Sorry. Lost my train of thought."

Fantasizing about him should be harder than this. I probably had a stupid grin on my face. Daydreaming is going to get me into some major trouble.

"Shall we start our meeting?" I question Gerry with a professional tone. "I think we'll make good progress today."

He leans over the desk and extends his hand to Thomas. "Nice to meet you. Enjoy the pretzels."

I wait outside Thomas's office, not paying attention to what he's saying to Gerry.

When he comes out, I motion for him to follow me. "Let's pick up our stuff at my desk."

As we walk down the aisle, I turn my head to the side and notice he's staring at my ass. My inquiring eyes meet his admiring ones. "Do you like what you see, Mr. Maier?" *I'm flirting. In the office, no less! Who* am *I?*

He stops short. "Sorry." He nervously points to my backside. "There's something on the back of your pants. It's a big sticker, I think."

I twist my waist to check it out.

He reaches out. "Do you want me to take it off?"

My hand flies up and smacks his away.

"Absolutely not," I say through gritted teeth. "I can find it myself, thank you very much." I pat my back pockets. Something tickles my fingers, so I yank it off. I hold it up in front of us. It's an extra-large sticky with a giant red arrow with the word *Attention* on it. Thomas uses these when he needs signatures on documents. He must think we're blind, because the sticky is huge. It must've been on the chair I sat on.

He smiles with flirtation oozing from his lips. "A red arrow. How appropriate. It was welcoming me to look exactly where I wanted to."

His comment is so wrong on so many levels, but I can't seem to address it, because I like it.

"My butt? Again, I hope it was worth looking at." We're having this conversation in the middle of the department floor. However, I don't think anyone sees or hears us, because their noses are stuck to computer screens. I glance at Thomas's door and sigh in relief when I see it's closed.

I walk away feeling a little less embarrassed. I'm confused instead. He'd said he wanted to look at my ass. I could claim sexual harassment. But from him, it felt like an innocent compliment, if that's possible.

His list of requests lies in front of us.

"I've considered several of your ideas for the website. Some will be no problem, but others need a little more work. I have some questions."

He props his hands on the table. "Ask away."

"Do you have a Facebook page for the restaurant? Or any other social media? There is nothing listed. We can put a direct link to them on the main page."

His demeanor changes instantly.

"I'm not a fan of social media, so I don't want anything connected to the website," he says with a pointed tone.

I raise my eyebrows. "Are you sure? We can set up at least a Facebook page. It could be good advertising for your restaurant."

He clenches his jaw. "No, thank you. It's not necessary. The restaurant will do fine without it."

My eyes widen in surprise. "Okay. If you change your mind, just let me know."

I hope the next thing doesn't annoy him even more. "Next question." I point to an item with my pen. "Do you really want the website to be translated into seven different languages?"

"People from all over the world travel to New York City for business or pleasure. Not all of them can speak English or German. It'll attract more customers because they can read our website and menu. We already have menus that are translated into these languages. You can use them for translation to speed up the process, or scan them."

"Good idea. It'll cut down on time." I jot this in my notes.

"Haven't you ever traveled to a place where English wasn't the main language?"

I never travel, and I'm embarrassed to say it.

He nudges my arm. "Haven't you?"

I pretend to search for something in my files. "No. For personal reasons, I've never been able to. The farthest I've gone is to Vermont for skiing."

"Really?"

Now I'm the one who's annoyed. I gesture to another item. "This is an exciting idea. I think it'd be great for someone to go on the website or load an app and be able to pick the table she wants to reserve. The website could have a video showing the restaurant inside and the beer garden outside, with the layout of the tables. The person can click on the table number, pick the number of people and the time they want the table."

He leans in closer, and I inhale through my nose. *Oh my gosh. He smells so delicious. I could bite him like a sandwich.*

He leans away. "Um, thanks." He chuckles. "Are you hungry or something?"

I squish my eyebrows together. "Thanks for what?"

"That I smell good and you want to bite me like a sandwich." His eyes crinkle on the sides.

No! I didn't just say that out loud.

My eyes dart to every part of the room except him. I pretend to look for something, anything. "Where's my pen?"

He reaches over and taps the pen in my hand.

"I obviously left my head at home." I cackle nervously.

He points his finger at the list in front of us. "I also want to include a statement on how customers pay the *Rechnung*."

Thank God. He let me dodge that one.

I look at him blankly. "The what?"

"Oh. Sorry. Sometimes German slips out when I'm speaking. I don't realize it. *Rechnung* means the bill or check."

"I'm learning a lot of German today." I smile at him.

"Do you want to know what the German word is for *sandwich*?" He grins.

I put my pen down and cock my head.

"*Sandwich*."

I set myself up for that one. "Ha-ha. You're a real comedian." I shove his arm with mine and feel my neck and cheeks burn like I just ate a jalapeño.

He shoves me back. "I'll be serious now. About the check. Maybe it's not necessary to add to the website. Back home you have the option to pay separately when you're finished. For example, if you only had an appetizer and two drinks, that's all you'd pay for.

"The server calculates each person's bill separately. I know there are times when everyone splits the bill evenly, but some people eat much less than others. That person shouldn't have to pay for someone else's food. This is something I don't understand about American restaurants."

"I agree with you there."

When I listen to him talk, he has so much pride for his country. Curiosity eats at me like a caterpillar on a leaf. "Can I ask you a personal question?"

He turns in his chair to face me and leans his chin on his hand, our knees almost touching. I tap my pen on the table. Man, he's handsome when he sits like that. He looks like a giant in this small meeting room. The white table only fits five people, but he takes up enough space for two.

"It depends on how personal," he answers with his sweet accent.

Who would ever think a German accent is sweet? Or maybe it's because his accent has a twang with both German and French.

I lean back in my chair and twist the lid off my bottle of Diet Coke. "Why do you live in the States? Your pride for your home country pours out of your mouth when you talk about where you're from. Why not stay there then? Don't you miss your family and friends and...girlfriend?" *I had to throw that tidbit in there.* "Do you have sisters or brothers?" I take a sip.

His eyes leave mine but return several long seconds later with steel seriousness. "First of all, I don't have a girlfriend waiting for me in Germany or in the US. I have no sisters or brothers."

No girlfriend. I cheer to myself.

"People ask me all the time why I'm here." He rests his elbows on his knees. "I came here to have a vacation. I worked nonstop and had no life. My job wasn't fun anymore. Your job should make you happy. Something happened that made me realize I needed an escape. My parents noticed I was exhausted and my heart wasn't in the right place. They suggested I take a break and go visit my family in New Jersey for a while. Since Mom comes from New Jersey, I vacationed in this area almost every summer ever since I was a child. I fell in love with New Jersey and New York City a long time ago."

My stomach drops. "Wait a minute. I'm confused. Are you only here temporarily? I thought you owned your restaurant?" *Please say you're staying.*

"I own the restaurant with my cousin. During my so-called break here, he approached me about investing in a restaurant together. At first, I didn't think anything of it. I went to look at it just to be nice. Once I saw its potential, I jumped at the opportunity. We both invested in it, but I control everything.

"I went to college for restaurant management. It was the change I needed. It's a lot of work, but it's different from what I did in Germany. Now I'm having fun again, and my stress level is much lower. However, there's always a miniscule chance I'll need to go back."

"Did you own a restaurant over there?" I swivel my chair toward the table and smash my Diet Coke against the side. In slow motion, I watch the bottle slip from my fingers and the soda erupt onto the edge of the table and his pants in the worst spot imaginable. A little bit splashes on my white pants too.

We both jump up, and almost bang our heads. He snatches the bottle off the floor.

I search around for tissues or napkins, and there's nothing. "I'm so sorry," I stammer. "I can't seem to do anything without making a complete ass out of myself in front of you. Let me run to the bathroom for some paper towels." As I spin to leave in a panic, he takes hold of my elbow gently.

"Tina, relax. It's okay," he says calmly. "They're only pants. I'm glad they're black. Let me go to the bathroom and clean up."

"It's out the door to the right. Again, I'm so sorry!"

Once he's out of sight, my anger returns. I storm off to the ladies' room, which is farther down the hall, to grab paper towels while grumbling to myself. I stomp back toward the meeting room. I'm such an idiot. I want to run to Thomas's office and tell him I don't want to be the project manager for this account anymore. No matter how professional I try to act, something stupid happens or I flirt with him. Maybe I'm not as equipped for this job as I thought I was. *Am I still being punished?*

I tuck my anger inside my bra and walk back into the meeting room. I stop short when I see him on his hands and knees cleaning the hardwood floor. Thank God it's not carpet. My heart clenches. Why? *He's just cleaning up the soda. It's a nice thing to do. But I made the mess.* I can't explain this pressure in my chest when he's around me. I want to wrap my arms around him—as if that's what colleagues do. *Snap out of it.*

"You don't need to clean up. It was my fault. I'll do it." I wipe down the edge of the table.

"It's no big deal. This is nothing compared to what I clean up at the restaurant."

"Gerry," I warn.

He looks up. "I said it's okay. I don't mind."

I ball my fists at my sides with frustration percolating under my skin. I hate this. I hate this. I've dealt with shittier situations. Why can't I handle this? Is it my pride? Is it him?

He stands up and wipes his hands off.

"This isn't working. We've met twice, and I've made a total ass out of myself each time. I've never had this happen before. I'm usually much more composed and professional. Maybe I should speak to Thomas and ask to be replaced."

He shakes his head. "No way. I won't allow you. I want to work with you on this project. Only you," he states firmly.

I cross my arms and stand straight. "You don't get it, Gerry. I'm the new Bridget Jones. Who knows what'll happen next time?" I close my eyes and pinch my nose. "Please tell me you know who I'm talking about."

"Yes, I know who she is, but that isn't going to change my mind." He puts his hands on my upper arms with a firm grip. "I have no doubt you can do what I'm requesting. You've suggested some brilliant ideas. I have complete confidence in you. Please stay on this project. Don't back out now over these little incidents."

His voice drips with desperation. How can I say no to him? Why does every part of my body ache for him and want to do anything he asks?

"Never once have I questioned your ability. Believe me—I've had my shitty moments with my job. I enjoy working with you and your quirkiness."

He caresses my arms up and down, which I'm enjoying way too much.

"I'm not sure I like to hear the word *quirk* connected to me in a sentence," I say.

"I see the wheels turning in your head. Maybe my English isn't as good as I thought. Let me say it differently so you understand." He rubs his jaw in frustration. "We haven't even finished our second meeting, but I'm already looking forward to the third." He lifts my chin up with his finger. "Do you get it now?"

Wow. My legs feel numb. I collapse in the chair and rest my head in my hands. It's heavy, like a bowling ball. I force myself to look at him again. "Why? You don't even know me."

He kneels in front of me and takes my hands in his.

I love his hands. Again, we shouldn't be touching like this, but I don't want him to let go. I inhale deeply. He smells like soda and... My head perks up. Is it licorice? He didn't smell like this a few minutes ago. I sniff around like a dog.

"What's wrong? Do I smell? I may be from Europe, but I use deodorant," he jokes.

I sniff again. "Do you smell licorice?"

His head falls back, and he lets out a guffaw. "Yes, I ate some between me coming back from the bathroom and you searching for something to clean up the soda." He shrugs his shoulders as he stands up. "You're not the only one who's hungry." His golden eyes pierce mine.

Do not react. I stand up and snoop around, as if I struck gold.

"Where is it? Hand it over! I love licorice." I giggle.

"Wow, a woman after my own heart. Not many people like it like I do." He reaches for his computer case and pulls out a large bag of black licorice.

"Eat as much as you want. Since it's my favorite candy, my family sends me bags of it every once in a while. I have a good stash at my apartment. I'm sure my teeth will fall out one day."

My mind goes back to Number One and licorice. Just like Alexa, most people would think I'm disgusting for finding that attractive. I guess I am quirky.

I lean my hip against the table. "For a European, you have nice teeth, so I wouldn't worry."

"Yes, I've heard that before, just as I've heard Europeans smell." He shoots his arms out to his sides. "I still don't understand why people say that. My mom was quite diligent when it came to dental and personal hygiene." He flashes a smile to prove it.

I push off the table and scoot near him. "I'm sorry. I hope I didn't offend you. It just slipped out. I've watched too many episodes of *The Simpsons* and other shows that joke around about that stuff, and have watched Austin Powers way too many times."

"You didn't offend me. I've heard it all before, especially from my American cousins. They pick on me about Europe, and I pick on them about the US. One day I'll tell you what Germans say about Americans."

"I can just imagine." I pop another piece in my mouth. "You know you can buy licorice here," I say between chews.

"This is my favorite kind, and it's made over there. I haven't found a brand here I like as much. I'm sure if you moved to another country, you'd have a list of items you miss. Especially food. My mom's is still peanut butter. Her family in New Jersey and I still send her packages with her favorite, and she's been living there for over thirty years. When she visits, she loads up on stuff to take back with her."

I reach for the bag, but he pulls it away. I try to grab it. He puts his large hand on my collarbone to keep me from moving forward. I use every ounce of my weight to push forward while laughing.

"No, no, no. You're allowed to have some, but only when you agree to stay on this project."

"Hey, that's not fair. It's bribery!" I break away from him while gasping for air. That was exhausting but fun.

He hangs the bag over my head.

He's too tall when I have my ballerinas on. I wish I could crawl up his body like a squirrel. I slouch in defeat, trying to catch my breath. "Fine. I'll give your project one more chance. But if something else happens, I'm out."

We stand there smiling at each other. I swear it's like he's my best friend. I can't quite pinpoint the unfamiliar emotions exploding in my body. It's as if all my senses have been sparked to life. Does he feel it to?

I'm analyzing…just like my sister, the therapist, always does.

I catch him off guard when I snatch the bag out of his hand. "Ha! I won. This bag's mine now." I dance around with my arms up in the air.

He laughs. "Hey, you caught me off guard, but you can have it anyway. Just promise you'll think of me every time you bite one."

I stop dancing when I grasp what he said.

He gathers his papers and shoves them hard into his computer case. "I'm sorry. I shouldn't speak to you the way I do. It just comes out. It's out of line and unprofessional." He zips up the case with force and turns toward the door.

As I've said to myself a million times, we shouldn't be talking to each other like this. "Gerry, we're both at fault."

He looks back over his shoulder at me.

"I've said some crazy things too."

In a more professional tone, he says, "I think the project is able to move forward. Please call or email me if you have any further questions."

"Sounds groovy, baby." I try to put a smile back on his face. Angry mode doesn't suit him.

A smirk grows on his face which erases all worries from my mind. "Quirky. Just the way I like you."

I walk him out, then head to Peggy's cube. I tap her shoulder. She removes her earbuds and turns in her chair.

"Hey there. Here's the list of requests for Gerry Maier's website. I made some notes on the side. I'll send you an updated version tomorrow. He has great ideas, but it'll be tough to meet that six-week timeline, so we need to get moving." I lay it on her desk.

She lifts the page up and traces it with one finger. "Did you spill coffee or something on it?"

My face begins to sizzle like bacon in a frying pan.

"You're blushing. What happened?" She points to her chair. "Sit down and tell me."

I relax my tense body into the chair. Definitely doing yoga tonight. Screw the gym.

She removes her black-rimmed glasses and remains silent as I explain how I spilled my soda on Gerry. Her hand covers her mouth the entire time. She's trying not to laugh, but her crinkled eyes betray her.

She removes her hand from her mouth and gives me an inquisitive look. "Gerry seems like a nice guy if he reacted like that. Handsome too."

Where's she going with this? I suddenly feel sweat trickle down my back. I try not to touch my necklace. Did she hear us?

"Yeah. He seems like a nice guy. I think he'll be easy to work with." I try to show no emotion and to keep my eyes from darting around the cube.

"I heard Gerry say something in French when I crashed your meeting with Thomas. Did he tell you what he said? I can speak pretty good French myself."

"Really? That's cool. Am I the only one who doesn't speak a

foreign language?" I grumble. "Gerry said *the pencil is yellow*. Why?"

She hesitates for a moment. "I wasn't going to get involved, but I thought I'd let you know that's not what he said. Far from it." Her mouth curves upward.

I sit up straight and lean my elbow on her desk. "What the hell did he say? Will it make me angry or embarrassed? Was it rude?"

She swivels in her chair. "It depends. You need to tell me what you think. Ready to hear it?"

"Yes, the anticipation is killing me." My voice squeaks.

She waves her hands for me to be quiet. "The exact translation"— she lowers her voice—"is *you're very beautiful*. I don't think he was talking about Thomas." She giggles.

Now I grab my necklace and press on the amethysts. "That's the last thing I would've guessed. Are you sure? You're not pranking me, are you?"

"I'm not twenty-one anymore. I don't play games. He's interested in you. If I wasn't married, I'd be interested in him. He's not hard on the eyes."

"I've only had two meetings with him. What exactly do you think is going on between us?" Why am I being so defensive?

She rolls her chair closer to me. "Hey, I met my husband at work. You spend so much of your time at work, the probability of meeting someone is very high. The only thing I can say is, be careful. You don't want it to affect your job or your performance." She whispers, "However, it can be a lot of fun trying to hide it from everyone." She winks.

"Don't be ridiculous. There's nothing going on between us." I stand up to leave.

"That's not what it looked like when you were sandwiched together in the entrance of your cube. You looked quite cozy."

What is it with sandwiches today? "You're crazy. Think what you want," I say nonchalantly. "Have a good night. See you tomorrow."

"Whatever you say. I'm here if you ever need to talk." She turns to face her computer. "See you tomorrow, Miss Beautiful."

"Shush."
Light chuckles follow me from her cube.

Chapter 6

Alexa drives like a madwoman. She cuts cars off left and right with her apple-red Beetle. My right hand has a death grip on the door handle, and my left hand presses against the roof.

"It shocks me you don't get speeding tickets. You drive like a speed demon." I watch her profile as I pray we'll get to the restaurant safely. You'd think I'd be used to her driving by now.

Alexa swerves one more time.

She grins just as we leave the tunnel. Her left blinker ticks. "You know I get pulled over all the time. Somehow, I'm able to convince most of the police officers to not give me a ticket. Some are harder than others. Especially if he's a she."

I shake my head and chuckle. "You amaze me."

Alexa yanks the wheel right and then left, almost snapping my neck.

"I don't know why you insisted on driving into the city tonight when we could've taken the PATH."

She slows to a halt and quickly reverses to parallel park. "Because here's a parking spot right in the front of the restaurant. Who needs public transport? Tonight's our lucky night," she exclaims.

I can finally loosen my grip from the door. "You're always surrounded by luck and guardian angels."

"Yeah, but not when it comes to good men. No luck there," she grumbles.

She puts the car in park while I pull my plum lip gloss from my handbag.

"There better be a ginormous amount of delicious food served tonight. I'm starving," I say as I coat my lips.

She checks her phone for messages. "You and your ferocious appetite. It's not fair. I hardly ate anything today, just so I could enjoy the food tonight. I avoided the gym because of Tony."

"Hey, I did Pilates when I got home from work. Don't act like I don't have to work for it." I rub my lips together and toss the gloss back into my handbag.

"Not as much as others anyway," she says.

"Have you ever heard of this place?"

She puts her phone in her bag and pulls out a tube of red lipstick. "No. Supposedly the chef's friend owns the restaurant. We have the place to ourselves. James mentioned it's in the basement, with a very cool atmosphere."

Months ago, I was living alone in a small apartment in rural New Jersey. My routine was the same almost every day. I worked, went home, and exercised in my living room. Sometimes I'd go out for drinks with my friends from work. During the weekends, I spent a lot of time at Lisa's so I could play with my niece, Felicia. Never anything to brag about.

Now I'm happily living in Hoboken. When someone asks me where I live, I'm so proud to tell them. I know it sounds childish, but I feel cool. Every day is different. I love my job, have a great roommate, and enjoy an actual social life. I'm finally living the life I've always wanted. But will this be enough down the road? I've waited so long for this. Will this excitement die down? Will it be what I imagined? I don't think I want to get married and have kids yet, but it would be nice later on. Maybe I should think about that when I actually meet a guy I'd like to marry.

Gerry.

I step out of the car and look at an old red brick building. Maybe it was a factory years ago. The entrance has large arched doors with glistening windows. The sign over the door says *Wine Cellar*.

Before I close my door, I toss my sweater over my arm and peek my head into the car. "Alexa, stop with the lipstick and get out of the car. We should go inside before we're late. It's rude. I'm looking forward to seeing Lisa and James and mingling with Kayla and Matt." I close my door and stand on the sidewalk.

I miss Lisa. Ever since she got married, her time is consumed with being a wife, mother, and psychologist. We don't see each other as much as we used to since I moved. I understand and am happy for her. Her husband is an ER doctor at the local hospital where they live. They are a true power couple. Felicia is my favorite—and only—niece. James and Felicia have completed Lisa's life. Once Lisa met him, her life changed for the better. She found her prince.

During her difficult years after the car accident, I was the one she opened up to. It was my shoulder she cried on. I cheered her up when she was down. Even if I was down or stressed, I played the peppy and positive one. I hid my sadness from everyone. But then again, no one seemed to care how I was doing. The focus was always on her and Dad.

One day, it would be nice to have someone to share my dreams with. Someone who'll push me past my limits. To finally let go and be spontaneous. Someone I can show all my moods to without judgment. The good things and the bad. Again, Gerry jumps into my mind. Even after my embarrassing moments around him, he's never made me feel uncomfortable. I don't know him, but he's had an interesting life already. I'm envious, but maybe that's why I find him so appealing.

I tap my shoe obsessively on the pavement. "Alexa, for the love of Pete, would you please get out of the car. You know I like to be punctual."

She finally gets out and walks over to me. "Pipe down over there. This humidity is a killer. My hair is like a fucking Chia pet. I need to look my best just in case the chef's a hottie."

"Speaking of hottie, I don't want to talk about Gerry or my job. Okay? I'm not in the mood to talk about my sunglasses fiasco, even if it is really funny. Let me enjoy myself."

"You never used the word *hottie* before when describing Gerry. Very interesting." She scrutinizes me. "However, if you don't want to focus on his hotness tonight, we can focus on the food. With blindfolds on, we'll be too busy spilling food on ourselves because we can't see anything."

I tense and clear my throat. "Remember, not a peep about what I told you the other day at the gym."

She crosses her heart. "I hope you can enjoy yourself tonight."

I shrug my shoulders. "I should be fine. Hopefully, the food will keep me distracted."

She weaves her arm through mine, and we walk inside. We're greeted with a staircase of creamy white exposed stone. Lovely shades of soft orange flow through them, giving off a natural tone.

"Wow. This staircase is beautiful," I say as I brush the stone with my fingers to enjoy the cool, rough surface as we walk down the stairs. It's a bit chilly in here but a nice change from the warm air outside.

Voices echo around us as we descend to the cellar. I hear Lisa's laugh among the guests. Alexa and I peek our heads into the room, and we're rendered speechless. The spectacular space is long and narrow, like a tunnel. Thousands of matching stones from the stairway cover the walls and the high, rounded ceiling. Several wine barrels are stacked neatly in two corners. Running along one wall is a huge wine rack filled with hundreds of wine bottles. I've never seen anything like this.

We turn to the right and are welcomed by a server with a tray of sparkling champagne flutes filled to the rim. Alexa and I look at each other and happily take one.

We clink the flutes together. "Cheers," we say in unison.

She didn't look at me, just like Gerry said. *Don't think about him, and don't tell her about the seven years of bad sex. She'd freak.*

I look around to see if there are any familiar faces. I wave to a couple of people I know. Then see James, Matt, and Kayla near the wine barrels.

"Isn't this place great?" Lisa says behind me.

I turn around with a big smile. She pulls me into her arms and gives me a tight hug. I almost spill my champagne down her back. Instead it flows onto my hand and drips onto the floor.

"Be careful, killer. I just spilled my champagne. There's no good reason to waste it." I shake my hand to get the bubbly off.

"Sorry. I couldn't help myself." She gives Alexa a big hug too. "I've missed you both so much."

Lisa flips a strand of Alexa's hair. "I've never seen your hair this long. It looks great."

She fluffs her hair. "Thanks. I've been growing it out for a while. Tina isn't the only one who wants to try something new."

"Well, I wouldn't know, since you haven't visited in so long." Lisa glances at Alexa and then to me. "You haven't either."

"Okay, Mom," Alexa mocks.

Lisa stifles a laugh and smiles. "I don't care. I'm just so excited you're both here."

"I've missed you too. My job is crazy right now. Alexa keeps our weekends entertaining." I nudge Alexa.

"How's little Felicia?" Alexa asks.

Lisa's shoulders droop. "She's home with Beth and hopefully asleep. It was hard to leave the house because she only wants her daddy right now. The terrible twos have arrived. It's not easy for Beth to deal with the dogs either. Speaking of James, he's over there with Matt. Go say hello. I need to use the bathroom."

I stroll over to the guys with Alexa trailing behind me. "Hey there, both of you," I say as I hug James and then Matt.

"It's about time you two showed up. You're the last ones to arrive," James teases.

Alexa hip checks him. "We're fashionably late by two minutes, big brother. That's not bad. I found prime parking right in front." She ruffles his hair.

"You're a pain in my ass." He smooths out his hair, then tries to do the same to her. She dodges him and rushes over to Matt while giggling.

"Thanks for inviting us, Matt. This place is awesome. I can't wait to eat," I say.

Alexa bumps elbows with Matt. "Hey, is the chef cute?"

He crinkles his face. "Alexa, I'm a guy. I don't think about those things. But from what I've heard, other women think so."

She beams. "I get first dibs on him," she says loud enough for the other women to hear. She's already marking her territory, and she hasn't even met him yet.

Kayla scoots near Matt. "Hey, girls. I'm so glad you could make it." She gives us both hugs.

She tugs on Matt's arm. "Sorry to interrupt, but we need to start."

"Sure." He looks our way. "Please take your seats."

"Lisa has a table for us," James says as he leads the way to our seats.

Matt taps his champagne glass a couple of times with a knife to get our attention. Kayla stands next to him with a smile the size of Texas. "Hello, ladies and gentlemen. Thanks for coming to this special taste-testing evening. I have a feeling most of you, if not all of you, have never done this before. Am I right?"

Silence.

"That's what I thought." He confirms with a smirk.

"We have a special treat for you tonight. So why don't you find yourself a seat so we can begin. There are six tables that sit four each."

As Lisa comes back from the bathroom, I hang my sweater over the chair and take my seat next to Alexa.

Kayla addresses the group. "Thanks for coming tonight. I'm really excited you're here. As some of you know, my German cousin is a famous chef in France and Germany."

"He's the one who introduced me to Kayla when she was visiting him in France," Matt adds.

What the hell is it with Germany or Europe in general lately? I'm surrounded by it. I try so hard not to think about Gerry or Number One, and they're practically thrown in my face.

Alexa leans toward me. "What's with Germany these past days?" she whispers.

"I was just wondering that myself."

Lisa taps my leg with her foot to be quiet.

"He graduated from one of the top culinary schools in France. He's considered one of the youngest chefs to reach executive-chef status with a Michelin star for his restaurant in Hamburg, Germany. He's a pure natural. He decided to visit the US to take some time off. He had so much fun he decided to stay for a while. It's a great honor to have him as our chef for dinner tonight and at our wedding too." She beams with pride.

Whispers and giggles echo off the stone walls.

"One of the things he's famous for is his blind taste testing. It's a unique way to enjoy your meal, even though it can be a bit messy." She giggles.

A woman I don't know raises her hand. "You keep saying *cousin*. What's his name again? Isn't it something strange?"

Kayla laughs. "It's definitely not a common name. Blame my aunt and uncle. I don't know what they were thinking. His name is Gervais Raphael. He'll introduce himself at the end of the meal. He's busy in the kitchen."

I lean over the table and ask Lisa, "Have you or James ever met him before?"

"I haven't, but James did once or twice. Matt's worked with him several times when he was training in Paris to become a pastry chef. I've heard he's very handsome. Maybe you can give him your number."

"Whatever. We both know that'll never happen, though I'd be his dream date since I love to eat. Alexa already called first dibs."

"I sure did," Alexa says as she wipes her red lipstick off her champagne glass.

Matt chimes in again. "Here's how the evening will flow. You'll be given a black velvet blindfold before the first course is served. Once you put it on, you'll notice a difference in your senses immediately.

Take your time and enjoy the food by smelling, tasting, and feeling the texture without seeing it. It'll truly be a different experience. Try to guess what you're eating. I'll tell you what it was after you've finished each course."

Kayla takes over. "We'll start off with a traditional French hors d'oeuvre that won't be served at our wedding. When the main course is served, you'll be given two different small portions to test. One is a traditional French entrée, and the other is a traditional German one. At the end of the evening, you'll be given a card to fill out with your choice. Matt has recommended a dessert for tonight, but he's not the one making it."

Boos ring out throughout the room.

Kayla lifts her hands up. "Sorry, everyone. Tonight's all on my cousin."

"I've never eaten true French or German food before. Well, maybe I have. Sauerkraut is German, right?" I say.

Everyone at the table chuckles.

Alexa crinkles her nose. "There better not be sauerkraut. It's so nasty. I came here for a gourmet meal."

Matt walks over to a table near him. He picks up black blindfolds and hands them out. I receive mine and inspect it. Pure black velvet. Very sexy. The blindfold I had years ago was a dishtowel. Nice upgrade.

"You can take your blindfold home with you," Matt yells over the loud group.

"I wouldn't mind taking these home. It could be a lot of fun," James whispers to Lisa.

Her face flashes bright red.

Alexa reaches over the table and smacks his arm. "We can hear you. Don't gross us out. We don't need to know what you two do in the bedroom."

James waggles his eyebrows. "Who says it would be in the bedroom?" he instigates.

Alexa covers her ears. "La-la-la. I'm not listening."

"Fight nice, children," Lisa jokes.

James and Alexa are always a riot when they're together.

Matt speaks up. "I hope you listened to our instructions and didn't wear expensive clothes. It's guaranteed you'll spill some food. I suggest laying your cloth napkin on your lap. Don't worry if you spill something. There's plenty of food, so you'll be served more if you'd like. As you can see, there are no candles on the table, to prevent a chance of fire."

Loud chatter fills the room.

"I'm serious. Once you're blindfolded, you'll become disoriented and want to shuffle your hands around the table." Matt walks between the tables toward the kitchen. "I've done this before, so I know what I'm talking about."

"Someone should film us," Alexa says as she shakes out her napkin and places it on her lap. "I can't wait for the wedding. It'll be fun to dress up for once. Maybe there'll be some eligible bachelors for Tina and me to pick from." She lightly jabs my arm.

"I thought you wanted the chef?" James baits her.

She taps her chin. "Oh, right. I already forgot about him. Let's wait and see when he introduces himself."

Matt returns from the kitchen. He claps his hands. "Okay, everyone. It's time for the first course. On the count of three, blindfolds on. One, two, three. Ensure you can't see anything. No peeking at any time. I'll be watching you," he says playfully. "Kayla and I wish you a memorable experience. The servers will wait a few minutes to serve the first dish so you can orient yourselves and figure out your silverware."

A glass topples over on our table. "Shit. First spill of the night. I hope it was my water and not my champagne," Lisa mumbles while laughing.

"Everyone ready?" Matt asks loudly.

Some say yes. Some hoot and holler.

I cringe as memories come flooding back from the time when Larissa put the blindfold over my eyes. I imagine I'm in that room right now, but then I'm happily distracted by Lisa's giggles and Alexa swearing like a drunken sailor every two seconds.

I'm adjusted to the darkness, so I proceed to carefully feel around for my silverware and figure out where my water and champagne are.

It's eerie how I can clearly hear the other guests. A couple of women worry they're going to ruin their clothes. Someone says they're scared of the dark. Why are they here then? Dishes clatter in the kitchen as one loud male voice yells commands. There's something familiar about the voice.

"The servers are now bringing the dishes. Please be careful, and sit still until you are served," Matt instructs.

"I'm afraid to move. He makes it sound so scary," Alexa mumbles. "I just want to eat."

A breeze tickles my neck as a server passes behind me and places our plates on the table. A slight scraping of a plate alerts me. "Bon appetite," says the happy server.

"Take it slow, and enjoy the process," Matt says.

The only thing I can think of is Number One's kiss and how he tasted and smelled. Nothing will beat that experience. But I need to focus on the food and not about what happened after the kiss. No need to ruin my evening.

I lean my head down to smell the food first. It doesn't have a strong smell, but I believe it's meat. "I don't think it's fish," I say to anyone who wants to listen.

"I'd have to say something with meat. Isn't France known for pâté?" James adds. "But what do I know?"

"Well, I hope it's not liver or snails. The thought of it gives me the willies," Alexa groans.

"Let's feel around and see if we need our forks." I hear shuffling of silverware.

My fingers trace the rough, peaked edges of three different pieces. Each one is about the size of my palm. My mind processes what my fingers connect with. The first guess is a slice of toasted baguette. The lumpy substance spread on the top sticks to my finger like paste. Then I feel a chilled compote of some kind. I bring my finger to my nose. It smells fruity.

"I'm eating it with my hands. I don't care if I make a mess." Without hesitation, I bite into it.

Crunching, moans and compliments circulate throughout the cellar.

"Ooooh. This is delicious. If this is what's considered pâté, I love it." My voice rises in excitement as I wiggle in my seat. "The fruity mixture complements it with a tangy sweetness. I think it's apricot. The crisp bread is perfectly toasted and buttery." I munch on the next piece.

"It tastes like pork," Lisa adds with less enthusiasm.

She never enjoys food like I do.

"I never thought I'd say something tickles my taste buds, but this dish definitely does," says Alexa. "I like the chef even more…"

"That's what we like to hear," interrupts Matt.

I twitch in response, as if his mouth is right next to my ear.

"Matt, you scared them. Behave," says Kayla at the table next to ours. Matt and Kayla aren't blindfolded.

"Sorry, baby."

Kissing noises fill my ears. I'm so envious. Will I ever have that?

"It looks like everyone's finished with the first course. I hope you enjoyed it. The servers are ready to take the dishes away. Again, be careful," Matt emphasizes.

"Keep your blindfolds on. The hors d'oeuvre you just ate was a type of pâté called pork rillettes with pickled dried apricots," Kayla explains.

"Ha! I was right. I said apricots. Now I can say I've eaten pâté."

Over the next thirty minutes, we're fed two luscious dishes. After we finish, Matt explains one dish was juicy beef roulade with a succulent red wine sauce. I never ate beef that melted in my mouth like that. The other dish was a tasty lamb extravaganza, but I didn't care for the consistency of the meat. The beef gets my vote.

"Now it's time for the finale. Again, this won't be served at the wedding, but I'm sure you'll love this dessert. It's one of my favorites," Matt says.

I hope this is a dessert I've never tried before. The scraping of a dish grabs my attention again. I'm cautious while touching this course just in case it's liquid or ice cream. My fingers glide over the slightly peaked surface. It's pretty large. There's a powdery substance on top. I rub my fingers together and then lick one. Powdered sugar. I inspect every angle until one of my fingers comes in contact with a fluffy cream sandwiched between two pastry-like layers. I imagine a huge cream puff. I taste the cream on my finger. It's light and airy. My first thought is a delicious vanilla cloud.

My fingers skim the bottom of the cream puff and touch a smooth, warm liquid or sauce. I dab my finger on my tongue and melt when I taste bittersweet dark chocolate sauce. I moan in delight. I haven't taken a bite yet, but I'm already in love.

I have no idea how to eat this. Like a sandwich or with a fork and knife? Searching for my fork, my hand brushes against something else on my plate. Stemmed bundles of smooth tiny balls lay in my hand. Berries of some sort. I lift them to my nose. They don't smell like anything. I pluck two of them and lay them carefully on my tongue. They burst in my mouth as I suck on them, leaving a sour sizzling twang on my tongue. I pucker in response. "Wow, these berries are sour." There are pits inside, which I take out of my mouth with my fingers. I hate pits in fruit.

The tartness makes my lips and tongue tingle and burn. I search for my water and take a big gulp. The burning sensation intensifies. I drink some more, but it doesn't help. This is more than being sour. I think I'm allergic. I begin to panic and automatically swiftly move my hands around, knocking over glasses. "Something's wrong with me. My lips and tongue are burning and swelling. Maybe I'm having an allergic reaction to these berries. I don't know what they are. I'm sorry. I need to take my blindfold off." My hands shake with fear as my stomach turns.

I pull my blindfold off, as do the others.

James's eyes bulge out of his head. "Holy shit, Tina." He jumps out of his chair and is at my side before I can blink. I push my chair away from the table. Some other guests rush over and surround me.

Kayla stands up and yells, "Gerry. Please come out of the kitchen. Hurry."

Gerry?

I hear quick footsteps stomping toward our table. "What's the matter, Kayla?"

There's no fucking way. I don't want to turn around because I already know it's him. My stomach twists like a screw. He walks quickly around the table, and our eyes meet.

He does a double take. "Tina?" he says in utter surprise. He rushes to my side and takes hold of my hand.

"Gerry? What are you..." I try to ask, but my lips and tongue continue to increase in size. Spit comes out of my mouth more than words. I grab my napkin and cover my mouth with it. "Don't look at me." I turn away as tears gather in my eyes.

"He's Mr. Clean?" Alexa's voice reaches a high octave.

I shoot daggers at her. She pulls back instantly.

Lisa's head darts to Alexa. "Mr. Clean?"

Matt cuts in. "Gerry, you know Tina? How?"

"Can we please focus on Tina? She's having an allergic reaction to the food," James, the doctor, yells.

Pure silence controls the room.

Gerry looks into my eyes. "Yes. I'm the chef." He directs his response toward me, not the entire group.

James interrupts. "Are you having trouble breathing? Does your throat itch? Does your stomach hurt?" he asks. "Your eyes are tearing. Do they itch?"

"My eyes are tearing out of embarrassment, not the berries," I sputter. "It's just my tongue and lips," I lisp.

"Do you have any allergies?"

I nod and point to the berries.

"They're called currants," Gerry says.

"Shit, I don't have medicine on me," James exclaims. He swerves around to face everyone. "Does anyone have antihistamines?" No one speaks up.

Of course, no one has anything. "You need to go to the hospital immediately to get some medicine, or at least to a pharmacy. Sometimes a food allergy can worsen within twenty-four hours after you ingest the food. I can take you." James stands up.

I pull my hand away from Gerry's. "No. Alexa." I elbow Alexa.

She grabs my hand. "Yes, I'll take her. There's a hospital not too far from here."

Gerry steps back as I stand up.

Alexa looks at Lisa and James. "Don't worry. She'll be fine. I'll call you later with an update. You need to get the train back to Jersey."

Lisa gives me a comforting hug. "Call us as soon as you can to let us know what's happening."

I nod.

Gerry tugs on my arm. "Let me go with you. I'm worried."

I shake my head. His shoulders slump.

"Fine. Let me walk you out then." He waits for us to move ahead of him.

We sprint up the stairs. Behind us, Lisa questions, "Alexa, are you sure there's a hospital nearby?"

She nods as we walk out the door. Her car lights flash as she unlocks the doors.

"Are you going to St. Michael's Hospital?" Gerry asks.

"Yes. It's only five minutes from here, and the traffic is quiet this time of night. I'll take good care of her. Thanks for tonight. The food was delicious." Alexa walks around to the driver's side of the car.

Gerry opens the car door for me. I slide into my seat and twist toward him, my mouth always covered by my hand.

He bends down. "I'm so sorry." His eyes filled with concern.

One tear tries to tip over, but I force it back just like I always do. I say as clear as possible with my swollen lips and tongue, "I said one more time, and I'm off the project. You know what this means." I pivot in my seat and grab the door handle.

He steps away. "Tina. Please don't."

"We need to go," Alexa urges.

I close the door before he can say another word.

Alexa speeds away as I watch him in the side mirror. His back is slouched, and his head is in his hands. I lean my head back on the seat and try to dissect what just happened. Every emotion shoots to my pulsating lips and tongue. Anger, sadness, disappointment, and embarrassment. Whichever the combination is, I can't stand it and want to hit something hard with a bat.

I open the overhead mirror but hesitate to look at myself. I'm scared to see how hideous I look. It'll only increase my embarrassment. I open my eyes and wince. "I look like a fish that lives in radiated water. How can my lips expand like this without exploding?"

"Stop talking. It's hard to understand you. We'll be at the hospital in a minute. How are you holding up? You aren't having trouble breathing, right? As long as you can breathe, I think you'll be fine." She taps my arm in sympathy.

My swollen lips and tongue aren't the problem. I can't believe Gerry is a famous chef. He knows Matt and is Kayla's cousin. What are the odds? He's not only my client but a friend of the family. There's no way I can avoid him now. This makes it worse. There's only one way out of this.

I need to get off this project. It's all too much for me. We don't have a normal business relationship. It's even more complicated now with the connection to Matt. I wish I could talk to Alexa, but I can't speak.

"Gerry's definitely a hottie. Especially in that black chef uniform. Good for you. I didn't know how to read his face when he saw you. He was shocked, but his eyes lit up until he realized you were swelling up like a tick. Panic took over then. He's definitely got the hots for you—I don't care what you say."

I grunt in response. First, I need to get this allergy taken care of, and then I'll worry about him. It's clear there's something between us. The question is, what am I going to do about it?

Chapter 7

Gerry

I stomp over to Matt. "How do you know Tina?" I'm angry, but I don't know if it's toward Matt, myself, or the damn currants. They have nothing to do with this.

He looks at me, perplexed. He gestures toward a woman. "This is Lisa. She's Tina's sister and James's wife."

I look at Lisa. It's hard to believe they're sisters. She's short, has light-brown hair and big blue eyes. Complete opposite of Tina.

I scrub my hands up and down my face, ignoring the fact we're surrounded by an audience. Maybe I need a necklace to yank on.

"The question now is, how do *you* know her?" needles Kayla.

James and Lisa inch closer with obvious curiosity.

"I hired the company she works for to create a new website for my restaurant. She's the project manager. I never told her I'm a chef. It never came up, since we just met. We were both caught off guard just now."

"What a coincidence," Lisa comments. "No wonder she acted the way she did when she saw you. But...why did Alexa call you Mr. Clean?"

A couple of guests behind her laugh. I'm not sure I want to know.

"Matt, can I talk to you in the kitchen? *Alone.* It's important," I say.

"Yeah. Sure." He turns to Kayla, Lisa, and James. "We'll be right back." He rests a palm on Kayla's shoulder. "Maybe it's time the guests leave and you add up their votes for the main dish."

She nods and walks over to one of the tables.

I move swiftly to the kitchen, with Matt trailing behind me. The crew is busy cleaning the dishes and wiping down the stainless-steel counters.

Matt leans against the counter and crosses his arms. "So what's up with you, man? James confirmed Tina will be fine. It's not your fault she had a reaction."

"I know but I can't help worrying about her," I say as I pace back and forth while pulling a dish towel through my hand. "But that's not what I want to talk about." I take a couple of deep breaths.

"Was it harder than you thought to cook tonight? I know you haven't done it in a while."

"Actually, it felt pretty damn good, but that's not why I'm upset." I stop pacing. "Do you remember the story I told you about how I came up with the blindfolded taste-test idea?"

A smile grows on his face. "Yes. The kissing game at Kayla's brother's frat party." He lets out a laugh. "Why are you bringing this up now? Did she have an allergic reaction to your kiss?"

I flick a rat's tail on his arm with my towel.

"Ow! What the hell is your problem?" His voice rises as he massages his arm. "You're acting like a fucking lunatic. What has you so pissed off?"

"I'm trying to tell you. Can you please be serious now?" I push up my sleeves.

"Sorry. Yes. But can you take your anger out on the dishes or pots, not me?"

I throw the towel on the counter. "Tina is the girl I kissed. My muse."

His eyes go wide. "What? No way. That can't be possible." He pulls his hands through his hair. "How do you even remember what she looks like?"

I put my finger over my mouth. "Keep your voice down." With good timing, one of my cooks drops a lid from a pot on the floor.

"Please wash it again," I yell to the cook. He sighs and puts it back in the sink.

"I recognized her instantly. She looks even more attractive now." I stuff my hands in my pockets.

"I can't believe it's Tina. Of all people. Are you sure? This is something you don't screw around with."

"One hundred fifty percent," I declare.

Matt throws his hands up. "Wait. Does she know you were one of the guys?" Now he starts pacing.

"I don't think so. She gives me no reason to think she does. But how would she? She never saw me after we kissed. I took off before she could. She only saw me once from a distance before the game. I've changed since then. I had more hair and was thinner." I stroke my shaved head with my hand.

Matt laughs. "I know what you mean. Becoming a chef doesn't help us stay thin, does it?" He pats his big stomach.

"Speak for yourself. At least I work out when I can."

"Back to Tina. Now you're working together and are both connected to me. That's just bizarre in itself. How's your business relationship?"

"We've had some really awkward moments. I'm more attracted to her now than I was all those years ago. I think she feels the same. Now there's no avoiding each other. To top it off, she told me outside she wants to be pulled off the project." I massage the back of my neck with both hands to relieve the stiffness.

Kayla walks into the kitchen. "Matt, it's getting late. James and Lisa need to get the next train out. We also have that large pastry order that needs to be ready by nine tomorrow morning."

He kisses her forehead. "No problem, babe. Just give us one more minute."

She smiles and leaves the kitchen.

To occupy my nervous hands, I polish one of the already sparkling stainless-steel counters. "Thanks for listening. Please don't tell anyone who Tina is. Not even Kayla. I'll need to tell Tina at some point. I want her to hear it from me. Only a couple of people know the *full* story of how I came up with the blindfold thing."

"You got it, man. My lips are sealed. If you need to talk, you know where to find me." We fist bump. "Good luck. Don't wait too long to tell her. It'll only make things worse. She might not be happy when she finds out who you are." He turns to walk out but steps back in. "But then again, maybe she won't care. It was only a college game."

I salute him. "Thanks. Talk to you soon. Sorry about the interruption tonight."

Oops. Which entrée won? I rush out of the kitchen. James is on the phone in the corner of the room, and most of the guests have left. "Hey, Kayla, you didn't tell me which entrée won."

Everyone looks at her. "The beef roulade was the winner. Not everyone likes lamb. Both tasted divine to me. Thanks again for tonight, Gerry," she responds as she squeezes Matt around the waist.

Just as I thought. That's my favorite German dish to make and eat. It's a traditional one that always takes me back to my childhood, when my grandmother would make it for me on a cold, rainy day. I'd walk into my house after school and glide into the kitchen, following the aroma of the delicious, bubbling sauce.

My passion to cook started at an early age. Since I was the only child, I'd entertain myself by watching my mother and grandmothers in the kitchen. They would let me make up my own concoctions. Some were immediately thrown out or fed to the dog. Sometimes the dog wouldn't even eat it. He'd whine and run to the corner of the room. Those recipes were thrown into the fireplace.

Despite my many errors, cooking came easy, like a chemist creating his potions. My family always ate roulade at Christmastime. I never heard anyone say they didn't like it other than vegetarians. Food critics always raved about it.

Matt's wedding will be the second event I've catered since I left the cooking scene in Germany a year ago. Yes, I have my own restaurant, but I'm not the chef. I give pointers and suggestions for the menu, but I don't run the kitchen. My employees don't even know

I'm a chef. But, man, did it feel good to be back in the kitchen tonight.

James puts his phone in his pants pocket. "That was Alexa. She said Tina's already received medicine. She'll be fine but was told to stay home from work tomorrow."

My shoulders relax. "That's a relief. I'm glad to hear she'll be okay."

This whole night is surreal. I haven't cooked for anyone like this in a year. Of all things, Tina's one of the guests. No matter the situation, something weird happens with her.

I walk them to the stairs. "Since the roulade won, Kayla, once you give me the final head count, I'll go ahead and order everything. Don't worry about a thing. The kitchen's taken care of for the first and second course. Matt is responsible for the dessert and wedding cake. I'd like to enjoy your wedding too. Now go enjoy being single for a little while longer."

"Sounds good. I'll email you the final count, including how many vegetarian requests, within the next week or so. Are you bringing a date?" Kayla asks.

I shake my head. "No way. I'll be too busy to take care of one."

Now that I know Tina will be there, my eyes will only be on her. Something tells me she won't make it easy for me.

Matt smacks me on the shoulder. "Thanks for everything. All the guests raved about the food and how fun it was. Some of the women asked if you're single. They might track you down at the wedding."

I wipe my brow. "Then I'm not leaving the kitchen."

We all laugh.

I shake Lisa's and James's hands. "It was nice to meet you, Lisa."

"It was a pleasure meeting you finally. I've heard a lot about you from Matt. We'll see you at the wedding."

"Enough talking everyone." Kayla motions for them to go to the stairs. "Lisa and James need to get to the train." She gives me a quick hug. "Thanks, cousin. You're the best."

Chapter 8

Tina

I can't hide in my bed all morning. I touch my face as I run to the bathroom to look in the mirror. I look normal, but I don't feel normal. The only thing that's on my mind is Gerry. He's a chef. A damn sexy, famous chef. Even as I was swelling up, I still noticed how he looked. I never thought I'd think a man dressed in a chef's coat could be that hot. But the black one he wore changed my mind. I swear, the noise in my brain is like a Formula One car competing in a race.

I send Thomas an email explaining what happened last night and that I'm not going to be in today. I need to think about what I'm going to do. Thankfully, I have a great team, and they'll be fine without me there.

If I ask Thomas to take me off the account, I'll disappoint him and mostly myself. He's counting on me. I need to prove myself, so I can't let my emotions or hormones interfere with my performance.

I'm supposed to rest today, but I'm too antsy. When I'm like this, I exercise or clean. After thirty minutes, the bathroom sparkles like a diamond. All due to the Mr. Clean products under the sink. Not helpful to keep my mind off Gerry.

My stomach churns when I replay the mortifying events of the past weeks since I've met him. As long as I do a superb job, I don't care if I look like a pirate or a raccoon or diseased fish. Well, I care a little bit, because I like being around him. We hardly know each other, but I can't ignore my desire to see him, talk to him, or touch him.

When he calls or sends me emails, I become giddy like a programmer who just downloaded a new app. Even if our phone calls are only business, I still get excited.

The doorbell rings just as I'm about to turn on the vacuum in the living room. Who can this be in the middle of the morning? I haven't even showered. The doorbell rings again, and I look through the peephole. It looks like a delivery guy of some kind. I crack the door open. "Hello. How can I help you?"

"I have a package for Tina Schmitt."

"That's me." I open the door wider.

"Please sign here." He extends the electronic signature machine.

After I sign it, he hands me the package and walks away.

"Thanks," I say as I shut the door.

The package is smaller than a shoe box. I flip it around. Only my name and address are on it. I can't find any scissors in the kitchen, so I opt for a steak knife. I cut through the tape and open it slowly. It could be a bomb for all I know.

Definitely not a bomb, but sweet enough to make my heart quake. Inside is a bag of black licorice, a purple rose, and a note. Even though I don't want to think about him, I can't help but feel warm and fuzzy. I lift the handwritten note. I wonder if he actually wrote it or if someone else wrote it for him.

Dear Tina,

I'm sorry about last night. Please don't back out of our project. Let's talk before you make any decisions.

I hope the licorice helps you feel better. The purple rose is to make you smile. You deserve your own roses. Not ones taken from your roommate who doesn't appreciate her own.

Thinking of you,

Gerry

Well, that doesn't make it any easier. How did he know I was home, and how did he get my address?

This is the third ring of his cell phone. I should disconnect before voicemail picks up. Maybe it's a sign I shouldn't speak to him. I guess one o'clock in the afternoon isn't the best time to call him at the restaurant. I pull laundry out of the dryer and put it into a basket.

"Maier speaking."

I twitch and almost drop the phone.

I hear his demanding voice and the sound of people in the background. Someone requests a table for four in the beer garden. Definitely a bad time to call.

"Hello. Anybody there?"

I hesitate one more second. "Hi, Gerry. It's Tina. Is this a bad time?"

His voice changes to soft and sweet. "No, not at all. Let me go to my office, where it's quieter."

I hear some shuffling and people talking to him. Then a door closes.

"Now I can talk. I'm glad you called. How are you? I've been thinking about you."

Butterflies whip up a storm in my stomach.

"I feel fine today. The medicine kicked in right away. I just wanted to call to say thank you for my little present. It was a nice surprise. I've never gotten something like that before. It brightened my day." I teeter back and forth on my heels and almost fall backward.

"I'm glad. It's the least I could do after what happened last night. I think we were both surprised. I can't believe you know Matt and Kayla."

"Funny coincidence, isn't it?" I lift the little vase to smell the purple rose. "And I can't believe you're a chef. You were the last person I expected to see last night, especially when I was swollen with hives."

I hear commotion in the background.

"Can't it wait? I'm on the phone," Gerry says firmly.

"No, it can't. A delivery is here, and it looks like someone messed up the order," a man explains.

Gerry grunts. "I'll be there in a second.

"Tina, I'm sorry. I need to go."

"No problem. It's obviously busy over there. We can talk in a few days. Have a good afternoon." I linger because I don't want to get off the phone. I wish I could see him, even though I shouldn't.

I'm about to swipe End, but hear his voice again.

"Tina, wait a second."

Excitement kicks in again. "I'm still here. Do you need something?" *Please ask me out.*

It's quiet for a couple of seconds. I press the phone hard against my ear in anticipation to what he's going to say.

"Can I see you this afternoon?" he mumbles as if he's in battle with himself. "Even if it's only for coffee. We need to talk."

Okay! Stay calm and cool. "Sure. But don't you need to work?"

"Yes, but I'm the manager. I can do what I want. The assistant manager starts in an hour. I can leave after that. I need to take a quick shower though."

Don't think about him naked in the shower! Think of cleaning the toilet again! "S...sounds gr...great. Would you like me to come into the city?" I say as I skip to my bedroom to see what's in my closet.

"No. I want to see what Hoboken's like. Do you want me to pick you up at your place, or would you rather we meet somewhere else?"

I think it's better to meet somewhere other than my apartment. Neutral territory. I don't know if I can trust myself. Maybe this is only a business meeting. My gut says it isn't. "There's a nice café down the street from my place, called Blue Moon. Why don't we meet there?"

"It doesn't matter to me. I just want to spend time with you without our jobs, families, or friends getting in the way."

Wow. This is definitely not a business meeting. I'm squealing in my head.

"I'll send you a text message with the address and what bus you can take. Unless you have a car. Just let me know what time." I hear someone else call his name in the distance. "You'd better go."

"I need to take a bus, so please send the information. I should be able to meet you around four. When I'm on the way, I'll send you a message. I look forward to seeing you." He hangs up before I can respond.

Did I just agree to go on a date with him? I shake my head. Nooo. We're two adults meeting for coffee. It's harmless.

Every day, I say I'll keep this platonic. Within seconds of seeing him or hearing his voice, that flies right out the window. I've been controlling my emotions for years. But when I'm with him, it's hard to hold back.

I'm playing with fire.

I love it!

Chapter 9

Gerry

Nothing has gone smoothly since I spoke to Tina. Deliveries were messed up, one of the cooks cut his finger and had to go to the hospital, and a large vat of pumpkin soup fell off the stove, which covered my jeans and half the kitchen floor. I hardly had time to shower and change my clothes in order to catch the bus I'm on right now. That's one benefit of living near the restaurant.

Tina and I need to talk. To discuss business. I have no idea if she requested to be removed from the project. However, I want to get to know her on a personal level. If she'd be off the project, it would be a lot easier for us to spend time together.

I took a big risk sending her that package today. If there's no connection between us, she could've easily been offended and complained to her manager. I just wanted to make her smile and let her know I was thinking about her. More than I should be.

I'm one stop away, I text her.

I'm already here. I look forward to seeing you.

Now that she has reappeared in my life, I won't let her go so easily. But how can I tell her who I am? Would she even remember the game? Maybe it was no big deal to her. I walked away without finishing it. Then again, maybe I wasn't the guy she picked. I really don't believe that. We exchanged something that couldn't possibly have been one sided. But it was just a ridiculous college game. Maybe I should never tell her. I'd grab my hair in frustration, but I don't have any.

My heart races as I ascend the stairs to the café's entrance. When I open the door, a bell clangs overhead. Not necessarily my way of entering a room. Now the entire world knows I'm here. I'm greeted with a smile by a young purple-haired barista.

The entire front is large windows. There's a wide white windowpane across the top third of the windows. Along the pane are thick white candles in different sizes and heights. When I look at them longer, they create an awesome illusion of the New York City skyline.

My eyes scan the room for her. The café is almost empty near the front. An older man with glasses on the tip of his nose reads the newspaper. He looks at me and then shuffles the newspaper loudly.

I proceed forward and look around a wall. In a quiet corner, she sits at a table for two. Head down, she's engrossed in a magazine. She hasn't noticed me yet. I pass a large table of girls chatting away while sipping on their frozen coffees.

I sneak up to her. "Hey there."

She twitches and almost knocks her phone off the table. "Gerry, you scared me."

She stands up, and this is when it gets awkward. I want to hug and kiss her.

"Sorry. I didn't mean to scare you."

"It's okay." She sits back down and pulls the spare chair close to her. "Come sit by me." She pats the chair. "My hives are gone."

"I'm glad to see that. I'll probably never give anybody currants again." I angle the chair to face her.

"You have my sweater." She points to the sweater in my hand. "I totally forgot about it last night. I realized I forgot it when I was in the ER. Thanks for bringing it back."

I hand it to her. "A server gave it to me and showed me which chair he found it on. It gave me another reason to see you."

I lean over. "What are you reading? You must like it since you were so distracted by it."

A server interrupts us. We both order double-shot latte

macchiatos and agree to share one slice of Death by Chocolate cake.

"Show me your magazine."

She slides it over to me.

"*Afar*. It looks like a travel magazine. Planning a trip?" I flip through it quickly and then push it back to her. "You like tropical beaches. I noticed the calendar on your cubicle wall."

Her face lights up. "You noticed that?"

"I notice a lot of things. You'd be surprised."

A corner of her mouth rises. "Yes, one of my dreams is to travel to beautiful tropical beaches. I'd love to fly to Fiji and stay in one of those little huts on the water. In Australia, there's Whitehaven Beach. It has one of the whitest sand beaches anywhere. Or maybe even the Maldives." She sighs as she rests her chin on her hands. "One day."

"It sounds awesome. Wearing nothing but a bathing suit and being lazy all day. I couldn't tell you the last time I was on a beach. Not even a Jersey beach."

She shoves the magazine into her bag and leans her elbows on the table. "Enough about beaches. Spill the beans. How did you know I was home, and how did you know where I live? I don't think Thomas would've given it to you."

"Spill the beans? I've never heard that before. Here I thought I'm fluent in English." I shake my head.

She swats my arm playfully. "Stop trying to change the subject. It means confess how you found my address."

"James told us last night you were staying home today. I called Kayla. She has your address because of the wedding invitations."

The corner of her mouth tilts up. "That's a lot of effort for someone you hardly know. You've earned some major brownie points."

I bite my lower lip. "Brownie points? You're killing me here. I'm not familiar with that phrase either."

"Come on. You never heard that from your mom or your cousins? I'm going to have to talk to them about what they're not teaching you," she teases.

"My parents and cousins will be at the wedding, so you can ask them then."

Her eyes flicker for a second.

I shift in my seat. "Enough small talk. Let's be serious. Did it bother you that I sent you a package? Be honest with me. If I make you feel uncomfortable, and you want me to back off, I will." I lift my arms up and lean back. "No explanation needed." I hold my breath, waiting for her response.

She touches the pendant on her necklace. "Your package made me really happy. Especially the purple rose."

I let out my breath.

"But..."

Scheiße. There's a *but*. I'm holding my breath again.

"But I don't know how to react to it. To you. I've never been in this situation before. *Ever*."

I take her delicate hand in mine. "Do I make you nervous? Tell me."

"Sometimes. But for good reasons." She squeezes her eyebrows together. "Why?"

"You seem to play with your necklace when you're stressed or uncomfortable. You've done it a lot every time we've been together."

She lets go of the necklace and shoves her hand between her knees. "Most of the time I don't even notice I'm doing it. My friends and family comment on it all the time."

"When we had our first meeting, I thought you were going to yank it off."

She cocks her head. "I think the mishap with the sunglasses gave me every reason to be nervous. Don't you think?"

"My gut says that wasn't the only reason. You weren't the only one who was nervous." I squeeze her hand gently.

She studies her hand in mine but doesn't pull away. "Why does it seem so natural for you to hold my hand? It makes me wonder what we're doing. I've never felt this level of comfort with any man before. Especially someone I work with. The day I met you, I wished you were an old man with a wart on your nose so I wouldn't feel this attracted to you."

I cup the back of her neck and graze her cheek with my thumb. "I'm not an old man. The man I am would tell you every day you mean the world to me. The man I am wants to pull you on my lap so I can kiss your plump lips. The man I am wants to touch you until you scream in delight. You have no idea what you do to me," I growl.

I take my hand away from her neck and sit back. "But unfortunately, I need to keep my hands to myself, because our business relationship is in the way."

She looks away but won't allow me to take my hand from hers. "No one has ever spoken to me like that before." Her eyes slowly return to mine. "What do you want me to say?"

I hesitate for a moment. "That you want it too."

Chapter 10

Of course I want it. What woman wouldn't? Look at him! I've been fighting it, but I can't anymore. I want him to kiss and touch me. I wouldn't mind doing a couple of things to him either.

"Look at us holding hands, and we hardly know each other. There's a magnet between us that keeps pulling us closer together. But I need to keep my distance from you because of my job. It's very important to me, and I don't want to jeopardize it."

The server arrives with our coffees and cake. My mouth waters when I see the creamy chocolate icing. He motions for me to eat some first. I pull the plate in front of me and cut a big piece with my fork. "One thing you should know about me is I love food. I'll try any type of food once. If you ever need someone to experiment new recipes on, I'm your girl." I sigh as the gooey madness melts in my mouth.

"Unfortunately, another reason to like you." He laughs. "Back to your job. It should be important. But why does it seem it's even more to you?"

He caresses my thigh, and I twitch with pleasure.

He pulls his hand away. "Sorry. I know I shouldn't touch you, but that magnet is pretty strong." He smirks.

I put my fork down and wipe my mouth with a napkin. He eyes the plate.

"Hungry, fella? Eat some."

He smiles and pulls the plate to him.

"Just don't eat it all," I warn.

"Since it's your turn to talk, I should try this and judge how it tastes. Matt's the best baker, so I need to compare."

I watch him munch away, wishing I was his fork.

"Enough interruptions. About your job."

"It's kind of sad."

"Do I need tissues?" he says as a wide grin with a chocolate crumb in the corner forms on his face.

I wipe the crumb off his mouth. "I see someone has a sense of humor. More brownie points."

He laughs while covering his mouth.

I spend the next few minutes telling him about the car accident and how my mom died. "I grieved, but I grieved alone." *Don't tell him everything.* "From the time I was sixteen until a couple years ago, I was like a mom to Lisa. My friends in college called me Mother Hen half the time; I watched over everyone. I was the designated driver, stayed sober to make sure nothing happened to anyone, and was the problem solver."

"I'm sorry to hear about your mom and Lisa."

"Thanks. I can't say I didn't enjoy life, but I couldn't let loose and do stupid things either." My eyes wander around because I can't tell him the full story.

"But things changed a couple of years ago when Lisa met James."

He interrupts me. "Actually, Matt told me a little bit about their story. It's pretty amazing they have a child now."

"Isn't it? Lisa's life changed in so many ways after she met him, and I've never seen her happier. She doesn't need me like she used to, because she has her daughter, Felicia, and James now."

"During the time you took care of everybody else, who took care of you?"

Nobody, because that's the way it should've been. I didn't deserve to be taken care of.

I shrug. "I never really thought about it. I did what I had to do. Yes, it would've been nice to have someone to lean on, but I've always taken care of myself and still do."

He nods but remains quiet.

"So now it's time to focus on me. I took the job at Modern Web to start over, take charge of my life, and to be almost selfish. It's time to spice things up.

"I go out with Alexa, but it's mostly to restaurants, bars, and stores. I live near the city, but I haven't been to a play since high school or gone to the top of the Empire State Building or even gone to one of the multiple museums or art galleries. There's so much I want to do, but I don't even know where to start. And that's just New York City.

"I want to travel more. I've had my passport for a while but have no stamps in it." I press my hand to my chest. Excited energy speeds through my blood.

He flashes his gorgeously crooked smile without saying anything. I could look at his face forever.

"Some of those destinations would be the beaches you mentioned."

"Not just beaches. I'd love to sit in a café with a view of the Eiffel Tower. I dream of Venice and Rome. Maybe Dubai or Tokyo when the cherry trees blossom. Or run through the lavender fields in Provence." I sigh as I envision myself lying in a field of lavender, high on the scent. "But they're only dreams.

"This job is the starting point, because I chose to move away. Granted, it's still my home state, but it's all new. It feels like another world because Hoboken is a big city compared to the little towns I've lived in. Believe it or not, I dreamed of going to college in Southern California. I'd already picked out schools I wanted to apply to...but I threw out the applications after the accident."

"Why California?"

"It was as far away as I could go without leaving the US. I liked the thought of a laid-back surfing lifestyle and beaches. I spent as much of my summers down the Jersey shore as possible. I was so different back then."

He pushes on his temples and closes his eyes.

"What's the matter? Do you have a headache?"

He stops. "I'm trying not to picture you covered in suntan oil and in a bathing suit."

"You're bad. Just think of me as an old lady with a wart on her nose. It works like a charm."

He crinkles his nose.

"Now about work. One of the things that made me really interested in this job is Modern Web has several clients in Southern California. Maybe I'll have the chance to go there for business meetings."

"Do you think that will happen?"

I shrug. "I have no idea. Thomas said there's a chance. The point I'm trying to make is, my job gives me freedom and the challenge I've been longing for. Thomas believes in me, and I want to succeed. That's why I'm so hesitant about us. I feel the strong connection between us, but I can't let that interfere with my job. Do you understand? I need to put *me* first right now."

His face gives nothing away.

I shake his arm. "Tell me what you're thinking."

"So you want to spice things up?"

I nod with interest.

"I just happen to love spice." He grins.

I cross my arms. "Who would've guessed?"

He becomes antsy with excitement. "I have a brilliant idea. Until my website is done, we'll remain friends. It won't be easy. But I'd like to spend time with you outside work. We can explore the city together. I've seen a lot, so I can be your guide sometimes. Something tells me we'd have a lot of fun together."

I pull my hands through my hair. "I've been living a train ride away from the city my entire life, and you've probably seen more of it than me. Won't you get bored showing me around?"

"Never. The difference is, I'll see everything through your cinnamon eyes. It'll be even more fun."

I pull my hair over my shoulder. "You have your restaurant to manage. Don't you work seven days a week?"

"Not if you say yes. I'll make the time. I need to stop working so many hours anyway. It'll give us a chance to get to know each other without getting involved while we work together. It's a win-win. Once our project is finished, we can take it from there." He drums his fingers on the table. "Even though I'd like more. Right now...just friends."

"It isn't easy for me either, but thanks for understanding. We need to be very careful in front of my manager and coworkers. My team's cool, but I don't want them to know we're spending time together outside the office. It's good we don't have a lot of face-to-face meetings planned."

"It's a deal. I'll take anything I can get. If this is the way I'm able to spend time with you and have fun, then I'm happy to oblige. Let's see how our calendars match up. Hopefully, we'll both have time during the weekends and maybe on weeknights. Let's be spontaneous."

I clasp my hands on the table. "Are you sure? I'm not used to being the focus."

"Well, get used to it. At least for the next few weeks. Maybe you'll be sick of me by the end."

"Maybe *you'll* be sick of *me*."

He cocks his head to the side. "Do you really think that'll happen?"

I move my head back and forth. His eyes never leave mine.

I wish I was still at my old company. I wouldn't care if I got fired.

Chapter 11

"Great job, Peggy and Tim. Thomas will be pleased. We're right on schedule for the website to go live the end of September. Let's keep up the momentum. I'm really enjoying this project."

We smile in unison as we close our laptops and push away from the meeting table.

I wish I had a basketful of flowers to throw around as I walk to my cube with my head held high. My team is awesome. As I walk to my chair, I'm surprised by a light-purple envelope placed in the middle of my desk.

I check behind me to make sure no one's looking. *I love being secretive.* My hands shake in anticipation as I open the envelope. Inside is a note and theater tickets for *The Lion King.*

No way! The date is for tomorrow. I open the note. There are no names on it, but I know it's from him.

I couldn't help myself. It's supposed to be great show. Call me to let me know if you have the time. I hope you can make it.

I want to scream out loud in excitement. I do a happy dance instead. After I've had my elated moment, I run my fingers over the tickets. He's the sweetest and so impulsive. Of course I'd love to see *The Lion King.* Other than Lisa, I'm probably the only person who hasn't seen it. She'll be so jealous.

I slip the tickets back into the envelope and put it in my handbag. I'm dying to call him, but I should wait until my lunch break. It's in thirty minutes. That feels like a week right now.

"What are you smiling about?"

I yelp when Peggy speaks next to me. "You just scared the hell out of me."

"Does that smile have to do with you know who?"

I put my finger to my lips. "Be quiet." I need to tell someone. "Do you need to go to the bathroom?"

"No. Why would you ask me..."

I give her a pleading look.

"Oh." She nods. "Yes, I need to pee like a racehorse. Let's go."

We check that all the stalls are empty. Paper towels lie on the floor. How hard is it for someone to throw them in the garbage? I hate litterbugs.

"Am I right? Is it about him? Details, please." She goes to lean against the counter but changes her mind because everything's so wet.

"Yes. Can you please, please, please keep a secret?" I beg her.

"Of course. As I've said, I was in your position once. Spill it."

I tell Peggy everything.

"Isn't it fun? Being a little bit sneaky? It brings back so many exciting memories."

"I love it!" I can't stop grinning. "We're only friends, but it's fun trying to remain just that."

I pretend to wash my hands when a woman walks in. "Hold on a second." I dry my hands and motion to leave.

Next, we hide in the copy room at the far corner, away from the cubes and offices. "I really like him, but I can't let anything happen until this project is finished. Am I being too cautious?" To mute out our conversation, I grab a piece of paper from the garbage to copy.

"Absolutely not. However, I think Thomas would be happy for you. I don't think you have anything to worry about. Unless you screw up this project. But keep it to yourself anyway. People love to gossip. Even though this department is dead, our group knows what's going on with other people."

Well, that doesn't help me feel any better.

She touches my arm. "There are times you just need to take risks. I don't regret meeting my husband at the office. We kept it quiet, but when our coworkers found out, they were thrilled for us. Granted, there were a couple who made their snide comments. But it doesn't matter. Do what is right for you. Either way, you can still have fun with him."

I look at my clock. "Do you need something for lunch? I'm going to the café across the street."

"Nope. I have my lunch at my desk."

Before we leave the room, I grab her arm. "Thanks for listening and for your advice. It's great to have someone to talk to. I'll give you updates as things move along."

"You'd better. I'd be pissed if you didn't. Have a good lunch."

Ten minutes later, I pay for a chicken salad sandwich and wait for it to be prepared. I pull out my phone and dial Gerry's number.

"Hi, Tina," he says, out of breath.

"Everything all right over there? You sound like you were running somewhere." I can hear the constant activity of the restaurant in the background. Why do I always call him during lunchtime?

"I was outside my office when I heard my phone ringing on my desk. Let me close the door. Give me a second." The door squeaks.

"I'm good now. How are you?" Before he closed his office door, he was all business. His voice is rough, as if he was yelling a lot. *Yummy.* As I've said, I'd rather eat him like a sandwich.

"Great because of you. Thank you so much for the purple surprise on my desk. Your brownie points are adding up pretty fast. I don't want to know how you delivered that envelope."

"I have my sources. Would you like to go with me?"

I feel like he just asked me to the prom, which I never went to. "Of course. Have you seen *The Lion King*?"

"I wanted to when I lived in Hamburg, but I never had the time. To get to the theater there you need to take a ferry. It adds to the experience."

I skim the floor with my foot. "It sounds great. Should I meet you at the theater?"

"If you don't mind, I'd like to pick you up and bring you home."

"Don't be ridiculous. It's out of your way. I can take the PATH."

"Just let me pick you up. We can spend more time together." A file cabinet slams shut in the background.

"Sorry. I know you're at work. I'll let you go." My number is called for me to pick up my sandwich. I swerve through the line.

"Never hesitate to call me. When I'm busy, I'll call you back."

"Thank you again. I can't wait to see the show and you," I admit without hesitation.

"I'll pick you up at six o'clock. We can have a drink before the show starts."

My appetite disappears from the excitement. I toss my sandwich in my bag for later.

"It sounds like a plan."

Chapter 12

Gerry

Just as I'm about to press the doorbell, the door swings wide open.

"Hi there. I saw you from my bedroom window." Tina beams. "Come in."

I stroll in and look around. Red curtains…several red and dark-purple pillows spread out along the large black leather couch. The walls in the kitchen are painted red. Interesting. A bit much, but I'm a guy. "I know you like purple, so I'm guessing your roommate loves red."

"Yes, Alexa loves anything red. It's bright like her personality. She has a business dinner tonight."

The cell phone next to her rings. She looks at the screen. "Let me answer this. It's Lisa."

I nod as my eyes follow her every move. Her flowing black skirt shows off her long golden legs. I wonder what she'd do if I trailed my finger up the back of one of them.

"Hey, Lisa. Everything's good. But can I call you back tomorrow? I'm just heading out the door. I'm going to see *The Lion King*. Isn't it cool?" She flashes me a giddy smile.

To distract myself, I scan the living room for clues about what Tina and Alexa are like. Something tells me I'll be able to tell what is Tina's. There's a vase full of dried lavender sprigs. She mentioned something about Provence. Marilyn Monroe coasters are stacked next to the vase. Definitely Alexa's. A rolled-up purple yoga mat leans against the wall next to the TV.

Think about walking on nails instead of how flexible Tina is.

"Who am I going with?" I glance at her. She turns to me with big eyes. "Um, a coworker had an extra ticket. I'll call you tomorrow and let you know how it was. Have a good night. Kisses to Felicia." She taps her phone.

I tilt my head as I move closer to her. "Why did you lie to her? You can say you're with me just as a friend."

"I didn't lie, because you are technically my coworker." She pulls her hand through her shiny hair and whispers, "Do you mind if we keep this a secret from our friends and family too?"

"Why are you whispering? There's no one else here?" I whisper back.

She cocks her hip. "I just want it to be you and me without outside interference. I think it's more fun this way. It's nobody's business what we do together. When she knows, then James knows... You get my point, right? I just want something for myself. She'll find out eventually, but just not now. It gives me a thrill." She bites her lower lip. "Does that make any sense?"

I move closer to her and touch her arm but stop and pull away. *Don't touch her.* "It makes total sense. You want to take care of yourself and do what you want without other people's remarks or opinions. I kind of like it myself. It'll be fun to go out and not worry about anyone around us. Our own little secret for now." I wink at her.

"All right. Let's skedaddle." She tosses a black sweater over her arm and opens the door.

I follow her out. She pulls my arm to go to the right when we exit her apartment building. "We need to take the PATH to the theater."

"What's the word? *Sketattle*?"

"No. It's pronounced *skedaddle*," she says slowly. "It's with *d*'s, not *t*'s. It's just another word or slang to say *let's get a move on.* I picked the word up when I was in college."

She's so adorable. I just want to put my arm around her and plaster her to my side. *These weeks better go fast.* "I should enter all these words and slang into my phone. You have your own language. Like emojis."

She searches through her bag and pulls out her MetroCard. "Do you have a MetroCard, or do you need a ticket?"

"I have one." I take it out of my wallet. "*Skedaddle* sounds too feminine. Tell me something more masculine," I say as we wait for the train.

The screeching of the train approaches in the distance. "Let's see..." She taps her chin and then snaps her fingers. "I got one. *Jonesing*. I'm jonesing for a beer tonight," she says in a guy's voice. "I'm craving a beer tonight."

I'm craving something else right now, and it's definitely not beer.

We arrive near Times Square, with a good hour to spare before the show starts. Since it's early September, it's still bright out and warm.

"Here's the bar I was talking about. It has a nice terrace in the back. We'll have some privacy there." I lead her through the bar and outside. We find a table in a corner and sit down.

She swivels in her chair while looking around. "It's like a little secret back here. The constant commotion of the city is blocked out. I love the brick walls covered in vines."

"The leaves on the vines turn blood red in autumn. My parents have the same vines in their backyard."

"How cool is that? We should come back here then. I'm sure it looks so pretty."

"The terrace is probably not open once it gets colder but we can try." If she still wants to be near me. In a month, things could be completely different between us.

I grab a bar menu off one of the empty blue mosaic-tiled tables. "Are you really jonesing for a beer, or do you want something else? By the way, I know the phrase *jonesing*. I learned that from my cousins."

Her eyes twinkle with mischief. "Let me see what they have. I'm not in the mood for wine." She flips through the menu. "I think I'll have a margarita. I'll wait for a German beer when I visit your restaurant again. With alcohol though."

"So you do plan on visiting me there? For business or pleasure?"

"For business obviously, but secretly for pleasure."

She scorches me with her burning eyes.

"You're not making this easy." I moan. "Two can play at this game."

Chapter 13

Tina

I know I'm bad. But I love to flirt with him to see how he reacts. We're supposed to play it cool, which makes me want to tease him even more. Maybe I feel this way because I'm not supposed to. What's that phrase? *You always want what you can't have.*

The server puts our drinks in front of us. We lift our glasses, tap them, and say, "*Prost*," our eyes never drifting from each other. *I hope this means seven years of good sex and then some...with him.*

"Since you are a 'star chef'"—I air quote—"do you like cooking for the Hofbräuhaus?" My tongue gets tied. "However you say the name."

He chuckles.

"You said you're there all the time. Is it because you're the chef and manager?"

His posture stiffens. "I don't cook anymore. Several chefs were hired," he says while staring at the wall behind me.

I take another sip and put it down. "Why not? Did something happen?"

He inhales deeply and exhales. The breeze that just blew through the terrace took his good mood away with it.

My body tenses. "Oh. I'm sorry, Gerry. Did I say something wrong?"

He shakes his head. "I usually don't talk about this."

I raise my hands with regret. "Then let's talk about something else. I didn't mean to pry."

"It's a fair question. You opened up to me the other day, so I should do the same." He pauses. "When I opened my restaurant in Hamburg, I already had a good reputation. Slowly the restaurant became well known. The Michelin star was a surprise."

"Wow, that's awesome. You must've been so proud. How do you receive a Michelin star? Do you receive the star, or does the restaurant?"

He circles the rim of his gin and tonic with his finger. "A star is awarded to a restaurant, but the credit is given to the chef of the kitchen. Inspectors are sent to a restaurant several different times to see if the experience is the same. The chef has no idea when the inspectors are there. They look at the quality and freshness of the ingredients. Presentation is also a major factor, which annoys me, and how the ingredients harmonize."

"How long had you had the restaurant when you received the star?"

He scratches his jaw. "About eighteen months. It was a dream come true, at the time. Think about it. I was thirty-two years old and had a star already."

"At the time?" I lean in closer. "You're not happy now?"

He rests his elbows on the table. "Once you receive a star, you have to work your ass off to keep up with the status behind it. I worked longer hours than I do now. There's always this pressure to create innovative modern dishes, which are about the size of my palm. The atmosphere of the restaurant had to be of high standard. I had complaints the waiting list to reserve a table was too long. On top of the pressure, it costs a lot of money. There was a profit, but not much. I made more money doing other things like cookbooks, cooking for social events, appearing on cooking shows...I've done it all."

"It sounds like you've lost your passion."

"Exactly. Some chefs refuse to receive stars or want to give them back. Several of my friends or mentors are divorced because they were never home. There have been chefs that have gone mental because they lost a star. Have you ever seen the animated movie *Ratatouille*?

The one about a rat who could cook?"

"Yeah. Great movie. Why?"

"It's vaguely based on a story of a French chef who might have lost a star and committed suicide because of it."

Where's he going with this? Is he suicidal?

I guess my face says it all, because he throws his hands up. "I'm not saying I'm suicidal. I just wanted to say it can make you nuts when you're trying to keep up with the pace and the reputation. I don't want to end up like them.

"One day, I was exhausted, and a customer complained about the presentation of his meal, among other things. Long story short, I didn't act like a gentleman. It's not something I'm proud of... That was the worst day of my career, and it's been haunting me ever since."

Should I ask him for the long version of what happened? Maybe I should just check the internet.

He swirls the ice cubes in his empty glass. "I gave back my star days after."

"Can you really do that?"

He shrugs his shoulders. "Not really, but I announced it to the media, so there wasn't anything they could do."

"What happened after you announced it?"

"I sold my restaurant a few weeks later and came here."

"It sounds more like you ran away," I say carefully.

He relaxes back in his chair but doesn't look at me.

"Am I right?" I dig.

He remains silent as he watches a couple sit down at a table near ours.

"Gerry. Look at me. You can talk to me."

Finally, his eyes meet mine. "Maybe at the time I did. I had no idea what I was going to do. Slowly, the months came and went, and I was still here. Just when I thought I had to go back, my cousin approached me about the restaurant. I felt it was a sign and agreed to invest. One after the other, I sold my apartment in Hamburg, my belongings, and my car. I like that no one knows who I am here. My staff doesn't even know I'm a chef. Was a chef." His voice drifts off.

"You aren't just any chef. Don't they recognize you by your name? Your family and friends don't say anything to people? I just find it hard to believe you can keep it a secret. What about at the tasting the other night?"

"I ask my friends and family not to talk about it. You heard my real name. That's what I go by as a chef. Plain ole me is Gerry. Why would they know a chef from Germany? There are a million chefs in the US. Let's put it this way. If people know who I am, they aren't saying anything."

I wait for him to continue as I play with the salt on the rim of my margarita.

"But I'm happy where I am right now," he says.

"And where is that?"

He watches me lick salt off my finger, which causes heat to travel throughout my body.

His golden eyes find mine. "With the most intriguing woman I can barely keep my hands or eyes off of."

Think of jumping in a pool of ice. Pretend you didn't hear what he just said.

"How did you take care of everything over there when you were already here?"

"My agent, Barbara, did everything for me."

The server takes our empty glasses.

I wave my fingers. "Ooooh. You have an agent. Aren't you cool."

He laughs, then puffs out his chest.

"I had to at the time. With my schedule, I needed someone to organize my daily activities so I could focus on the restaurant. She still works for me. From time to time she calls me with different offers to encourage me to move back there. Nothing's interested me yet. Maybe I'm only meant to run a restaurant."

"Is she pretty?" I blurt out, then instantly cover my mouth.

"Barbara?" The corners of his mouth slightly rise. "Is someone jealous? Would it help if I say she's old and fat with a wart on her nose?"

I fold my hands on the table and lean forward. "Maybe, or I'm curious if you act toward other business associates the way you do me."

"She's fifty, happily married, and has three kids. And by the way, I've *never* been attracted like this to someone I've worked with until you came along."

My eyes avoid his as I pull a piece of imaginary lint off my shirt.

"Back to the Hofbräuhaus. Are you satisfied with just running the restaurant? What about the blind taste testing? You can do that here. I'd love to hear how you came up with the idea."

He suddenly looks nervous, wiping his forehead with the back of his hand. I've obviously asked the wrong question again. It sounds like he has a skeleton in the closet, like me.

"What do you really want? Do you have a dream job hidden in that noggin of yours?" I reach over and pretend to knock on it.

He shakes his head. "*Noggin*? Another word to add to *Tina's Dictionary*."

"Your peach fuzz is soft, like a pussy willow. I've been wanting to touch it since I met you."

He closes his eyes and leans his head forward for me to do it again. I massage it slowly with both hands this time.

He mumbles, "I like it when you touch me. But I guess I'm not allowed to say that since we're *just friends*."

He lifts his head and opens his eyes again, and I slowly take my hands away.

"I like it too," I mutter. "But we both know we have to avoid it." I lean away. "I'll try not to do it again."

He sighs and leans back in his chair.

"Why can't I be at my old job? I wouldn't care if we got involved or if I was let go."

"I'm not sure about that." He looks at his watch. "Even though I'd love to continue this conversation, we need to get to the theater. It's seven thirty."

"I'll pay for the drinks since you paid for the tickets." He lifts his hand to refuse, but I cut him off before he can speak. "No. You aren't paying for everything."

After I pay the check, he leads me out of the bar toward the Minskoff Theatre. You can't miss it with the giant yellow lion's head on the marquee.

I tug on his arm. "I'm so excited. Thank you again. See how easy it is to please me."

He leans close and whispers, "No touching, remember?" His breath tickles my ear, making me shiver. He steps back and flashes me a wicked smile.

"Come on. Let's go inside and find our seats." He reaches out to take my hand, then freezes.

"Not so easy, is it?" I say as I step away from him.

He shakes his head and clasps his hands behind his back.

I saunter through the golden doors and don't look back. I purposely sway my hips, but he probably doesn't even notice.

"Was that little dance for me?" he says from behind.

I play it cool. "I don't know what you're talking about." I swing my hair over my shoulder.

I spin around in the golden hall leading to the ticket checkpoint. Overhead is a crimson-red wall with a massive lion's face. "It's beautiful in here. It's sad I haven't been to a show in so long. Let's take a selfie with the lion in the background. Want to?" I smile ear to ear.

"How can I say no to such a gorgeous smile? Give me your *handy*."

My eyes bulge out of my head.

"What's the matter? Give me your phone."

"You said give me your *handy*." I cover my mouth to stifle my laugh. "Is that some kind of subliminal message?"

"I think your mind is in the gutter. *Handy* means cell phone in German."

"Hysterical! Just never say, 'Do you want a handy?' You'll get punched in the face or kicked in the balls."

"Thanks for the tip. My German seems to pop out only when you're around. Anyway, can we get on with the selfie before you make us late for the show?"

"You started it. Pull out your handy," I instigate.

He scowls, which makes him appear even sexier.

"It just flew out. Sorry, I'll be serious now." I zip my lip to stop talking.

He whips it out, and we must've looked like two idiots. He takes several shots before a decent picture turns up, because he always makes a stupid face. A couple of people photo bomb us. We can't stop laughing as we flip through the images.

I freeze on one. "I'm going to post this one on Facebook."

"No. I told you I'm not a big fan of social media." His voice is suddenly tense.

I raise my eyebrows. What is his issue?

"Also, didn't you want to keep this between us?" His tone is softer this time.

I bang my forehead with my palm. "You're right! Forget it."

He gives the tickets to the doorman, and we proceed through. I fold my arms over my chest. It's so damn cold in here. Air conditioning sucks. No one seems to know what temperature to put it at. It always seems to be on freezing. I put my sweater on but wish it was Gerry warming me up.

I turn around to face the rows of seats. "So where are our seats? In the back row?"

He shakes his head. "Absolutely not. This is practically your first time, so we have the best seats. Middle, orchestra."

My jaw drops. "That's way too generous. They must've cost a fortune. I—"

He presses his finger against my lips.

"Don't talk about money. This is my pleasure. You're worth every penny," he says with a firm tone that would turn on any woman. When he removes his finger from my lips, I press my fingers there.

Will my pulse always kick up when he touches me?

"Fine" is all that comes out from behind my fingers.

He motions for me to follow him. It's hard not to stare at his ass in those black jeans. I look up and see a smirk on his face as he glances at me over his shoulder.

"Is there a sticky back there flashing *attention*?"

I clear my throat and fiddle with my necklace.

He motions to the eighth row and scoots sideways to the middle two seats. We sit down, and my eyes spring wide open.

"Great, huh?"

I just nod because I don't know what else to say. A frigid breeze blows across my shoulders. Above us is the air conditioning vent. *Great*. I stuff my hands between my knees to warm them up.

He turns toward me. "Are you really that cold?"

"Yes. My hands and feet, and usually my nose, are always cold." I feel my nose. "Yep, my nose is also. I'm not a fan of AC when it's so low. There's always a pair of socks stashed in my desk drawer in case my feet freeze when I wear sandals to work. My lunch hour usually consists of me defrosting outside the office."

He touches the tip of my nose and laughs. "You'd think it were winter. Give me your hands so I can warm them up." He grabs them before I can answer.

"You're like a furnace," I say as I scoot as close as I can to him in my seat. At least there's an armrest between us. "I know this is off limits, but I'm too cold."

He puts his arm around my shoulder and pulls me closer. "I can warm you up, but you'll need to cool me down."

Just his flirty words alone increase the blood flow to special parts of my body.

We exit the theater. "That was so epic when the animals came down the aisles in the beginning."

"I loved it too, but more so because of the amazement on your face. You're so beautiful when you glow like that. I hope I get to see it again soon."

He said I'm beautiful, just like he said in French.

"Speaking of beautiful. A little birdy told me you didn't say 'the pencil is yellow' in French or German the other day in Thomas's office. You said something else. Would you like to tell me what you really said?" I raise an eyebrow and cross my arms while people funnel around us.

He pulls me to the side away from the crowd. "Okay. I confess. I really said, 'You're very beautiful.' You are, but I love it that you don't realize it."

I'm ready to melt into a puddle on the ground, and it's not from the heat in the city.

I approach my apartment door with Gerry trailing behind me. He insisted on walking me to my apartment.

I prop my back against the door. He leans against the wall opposite me. We gaze at each other. Every new minute I spend with him, the more gorgeous he becomes.

"Thanks for coming with me—I really had fun. A bit too much. I love being around you. I don't want to leave yet."

I purse my lips while I mentally battle between what's right and wrong. In the end there are more pros than cons...but I have to do what's right.

"I'd ask you to come inside, but I think it'd be safer to call it a night."

I feel the door give way as I fall backward, but I catch myself on the doorframe. Gerry leaps to catch me at the same time.

"Hey there!" Alexa exclaims.

"What the hell, Alexa?" *She did that on purpose.* I give her a dirty look.

"Whatcha doing? Working late?" she says with her never-ending peppiness.

I smooth out my shirt and stand tall. "Gerry had an extra ticket to *The Lion King*. He asked me if I wanted to go."

She nods her head with a mischievous grin.

"How convenient. It's pretty dark in the theater. Did you actually watch the show?" She stifles a laugh.

I'm going to kick her ass.

I yank on her arm. "Can you please give me a minute with Gerry? Alone."

"Sure. Bye, Gerry. I look forward to seeing you at the wedding, or maybe some time sooner." She winks at him.

I shove her away and close the door.

"I'm sorry about that. I guess there's no way of keeping this from her."

He moves closer to me. We're only inches apart. I look up to his enticing face and then at his lips. They look so kissable. All I want is one taste of him right now. Or maybe two. But then it'd lead to three...*damn*.

"Just in case Alexa's listening, I'll whisper. This was the best *just friends* date I've ever had. Especially while keeping you warm in the theater."

He inches even closer, and I can feel the heat from his lips. I inhale deeply through my nose to smell his enticing musky scent.

"This *friends* thing is going to be harder than I thought."

"I know," I whisper.

He pulls back slowly while his gaze caresses my face. "Sweet dreams, Tina. Talk to you soon."

He walks away and doesn't look back. What a tease. I need to defuse my body. I wilt against the door and try to focus. My hand finds the knob and turns it. Alexa's by my side in seconds, with a huge grin, no less.

"What have we here?" she says. "A date with a client. I thought that was taboo. I want to hear every juicy detail." She waves me over to the couch. "Do we need alcohol for this?"

"I wouldn't mind a glass, even though I'll probably get drunk from one." I drop my handbag on the floor and take off my black espadrilles.

She comes out of the kitchen and opens a bottle of white wine. "Only a little bit for me," I say.

She pours us some and places the bottle on one of the coasters on the coffee table. We get comfy on the couch.

"I like him. A lot. He's so interesting and has a great sense of humor. But we agreed to be friends while we work together." I explain how he surprised me with *The Lion King* tickets.

"We had such a great time tonight and couldn't stop laughing. It was impossible to keep my hands off him because I was freezing. He offered to warm me up, and I couldn't refuse with the freaking AC right over our heads."

"Excuses, excuses."

"Seriously, it was freezing. Just like in here right now. I'm surprised it's not snowing." I get a chill.

"Oh, please. Don't try to convince me it was all innocent. I bet you were still all snuggled up even when you weren't cold anymore."

I fight the smile that's close to breaking through...and lose. "I tried to move away to play by the rules, but he kept a firm grip on me the entire time. I gave in because he's so warm and cuddly. Do you have an extra calendar I can use to cross off the days until this project's over?"

She giggles. "I know a month or so sounds like a long time, but it'll go fast. You know the saying—all good things come to those who wait." She pats my leg. "It also gives you time to get to know each other without sex getting in the way."

I angle myself so I'm facing Alexa and cover my legs with a blanket. "Why would he ever want someone like me though? He speaks several languages, comes from Europe, famous chef, blah, blah, blah. I'm so boring compared to him. How am I at all interesting? The closest I've come to leaving this country is losing myself in travel magazines."

"Just because you haven't traveled out of the country doesn't make you boring. I've never done it. Do you think I'm boring?"

I huff. "Absolutely not."

"Exactly. You said it yourself. You feel your life's starting now. Maybe he's the one you're meant to explore the world with."

"I wouldn't go that far." I massage my sore feet out of frustration.

"Why do you say that?"

Because I don't deserve him.

"He brings the excitement into your life you've been craving. Have fun for the next few weeks. Maybe he'll surprise you again with a little outing. Once the time's up, you'll both know what you want."

"I'm being realistic and don't want to get my hopes up."

Her phone vibrates on her lap. She reads it and rolls her eyes, then tosses it next to her on the couch.

I eye her. "Was that Tony the Tiger? Or another one of your admirers?"

She groans. "I told Tony I'm not interested, even after he sent me those stupid roses. He thinks I'm playing with him. Why the hell would he send me roses after that god-awful date?" She places her wine on the table and reaches for her phone. "He can kiss my ass. I'm blocking his number as we speak." She taps her phone with speed, then places it on the coffee table. "Done."

She snuggles into the couch. "It is too cold in here. I'll turn the AC down tomorrow."

I give her a desperate look.

"You know I like it cold when I sleep." She pulls part of the blanket from me and lays it on her legs. "So back to Gerry. Does he want to meet up again?"

"We didn't make any plans." I sip my wine, but I'm really not in the mood for it anymore.

"As I said, maybe he'll surprise you with something else."

"Should *I* initiate something?" Nervousness kicks in. I've never asked a guy to do something. But it wouldn't be a date. *Keep lying to yourself.*

"I don't know. You said you want to take more chances, but I don't want to see you regret it. Don't jump the gun. Wait until after the weekend. See how you feel then. Why don't we go shopping in the city on Saturday to distract you? Buy some new clothes for the fall. What do you say?"

"Sounds good to me," I try to say in the middle of yawning. "I could use a few nice new things to brighten my wardrobe. Let's avoid Fifth Avenue this time though. I make good money, but not enough for shopping there. Window shopping is about all I can do. Remember what I always say?"

Alexa huffs. "Yes, I know. Bargains are your friends."

We stand at the same time and drink the last drops of our wine.

"I've got to take my contacts out. I'm dead tired," I say.

"I'm sure you are, with those raging hormones zipping through your body. Get some sleep, because I've a feeling you won't be getting much during the next few weeks."

Beauty sleep versus Gerry? Not a hard decision. Definitely Gerry.

Chapter 14

Tina

Century 21 on Lincoln Square is massive, with a buzzing crowd already at 10:00 a.m. "You wanted to come here and promised me some good sales. Where do you want to start?" I ask Alexa while scanning the store directory. It has everything from discounted clothing to home furnishings. I love bargains, but this store is packed. There better not be any cat fights over something on sale.

She points to Bridal and Formal Wear. "I saw a red dress on the store's website. It's on sale, so I want to see if I can find it. I printed out some coupons for us."

I pull my head back. "But you already have a dress for the wedding."

"Who cares? If I find it, I'll try it on. If it doesn't scream *take me home*, then I won't buy it."

"Whatever you say. Just don't steal the limelight from Kayla. Your day will come." I smirk.

"No sign of marriage in the near future. I'd never do such a thing to Kayla, unless she hated me, of course." She spins around and points. "It's on the second floor. The escalator's over there to the right. Let's go, chica." She drags me by the arm.

"What's the rush? Let's take it slow. It takes time to find a good deal."

We arrive at the second floor and make our way to the department. I notice a woman wearing a beautiful wedding dress in the distance. Her smile reflects in the giant three-piece mirror. We watch as she twirls around. "You look stunning in that dress," I say to her as we approach her.

She sees me in the mirror and turns around. "I know. Thank you!" She giggles in delight. A saleswoman spreads the train on the floor.

"What do you think, Mom?" she says to an older woman sitting in a chair near her.

Her mom dabs a tissue under her eye and sniffs. "You look simply gorgeous. Out of all the dresses you've tried on, this is the one." She stands up and gives her a motherly squeeze.

My heart clenches. My mom will never see me in a wedding dress, and it's my fault. I ruined everything. Tears well up in my eyes, and I squeeze the pendant until my hand hurts.

Alexa grabs my elbow. "Hey, are you okay? You have tears in your eyes."

I pull my arm away as I search in my bag for a tissue. "I'm fine. That woman has too much perfume on. I need to sneeze, and it won't come out. My eyes always water when that happens." I pull one out and wipe my nose.

"Funny. I don't smell any perfume. Your nose is so sensitive."

Seeing the woman with her mom guts me. I'll never do that with Mom. I have my stepmom, Beth, but it's not the same. It'll never be the same.

I follow Alexa to the formal-dress section but glance back at the bride one more time. She has no idea how lucky she is to be there with her mom.

Alexa rummages through the racks full of red dresses. She squeals. "Ha! I found it. It's even more beautiful than on the website, and it's in my size. It's a sign. I have to try it on." She holds the dress in front of her.

"Let's have some fun and find some dresses for you. Where are the purple ones?" She scans the racks.

"You know I already have a dress for the wedding."

"So what. It's fun to play dress up!"

I need to shake this shitty mood. This is supposed to be fun, and I've paid for what I did. Time to put on the mask of happiness. "Sounds great. There are some purple ones over there."

"Let's see. This is a fall wedding. Darker purple would be better than pastel." She flicks the hangers across the rods like a pro and lifts a dress off. "Look at this one. What a cool color, a little lighter than plum."

"It's called Mardi Gras purple," says a saleswoman, who appears out of nowhere. "Who's this dress for?"

I raise my hand.

"This color matches your skin color beautifully."

Sure it does. It could be the color of vomit and she'd say the same thing just to make a sale.

Alexa looks at the tag. "It's your size." She grabs my hand. "Try it on. It's so pretty, and fifty percent off, and I have those coupons."

It's not possible to be in a bad mood when she's so excited and the dress is so cheap.

I take the dress from her. "Where's the dressing room?"

We exit the store with two new dresses and matching shoes for the wedding. "Let's go this way," Alexa says as she points to the right.

There was no question about it once I tried on the dress. I've never owned one so extravagant. It has spaghetti straps with a triangle bodice and sexy V-neck. I'm thankful I have the boobs to fill it. The chiffon layers flow to the knee, then dip to midcalf at the back.

"This wasn't the type of bargain I was looking for today, but I'm ecstatic. It's so gorgeous." Retail therapy cheers me up every time. "I'm not sure what I'll do with the other dress I bought for the wedding."

"I'm sure you'll find somewhere to wear it. It isn't as fancy, so you could wear it to a nice restaurant or business dinner," she comments. "Mr. Clean will fall over when he sees you in this. The only food he'll want to eat is you."

I tap her on the butt with my bag. "Speaking of eating, I'm starving and thirsty. Do you know a good restaurant or café nearby?"

She stops and looks down both streets. "Let me get my bearings." After a few seconds, she snaps her fingers. "You know what? I think Matt's bakery isn't too far from here. Let me look it up on my phone. I've always wanted to check it out, but I've never had the time." She types away. "We're in luck. According to Google Maps, it's only two or three blocks from here. Let's go and surprise him. I don't mind eating fattening pastries for a late lunch."

"You don't have to convince me. Lead the way."

Chapter 15

Gerry

Do I need to take a number or something? Matt's bakery has a line to the door. I squeeze my way through the crowd and walk behind the front counter. I look in the far back and see Kayla fighting with a bag of flour.

"Kayla?" I call.

She turns her flour-covered face in my direction. "Gerry. Come on back." She wipes her forehead with the back of her hand.

"It's a madhouse out front. Business seems to be running well."

"Almost too well. We're exhausted, and my back's killing me from standing over this counter all morning. I can't wait for the honeymoon."

"Where's Matt? Can I help with something?"

"He's on the phone taking an order. It sounds complicated." She points with her elbow at a tray full of fresh éclairs. "Can you check the case in front if we need to put more out, and which flavors? One employee called in sick, so it's more hectic today than usual."

"Sure." I walk over and check out the case. On the other side of the glass case, a pair of familiar cinnamon eyes is looking at the éclairs. Tina's eyes pop open when she sees me.

She peeks over the counter. "Gerry? Wow. What a nice surprise." She grins ear to ear.

"It definitely is."

"Mr. Clean?" Alexa asks and follows Tina's eyes. Her face turns bright red. "Sorry. I meant Gerry."

Before I can ask why Alexa calls me Mr. Clean, Kayla comes up from behind me. "Gerry, do we need more éclairs or not?" she says impatiently.

"Your bakery is quite popular today. Look who's paying a visit."

Her face brightens. "Hey, girls. What a nice surprise. I'd give you both a hug, but I'm full of flour and icing. Take a look around. If you want anything, Gerry can help you out. We're swamped today. Since it's your first time here, take whatever you want. It's on the house." She walks over to the worker at the front counter and whispers something in her ear. They both look over to Tina and Alexa, and she nods. Kayla walks to the back, but she turns around again. "Tina, I'm glad those currants didn't do any permanent damage. I would've killed my cousin!"

We laugh in unison as she disappears into the back.

I rest my elbows on the case. "So what are you two beauties doing here? No good bakeries in Hoboken?"

"We went shopping nearby. I suggested we come here to check it out," Alexa replies.

"Hungry?" I glimpse at Tina.

Her eyes twinkle with mischief. "More than you can imagine."

"What can I get for you both? I saw you eyeing the éclairs. Matt's are the best. He has some crazy flavors. Why don't you try one?"

"Do you see something you want, Alexa?" Tina asks.

"I sure do. That fat chocolate mousse one all the way in the back has my name on it."

I open the case and point to one. "This fatty right here?"

She giggles and nods while looking at the other ones.

"Anything else?"

"How about one of the mini salted caramel ones?"

I put them on a plate and hand it to her. "Good choices."

"There's one small empty table in the corner by the window. I'll go and save it for us. Can you get me a bottle of water please?" she says to Tina.

"Sure. No problemo." Alexa takes her bag from her and walks away.

"Nice seeing you here. Makes my day off even better."

"Wow. You actually took a day off. What did your boss say about that?" her voice plays with me as she moves closer to the case.

"He told me it was about time I took an entire day off. Not just a couple of hours."

"An entire day? What will you do with your time? Buy more blindfolds?" she jokes.

I flinch in response. If she only knew how horrible I feel when she brings up anything remotely related to our long-ago kiss.

"Gerry, please move." Kayla elbows me. "I need to fill someone's order. You're in the way. Please get Tina what she wants and go sit with them. Matt will be out in a minute."

I look at Tina. "Let me pick two éclairs for you to try. If you don't like them, I'll eat them."

"Sounds like fun. I can only imagine which ones you'll pick. Can I please have a water too?"

I nod. "Go sit down. I'll bring your food and drinks."

A few minutes later, I place her éclairs and the water bottles on the table. "Here you go. I feel like I work here. Can I sit with you two?"

Alexa answers first. "Of course. It's so funny you're here today. We were shopping at Century 21. You should see the dress Tina bought for the wedding. S-E-X-Y."

"It sure is," Tina taunts me.

I find their bags at their feet. "What have we here?" I say as I grab a bag.

Tina yanks it from my hands. "No way, José. That's for the wedding. You'll have to wait."

I throw my hands up. "Hey, I'm a patient man, but at least give me a hint."

She lays the bag on the other side of her, out of reach. "It's purple." She giggles.

I squint my eyes. "Really? I thought it'd be red."

Alexa perks up. "I'll be the lady in red at the wedding. She's the one who loves purple."

"I know. I'm just kidding. Since you won't show it to me, at least eat the surprise éclairs."

"No blindfolds this time?" Alexa mentions, then bites into the chocolate mousse éclair.

My stomach jumps. Time to leave. Why do they keep bringing it up? I never talk about it to anyone. "I'm fresh out of blindfolds. I think she had enough of that the other night."

"Yep. Now let me eat one of these."

"How did you come up with the whole blindfolded taste-test thingy anyway?" Alexa questions.

Tina stops midbite. She covers her mouth and mumbles, "I'm curious too."

Scheiße, I say to myself.

"Well, I, um..."

"Hey, guys." Matt interrupts. "Great to see you here. Gerry, why aren't you at work?" Matt gives the girls a hug.

Perfect timing.

"No hug for me, big guy? I feel left out."

"I'll give you a big kiss." He bends over and smacks a long, squeaky kiss on my cheek.

The last woman in line turns around to see what we're doing.

"Man, you've got to trim that scruff. That's painful." Matt covers his lips.

I push him away. "Get away from me. You're the disgusting, annoying brother I never had." I wipe my cheek.

He grips the back of their chairs. "What do you think of the éclairs? They're selling like hotcakes today."

Alexa kisses her fingers. "The chocolate mousse one is divine."

"There will be a buffet of desserts and wedding cake at the wedding. Éclairs will be included—made by me, of course."

"I have no idea what this one is, but it's delicious. It's spicy, if that's possible for an éclair, or I'm allergic to this too."

Matt leans over. "You have the chocolate chili one. It's not that spicy. It just gives it a little kick."

"I thought I was going to need the medicine in my bag." She looks at me from the corner of her eyes with a slight grin.

"I can already see this'll be a never-ending joke for the next twenty years."

Tina rubs my knee. I grab her hand and hold it there. She doesn't pull away. Maybe it's because she's freezing again. I take advantage and keep it there to see how long it takes for her to pull away. Matt looks at our hands and then at me. He nods with a slight grin.

"Matt, we need you back here," yells Kayla over the noisy room.

"Sorry, guys. I need to get back to work. Kayla's stressed. It seems people are addicted to éclairs today. I can't seem to make enough. Say goodbye before you go." He greets customers in line as he walks behind the counter.

"What are your plans for the rest of the day? Are you going shopping somewhere else?"

Alexa responds quickly. "We were going home, but Tina mentioned you have the day off. Why don't you two go and do something? The weather's great, and Central Park isn't too far from here."

I squeeze Tina's hand. She looks down and slowly pulls it away. That hand goes straight to her necklace.

"Why not? It's early afternoon."

"I'm game," Tina says. "I've always wanted to walk through Central Park. Alexa, come with us."

Please say no. Not that I don't like her, but I want Tina to myself.

She waves her hand. "No thanks. I'd rather go stare at myself in the mirror with my new dress and shoes on." She wraps the caramel éclair in a napkin and puts it in her handbag. "I'll eat this on the bus. Give me your bag. I'll take it home so you don't have to worry about it."

"Are you sure? You don't have your car today."

"Stop the mother-hen act. I'll be fine." She stands up. "I'll see you later." She gives us both hugs. "Toodles. Have fun!"

I turn to Tina. "I'm so glad I took the day off."

Chapter 16

Tina

Take a deep breath and count to ten. The last several minutes weren't easy to stay calm and cool. I want to scream in excitement that he's here. It's proof that something is pushing us together.

"And I'm glad Alexa wanted to come here. I wondered when I'd see you again," I admit.

"I've been thinking about a lot of things since I saw you last. It made me realize what I've been missing these past years. The assistant manager works today, so I don't need to be there."

I bounce in my chair with excitement. "Then today's *your* day. What would you like to do?"

"Alexa's right. The weather's great for a walk through Central Park. Let's sketattle."

"It's *skedaddle*...but you're right." I crinkle my nose and shake my head. "Too girly. Don't say it again."

He takes my hand and pulls me up from the chair. Every time he touches me, I turn into a gooey mess. When he held my hand a few minutes ago, I didn't have the willpower to pull away. Our hands fit as if they were made for each other.

I want to be attached to him every second we're together, just like Sylvester the Cat or Tom from *Tom and Jerry*. I can't remember which one, but there are episodes when a cat is tightly wrapped around a man. To get the cat off, the person needs to push it down and take it off like a pair of pants. That would be me. It's been years since I've craved such a connection with someone.

I push my chair in. "Should we say bye to Matt and Kayla or pay for our food at least?"

"Nah. They're too busy to notice we're gone. Kayla said it was on the house."

He looks at my feet. "Good. You're wearing shoes you can walk in for a while. I want to show you something in Central Park, but it'll take some time to get there from here. Most people don't realize how big the park is."

"What a gentleman," I comment when he opens the door for me.

"Not everyone has that opinion," he mumbles.

"I find that hard to believe. Why would you say that?"

"Never mind. Let's go and have some fun."

I let it pass, but there's something he's not telling me. It's probably connected to the incident that made him come to the US. I can't push him to tell me, because I don't want him to push me. I've thought about snooping on the internet, but I feel like I'd be invading his privacy.

I search for my sunglasses in my handbag. "You'll be happy to know I bought a new pair of sunglasses. I promise not to embarrass you while we walk through the park." I take them out of the case and put them on. "See?" I say as I strike a pose.

"I think I like them better with only one lens."

For a second I think he's serious but then he bursts out laughing. Good acting.

I swat his arm. "You're cruel."

He puts his sunglasses on, which makes him look even hotter. *Damn!*

Fifteen minutes later, we pass Tavern on the Green. I've seen it on TV but never in person. "Have you ever been there before?"

He shakes his head. "Never had a reason to go, but maybe that'll change in the near future." He glances my way.

With a big smile on my face, I wave my arms back and forth. "Where are we going? Not that I have a clue about what people do here."

"It has something to do with water."

"That could be anything. One more hint."

He walks ahead of me while walking backward. "It's a house."

"Those are stupid clues. Fine. I'll just wait."

He wiggles his eyebrows and then turns forward again. "It's more fun when it's a surprise."

I see a baseball field to the right. "Have you ever played baseball? Do they even play baseball in Germany?"

"Actually, yes. A town not too far from my hometown has its own baseball team. It was in the first league for a while but went down one level. They don't have the big stadiums like here. But it's popular in certain areas. I've been to a couple of Mets games here. When I was younger, I always went to batting cages with my cousins. I loved it."

"It's good for anger management." I pretend to swing a bat. "I cracked many balls into the field when I was younger."

He stops me from walking. "Are you telling me you have anger issues? I'd never believe it."

"And I can't imagine someone said you aren't a gentleman."

He looks away from me.

I continue. "Only the baseballs knew. I'm good at hiding things. Believe me—I've had moments when I needed to expel some major negative physical energy. No one knows I used to do that. I'm pretty strong, ya know. Feel my bicep." I flex it for him and tap it.

He squeezes it. "Wow, you're like Popeye. Maybe there was some spinach in one of those éclairs."

I punch him in the arm.

"That was nothing. Try again." He smacks his arm and braces himself.

I punch him harder, and he flinches.

I cover my mouth with my hands. "Oh my gosh. Did I hurt you?"

He bursts out laughing. "Hell no."

"I'm gonna get you for that." I rub his peach fuzz on his head and run away. He chases me until I can't breathe anymore. I'm laughing too hard. He runs up and puts his arm around my shoulders, and then he gives me, of all things, a noogie. *He's so freaking cute.*

I scream and pull away from him, panting. "I can't believe you just gave me a noogie. What are you, two years old?" I pat my hair down.

He moves closer. "Want me to do it again?"

I back away from him. "No. We aren't even supposed to touch each other. Remember? Unless you want an atomic wedgie."

"An atomic wedgie. What the hell? You started it first." He steps closer.

I take a step back with my hands up for protection and then stumble and fall on my ass on the grass.

He kneels next to me. "Tina, I'm sorry. Did you hurt yourself? You fell over a rock. I didn't see it behind you." He takes my hand in his.

I laugh out loud. "I'm fine." I don't care anymore if I make a fool out of myself. "You act like I'm gushing blood. I'm a lot tougher than you think. It's nice to sit here for a second though. We've been walking for hours." I pretend to whine to annoy him.

He looks at his watch. "You mean forty-five minutes. Don't exaggerate."

"Where's this house we're walking to? I'm dying of thirst."

"Do you always complain this much?" He holds his hand up and flashes five. "Five more minutes."

I tilt my head to the side. "Does that mean thirty minutes in German?"

His crooked smile appears. "You're quite the smartass. I promise you'll like where we're going."

I stand up and dust off my pants. "It better be that building over there in the distance."

"Yep." He turns his back to me. "Get on my back, my little *Schnecke.*"

I crinkle my face.

"Sorry, my little snail. You're taking forever. I'll give you a piggy back." He bends at his knees. "Jump on."

I inch closer to him and place my hands on his shoulders. "You're pushing the boundaries, Mr. Maier."

He huffs. "Just do it and stop being such a baby." He inches closer to me.

I jump on, but only because I want to know what it feels like to have him between my legs.

We finish our drinks in the outside bar of the Loeb Boathouse, which overlooks the lake. "What a great place. It was worth the walk. If I ever come back here again, I'm definitely renting one of those boats on the lake."

"Let's go check it out. Let me pay first." I lift my hand but he cuts me off before I can protest. "It's my turn to pay."

After he settles the bill, we walk around a little bit and watch the boats glide by. "Come on." He pulls on my sleeve. "Let's rent one."

I clap my hands together. "Seriously? Don't do it just for me."

"I'm not. It looks like fun. Let's take a selfie with the water and boats behind us." He takes out his phone.

We sift through the several pictures we took. "Can we be any more stupid when it comes to taking selfies?" I point at one. "We can see right up my nose."

He pulls it closer. "Wait a second. Do you have nose hair?"

"Do I?" I cover my nose with my hand and look closer at the picture. His laugh radiates through me. "You're mean." I smile but jab him in the stomach with my elbow.

We walk to the counter. "I hope you know how to swim," he says.

"Of course. I swam in the ocean any chance I could when I was younger. Do you know how to row a boat?"

"I think so. I've rowed some boats back in a day."

"Back in *the* day," I say.

"That'll be twenty dollars," says the boat controller. Gerry hands over the money, and we head to the dock.

"This boat is huge for two people. Are you sure you know how to work the oars?"

He steps into the boat and turns around to help me get in. "Stop worrying and get in the boat."

The boat wobbles, so I sit down before I fall off the side. He follows and takes control of the oars with precision, steering us away from the dock.

"How do you know how to control the oars so well?"

"I was a rower and a swimmer in high school and college."

Yummy!

"So that's why you have such broad shoulders. Do you still do it now? Is that how you stay fit?"

"I hate going to the gym, so I bought a rowing machine when I moved here."

"I hate it too. I can't get past the smell." I wave my hand in front of my nose.

He paddles away from the other boats. "I don't swim anymore. My mom insisted we have a built-in pool put in years ago because she was an avid swimmer. She also gave swim lessons to the local kids. I use the pool when I visit. Since I did both sports for so long, my body is shaped like this. I can always spot a swimmer because their back is V shaped."

"No complaints from me. You look good, but I don't know how you stay fit when you're surrounded by food all day." I gesture with my hand toward his body.

"You love food and have a great body."

"Excuse me." I point my finger back and forth between us. "Just friends, remember?"

"What? You just said the same to me. Friends can't say that?"

A boat passes us a little too closely, and I say to the couple, "We're just friends."

"It doesn't look like it to me," the woman says. She winks at Gerry.

He stops rowing. "Oh. I'm sorry. Should I have said you're as hot as the chili in the éclair you ate? Or as hot as the Sahara Desert? Or so hot that I'm counting the days on the calendar until my hands and lips can burn on your bare skin." He clenches his jaw.

I can't see his eyes through his sunglasses, but I can feel them.

Holy shit. He's serious. My hormones are screaming *let him.*

"You're thinking about it too. Admit it."

I remain silent and look out at the water. No way am I admitting that. *Hide your emotions.*

"I guess it's going to be a long night. I'm not moving this boat until you admit it." He lets go of the oars.

I jump up and step closer to him to grab them.

"Don't jump up like that. The oars are attached. We're fine," he says as he tries to stabilize the boat.

It wobbles enough that I lose my balance, falling face first into his lap. *Your face is in his lap. Get up! But what if I like it? Get up!*

I push off him to escape the awkwardness. His arms wrap around my waist, preventing me from moving away. We're face to face as I rest on my knees. I take his sunglasses off to reveal his heated eyes.

"Why couldn't you just admit it?" he says with a low voice, his eyes glancing at my lips. "Now look what happened. Not that I mind."

I whisper, "I think about it all the time. *You* all the time."

He dips his head closer.

"Are you both okay over there?" interrupts the controller in a boat next to us.

We jerk apart.

"I saw you almost fall off the boat. Do you need help?"

I carefully push off Gerry, my eyes never leaving his. I sit back in my spot. I'm suddenly nervous, like we've been stopped by the police. "I'm okay. No worries. We were just, um, discussing something."

Gerry snickers.

"It didn't look like it to me." He tips his sunglasses so he can show us his knowing eyes. "No more standing in the boat or pawing each other. You have fifteen minutes left on the water."

"Yes, sir," Gerry says with a small smirk as he slowly rows away.

As soon as we're away from other boats, he slows down and looks at me with such sincerity.

"What's the matter?" I ask as the boat calmly drifts along the water. "I'm sorry I fell on you."

He shakes his head. "I've had more fun these past couple of weeks with you than I've had this entire year. I'm so thankful I found you."

My heart grows three times the size. "Me too."

Chapter 17

Gerry

I look up from my computer when I hear a knock on my office door. "Come in."

The assistant manager, Joel, peeks his head in. "Someone's here to see you. Should I let her in?"

Maybe it's Tina. My stomach twists, and my hands shake. Since when does this happen? I roll my chair back and stand up. "Yes, please." I pat down my shirt and check if it's dirty.

"Here she is."

My chest sinks because it's not Tina, but I'm happy to see the familiar face anyway. "Barbara! What the hell are you doing here?" I hug her tightly, then raise my hand. "Thanks, Joel. I can take it from here."

He nods and leaves the room.

She looks me up and down. "Wow, you look great Gerry. America is doing you good."

"Thanks, I guess." I motion to a chair and close the office door. "I can't believe you're here. Why didn't you tell me you were coming?"

She pulls on her earlobe. "My assumption was correct. You don't read my emails. I wrote you saying I'd be in New York this week. The kids have a week off from school, so I convinced Stephan to vacation here."

"It's great to see you. Why didn't you bring the family with you tonight? I would've liked to see them. They could've had dinner here."

She chuckles. "Seriously? They eat German food all the time. There are too many restaurants to try out here. They went for pizza at John's of Times Square."

"Good. You can't visit New York without having pizza there. Where are you staying?"

"I rented an apartment through Airbnb. It's small but near Times Square. You can't beat the location."

We catch up on our families and her business back in Hamburg. It's strange to speak German with her. I speak English ninety-five percent of the time now.

She sits straight up on the edge of the chair and folds her hands nicely on the desk. She's switched to business mode. I don't like it.

"Gerry, I'm not in New York just for pleasure. I'm here to discuss business with you. As I've said, you don't respond to my calls or emails most of the time. You haven't come back to Germany. So this is what I had to do to get your attention."

I sit back and cross my arms defensively. "Then say what you came here to say."

"I've received several requests for your taste testing. The people requesting are willing to pay whatever you want. I'm talking politicians, the CEO of Mercedes, and a couple of actors."

"Not interested," I say flatly.

She squints her eyes with annoyance. "For the millionth time, why?"

I clench my jaw. "You know why."

"That was over a year ago. The news has moved on to other ridiculous stories. That jerk got what he deserved. He was and still is a liar. You aren't the only chef he did that to."

I put my elbows on the desk. "He wasn't the only one who jeopardized my reputation—I did too. I took a bad day out on him. And what he said after that was a bunch of bullshit." My heart beat pulses in my ears. "You make it sound so easy to forget what happened. Just remember—it happened to *me*, not *you*. Your name wasn't plastered all over the French and German media."

"Your fans and fellow chefs know you and know the truth. It's been a year, and they're still calling me, questioning when you're coming back. But you continue to hide behind this restaurant." She looks around my office like it's shit. "Pretending it's what you want to do. I'd understand a bit more if you were the chef here. But you're not. I've known you for years. A part of you aches to get back in the kitchen."

I grimace. "What's wrong with what I'm doing now? This restaurant is a huge success. I held a taste testing days ago and I'm catering my cousin's wedding in a couple of weeks."

"Are you satisfied with that? Do you still dream of running your own cooking show?"

"That's about the only thing I'd consider at this point." I squint my eyes. "Why? Did you hear something?"

"Let's just say I had a conversation with one of the executive producers from VOX TV network. He wants to meet with you and discuss in detail your ideas for the cooking show you want. I gave him a basic overview of your ideas. He's interested."

I let out a deep breath. "I've heard it all before from several other channels. You know that. They all end up cutting the cord right before I sign the contract. Giving me bullshit excuses like budget cuts. Look where it got me a year ago."

"But this time it's different. I have a good feeling. The least you can do is meet with him. Can you fly home soon?"

I stand up, my hands planted on the desk. "Barbara, my home is here now."

She leans back as her eyes spring open.

"Sorry. Let me correct myself. A trip to Germany."

My phone rings on my desk as I sit back down. It's Tina. I shouldn't answer, but we haven't spoken in a couple of days.

"Let me take this call."

"Should I leave?"

I shake my head.

"Hi, Tina. Can I call you back?" I avoid eye contact with Barbara and make it sound like a business call, even though it's after work hours. She'll pick up there's something going on. "Sounds good. Talk to you soon."

"So, where were we?" I say as I shuffle papers on my desk.

She closes her eyes and sighs. "You've met someone, haven't you?"

"I'm interested in someone, but we're not dating." *Yet.*

"Is she why you won't go back to Germany? Will this influence your decision about this opportunity?"

I shrug. "I haven't really thought about it because we aren't together." *Liar.* "But if there's a good chance to produce and direct my own show, I'd consider going back. Only if all my conditions were met, which they never have been."

"If I can set up a meeting with the executive producer, are you in?" She pauses. "I want a yes or no. *Maybe* doesn't work here. If you say yes and I set up a meeting, you *will* show up. Do you understand?"

"If I say yes, I'd never back out. But it has to be mid to late October. I'm too busy here. Also, if I meet with him, I want to meet in Freiburg. Then I can visit with my family for a week."

A smile grows on her face. "You have a deal. I'll work on it and get back to you. It might take some time to set a date because he's busy. After our meeting here, I'm not working. I want to enjoy my vacation with my family."

We both stand up. "Sorry I haven't been easy. I appreciate you sticking by me this last year. I won't ignore your calls or emails anymore."

"You just agreeing to a meeting makes it all worthwhile. My gut tells me this is what you've been waiting for. It's your big chance to get back into the arena."

"We'll see about that," I say as I lead her to the exit, just as Matt walks through the door.

"Hey, buddy. I wasn't expecting you." We shake hands. I introduce Matt and Barbara, who both know about each other.

"Nice to meet you, Matt." Her phone beeps. "Stephan's asking if

I'm on my way to the pizza place. I need to run before all the pizza's gone." She puts her phone in her pocket. "I'll keep you posted on everything. I'll try to stop by with the family before we go."

I hug her, and she's out the door.

Matt waits for me at the bar, looking exhausted.

"So what's up? You rarely have the time to come here."

"Why was your agent here?"

"You answer me first."

He hands me an envelope. "Here's the final head count, including vegetarian requests."

I rest a hip against the bar. "Cool. Let's sit and have a beer. Do you have time?"

"Sure. I need a break from all this wedding planning. I'll have a *Weißbeer*." He points to the large mugs.

I fill two mugs and hand his to him. "Let's go to the beer garden. I need some fresh air."

We find a table in the corner. Unfortunately in the smoking section.

"You could've emailed me the numbers. Things stressful with the wedding?"

Matt sits on the bench and lets out a big sigh. "The wedding and the bakery. Our business is booming. More than we anticipated. I was asked to do an interview for *Pastry & Baking North America*."

"Wow. That's huge. Great advertising. Congratulations." My gut tells me there's more to his visit. "What else is going on?"

He groans. "On top of working ridiculous hours, Kayla's also stressed about the little wedding details. She has a massive spreadsheet listing every tiny thing we need to do. How many white rose petals and little bottles of bubbles do we need for the church ceremony and after. Or get this one—for the place cards at the reception, she's writing each one herself. Every *i* in someone's name has to have a red heart instead of a dot. We have over two hundred guests coming. Who would even notice it?"

Tina would.

He shakes his head. "I just want to get married. I'm glad we only have a couple of weeks left. When the time comes for you to get married, elope." He takes two big swigs. "I didn't come here to talk about the wedding. How are things going since I saw you all at the bakery? Did you do something with Alexa and Tina?"

"Alexa made up some excuse to go home so Tina and I could do something alone together."

"Something is pushing you two together. You finally take a day off, and she ends up at the bakery."

I nod in agreement. "We walked through Central Park. But it wasn't a date. We've decided to stay friends for now."

His mouth rises up on one side. "How's that working out for ya? I didn't know friends hold hands."

I groan. "It's the worst, man."

He pulls out a pack of cigarettes. My mouth flies open. "Since when do you smoke?"

"Since I asked Kayla to marry me. With the constant stress from the wedding and the long hours at the bakery, we're fighting a lot. There's no downtime. We fought about the damn seating chart tonight, so that's why I'm here. I needed a breather. Want one?"

"Not me. I can't get past the taste. I'm sure Kayla *loves* it when you smoke."

He flicks his lighter several times. "Why do you think I'm smoking here? She hates it and despises the way I smell afterwards. I'm not allowed to touch or kiss her. It's a sure sign of stress when I smoke."

"I guess there'll be no make-up sex for you when you get home."

A regular comes up to me and gives me a high five. That's what I love about this place. It's casual, and regulars come and go.

"That's what a shower and toothpaste are for." He grins. "I'm assuming Tina still doesn't know who you are. I think I would've heard something from you or James by now. You know I'm going to get in trouble for knowing who Tina is."

"I know. Thanks for being quiet about it. I haven't said anything to her, and I'm not sure I will."

He shakes his head. "No way. You need to tell her. How long are you going to wait? Don't you want to get it off your chest?" He takes a long drag of his cigarette. The tip glows brightly, like a firefly. He exhales long and slow while the smoke glides behind him like a ghost in the breeze. "It's really not a big deal."

I hunch over the table without lifting my head. "Maybe it isn't a big deal, but my gut tells me it won't go over well. I don't want to say anything while we're working together. It would make things really awkward if this becomes negative. Why does it have to be so complicated?" I yank myself back up. "I can't let her go this time. We're meant to be together. She's mine."

He bursts out laughing. "She's yours. What are you, a caveman? Do you have a club at home?"

"I can't tell you the last time I've been this happy. When I'm around her, nothing else matters. We had a blast in Central Park. She makes me laugh. I want to be with her all the time, and we haven't even kissed yet."

"It was good to see you took a day off. You need a life outside of work. It was the same in Germany. All work and no play. You've been like that since you opened this restaurant. Maybe the change in pace will inspire you again. What happened that one night at your restaurant in Hamburg is long gone. It shouldn't bother you anymore."

"What is with you and Barbara tonight?"

"Hey, why was she here anyway?"

"She basically confronted me and said what you just said." I look over his shoulder to observe how one of the servers is speaking to a customer. By her body language and the scowl on her face, she's not happy. Something I need to discuss with her.

I return my focus to Matt when he starts talking. "You need to hear it. Don't you miss cooking? The night at Wine Cellar was excellent except for Tina's allergy. Kayla said the guests couldn't stop talking about the delicious food and how fun it was."

"It felt unbelievable being back in a gourmet kitchen like that. It was fun. That's what I miss about cooking. The fun part."

"Are you sure you want to cater the wedding? I'd kill you if you backed out though," he says with a fake laugh.

"If Kayla didn't kill me first. But of course I want to do it. You're crazy if you think otherwise." I swirl my beer in the glass. "Sure, I miss cooking. I just don't want to get caught up in the stress again. Life is too short to aim for constant perfection. Why do you think I gave my star back right after the incident?"

"Doesn't this restaurant take up most of your time?" He stamps out his cigarette in the ashtray.

"Yes, but I'm not the chef, and I call the shots. I have people I can count on when I'm not here. We serve good home-style German food. None of that fancy shit I was caught up in back in Hamburg. Now that I've met Tina, I need to live a little." I finish my beer and think of Tina with her beer mustache. I smile to myself.

"You know how I've always dreamed about having my own cooking show."

He nods.

"That's why Barbara was here." I explain what Barbara and I discussed.

"If this works out, are you sure you want to get involved with Tina if there's ever a possibility of you going back? If you even want to go back."

"I don't know. I can't think so far ahead. Every time I get close to a deal, it never works out. I'm not going to push Tina away for something that most likely won't happen."

"Who knows how Tina will react when she finds out who you are. But if you're meant to be together, things will work out in the end. It just might be a bumpy road to get there."

He stands up and shoves his cigarettes in his pocket. "Well, I'm here for the next couple of weeks if you need to talk. After the wedding, we're gone for two whole weeks. I can't wait to get the hell out of here and fry ourselves in Hawaii, among other things." He waggles his eyebrows as he pulls money from his wallet.

"Stop bragging, and don't even try to pay for your beer."

"Hey, don't forget about my bachelor party. Kayla and I will meet everyone here for the first drinks and then go our separate ways to party."

"Don't worry. It's already on the books. Several tables have been reserved. I hope I can take that night off."

"Thanks, man. I owe you one. Talk to you soon." He turns and walks away.

I sit alone and finish my beer. What if VOX does offer me a deal? I'd need to move back to Germany. Now that Tina's in my life, I'm not sure that's an option anymore. What if I asked her to go with me? But we've only known each other for a couple of weeks. She wants to explore different countries, not live in them.

I massage my tired eyes. I'm getting way ahead of myself when it comes to Tina.

<h1 style="text-align:center">Chapter 18</h1>

I'm running on zero right now. This day was loaded with nonstop action. Spending time with Gerry has pushed us to a new level of friendship. We act like goofy teenagers without a worry in our minds.

"I still can't believe you had these T-shirts made for us." I bump him with the grocery bag I'm carrying.

He laughs. "Hey, I couldn't resist. My friend makes T-shirts. I want everyone to know we are *just friends*, so why not make T-shirts that say it? Now everyone in the city knows I'm not your boyfriend, and we look like two idiots."

I swerve out of the way before I bang into a guy who's playing with his phone without paying attention to where he's going. "How convenient for you that my T-shirt's a bit snug in the chest." I glance at him and see that sexy smirk thing he does so well. "At least I can thank you that mine's purple." What's nice for me is his shirt is snug too, but black with purple lettering. I can see the defined curves of his muscles. My hormones skitter into a frenzy when I gawk at him.

After Central Park, we've been talking as much as possible. Sometimes it's for business, but most of the time it's personal. Did I ever have braces? Does he have any tattoos or piercings? Did I ever smoke? Did he ever skinny-dip or ride a motorcycle? He has skinny-dipped, because his parents have a pool. That wasn't an easy conversation since it made me think of him naked in a pool. But I don't want to know who he skinny-dipped with. As for riding a motorcycle, he never answered, because we got distracted by something else. I can just imagine how mouthwatering he would be on a motorcycle.

He always finds something for us to do. He makes it sound so casual and random, but I wonder if he thinks about it beforehand. Today, we went to the Statue of Liberty, walked over the Brooklyn Bridge, and had lunch in Chinatown. Every second I'm with him, the more I want to be with him.

Instead of going to a restaurant for dinner tonight, he offered to cook for me. At *his* apartment. Since we started this *just friends* thing, we've not spent time in each other's apartments. I was surprised he asked, since he says he rarely cooks for other people now. Maybe his desire to cook is coming back. We agreed on plain old spaghetti and meatballs.

"I can't wait to sit down. My dogs are barking."

"You and your sayings," he mumbles. He unlocks the apartment door. "I know we did a lot today, but we need to take advantage of this awesome fall weather."

"I can't wait to look at our selfies from today. Can we download them onto your computer?"

"Sure. I've downloaded the others already. We can do it after we eat. I want to frame the picture of you shoving a huge handful of peanut M&Ms in your mouth," he adds smoothly.

"Oh, and you shoving almost an entire hot dog in your mouth was any better? Ketchup-and-mustard face. Disgusting!"

"*B*uuut, we don't have a picture of it."

I crinkle my face in annoyance as he gestures for me to go inside.

He chuckles behind me. "Someone gets cranky when she's hungry."

I step into a narrow, compact kitchen to the right. The appliances look top-notch. I almost need sunglasses—the room sparkles, it's so clean.

"Your kitchen looks like a showroom. Is it because you're anal or because you don't use it often?"

"Probably both. I never really wanted to cook for anybody here until you arrived looking like a pirate. Hey, maybe we should watch Pirates of the Caribbean tonight." His eyes crinkle on the sides and his lips fold in to hold back his laughter.

"Don't start Mr. Instigator over there. You're lucky my hands are full. Are you lacking sugar, or did you drink a can of sarcasm today?"

"I think you're the one lacking sugar." He's right.

As we move farther in and put the groceries down on the tiny kitchen counter, I'm surprised to see the apartment as a whole isn't so small, the way people claim city apartments are. It isn't huge, but it's the perfect size for one person.

He points to the left and taps a door. "Here's the bathroom when you need it." He walks out of the kitchen which is immediately the living room and then he turns to the right. "Here's my bedroom."

I peak in. There's a king-size bed with a fluffy black-and-white checkered comforter. It taunts me to take a nap after all the walking we did today. *I love naps.* There's no space for a dresser or any other furniture except one small black nightstand. Ceiling fans spin in lazy circles in each room. The wall connecting the bedroom with the living room is red brick. "I like the red brick walls. It's unique and adds some color to your place."

"When I go to bed, I close the folding doors. It blocks some of the noise. You'd be surprised how loud it still is during the night. Even with the windows closed." He opens and closes the black, squeaking doors.

I turn slowly in the living room which includes a tiny kitchen table for two, a couch, small TV and a desk. I do a double take when I notice a staircase going down. "Do you have a basement?"

"Not a basement. It leads to another bedroom and guest bathroom, but I use it for my rowing machine and storage. As you can see, I have no space up here for any big furniture."

"Two bathrooms and two floors in this small apartment, and you live so close to work. You're spoiled rotten."

He opens the bags and puts the items on the counter. "Sit down and rest your feet while I cook. I don't keep beer here, but I have wine. What will it be? Red or white?"

I put my hand on my hip. "And who said I wanted to drink tonight? In case you don't remember, I need to go home later."

He snaps his fingers. "That sucks. I was hoping I could get you drunk and take advantage of you. You ruin all the fun." He pouts. "You said Alexa's away this weekend for sales training. She'd never know."

"You're funny. Maybe I want to take advantage of you. What do you think of that?" I poke his arm.

"Let's go!" He pretends to pull me to the bedroom.

I tug him back. "You're a real riot." I tickle his ribs while he tries to wiggle away. "Red wine sounds good."

"I want to get everything ready now so we can relax while the sauce and meatballs simmer. You can sit and talk to me while I chop away. But first let me get the wine."

He goes downstairs and comes back with two bottles. He hands one to me with a corkscrew. "Can you open this for me please?"

I'm not good at opening wine bottles, so it takes me several seconds. I don't want to break the cork. I let the bottle sit open for a few minutes.

"Want to listen to some music? I can plug in my *handy*." He clears his throat. "Um...iPhone. Who's your favorite band?" he asks while chopping the hell out of fresh parsley.

I'm waiting for pieces to shoot over his shoulder like Edward Scissorhands.

"One Republic. I'm not a fan of concerts, but that's one band I'd love to see. Ryan Tedder has a voice I could listen to all day long. If he sang to me, I'd cry just like his groupies." I close my eyes and smile.

"A famous German actor wrote and directed a movie that had the remix of 'Apologize' on the soundtrack. The song became a huge hit in Europe. That's how I heard of them the first time."

"That's my favorite song by them." I don't push him to turn on music. I enjoy talking to him. Granted, I can still hear the muffled sounds of the city outside. Being here alone with him in his apartment is more exciting than anything else we've done. My craving for him increases every day. It's hard not to hear his voice at least once a day.

He stops his chopping madness and wipes his hands on the dishtowel hanging from his belt loop. He reaches for some onions.

My eyes spring open as I watch him. "It's amazing how fast you chop onions. I'd be so afraid to cut my finger off."

"Practice makes perfect. Believe me—I've cut myself plenty of times. Some of them needed stitches." He points out one noticeable scar on his finger.

I lift my hand up. "No need to share the details."

I pour us wine, and I giggle.

"What's so funny?" he says.

"I'll never be able to toast my friends, family, or you, for that matter, without locking eyes with them again. No need for more bad luck in the bedroom. Maybe that's why I've had such a dry spell these last years." I giggle again. "I have the giggles, and I haven't had a drop of wine yet."

"I like you this way. Start drinking. Maybe you'll tell me your deepest, darkest secrets."

"If I do, then you need to spill yours too. There's no one way here." His gaze slips from mine, and his good mood shifts for a moment to something I can't name but returns within seconds. So he does have secrets.

"Cheers!" he says. Our eyes connect, knowing our luck in the bedroom will be far from bad. I can't wait.

I smack him on the butt and lean against the counter. "Get back to your duties, my giant chef. I'm starving. I need food if I'm going to drink this wine."

He cuts up a baguette and puts the pieces in a basket.

"Aren't you going to wear your chef hat?" I say, only half kidding. I kind of want to see him with one on.

"Why? Do you think it's sexy?" He growls.

I cock my head to the side. "I don't know. I never thought

watching a man chop vegetables would be attractive, and you proved me wrong there a few minutes ago. Why not add the hat to it?"

"Obviously I don't wear it at home. If I did, I'd suggest you walk out the door right now." He aims his chin toward the door. "I'd brand myself as crazy."

I spread a gob of butter on a piece of baguette. "You didn't have one on when I ate those currants."

He shrugs. "I took it off in the kitchen before I went to your table."

"One more question. Why do you always wear black?"

"It's only out of habit. A chef is always covered in food by the end of the day. I'd rather not see it. Working in a restaurant is the same."

He sautés onions and garlic as I munch away. "Hey, not too much garlic. Alexa will kick me out of our apartment when she comes home tomorrow morning. She hates when someone smells like garlic. Her nose can detect it from a mile away even a day later. It's hysterical how angry she gets. And people say my nose is sensitive."

He points to the fresh parsley. "I'll give you a bunch of parsley to chomp on when you go home. That'll help. Or you'll just look like a rabbit."

As he prepares the meatballs, I roam into the living room. I place my wine on the end table and plop onto the couch. "Phew. It feels good to sit." I could get used to someone cooking for me. I love to eat food, not cook it. "Thanks for cooking, good looking. No one—well, no guy—has ever cooked for me. This is a real treat."

He drops the last meatball in the sauce. "I love how you talk. You make me laugh and teach me new ways to say things."

"What can I say? I love to entertain." I lay my arm on the back of the couch.

He washes his hands. "Good. Now this needs to simmer for about thirty minutes." He sets the timer that's on the counter. "I think the baguette will hold us over for now."

"It soaks up the wine, so I need to eat some more." I scoot over to the left. "Come sit on the couch with me and relax. You deserve it."

He takes his wine and sits down. "Ahhh. That does feel good. I guess my dogs are barking too." He cracks up.

He takes my sneakers off, then lays my feet on his lap and begins to massage them. At first, I'm embarrassed he's touching my feet. What if they smell? But no way am I pulling them away. "That feels *so* good. I love to have my feet and hands massaged." I moan as I lean my head back on the couch to savor the moment. "I could get used to this. You making me dinner and now a foot massage. Doesn't it gross you out to touch my feet? Feet are disgusting. Garlic to Alexa is what feet are to me." I crinkle my nose.

"I'll never be grossed out by your feet or anything else on your body."

I lift my head up and notice the sweetest smile on his face. My heart quickens, but I lay my head back again before my hormones insist I do something I shouldn't.

"Where did you get your necklace? You wear it every day. You haven't been playing with it as much lately. Does that mean you aren't as nervous when you're with me?"

I touch my necklace softly and look at him again. "My nervousness decreases every minute I spend with you. You're always so relaxed, which calms me down."

"Is there a special story behind it?"

Should I tell him? He'd be the first person to know. The urge to tell him everything about me is intense. I inhale deeply. "My mom gave me this necklace for my sixteenth birthday. She sat me down on my bed and gave it to me when we were alone. When I opened the jewelry box, I cried. My parents never gave me something so expensive. Mom didn't work, and Dad was a mechanic. We didn't have a lot of money."

"Is that why you love purple so much?" His strong hand massages a spot that makes me want to melt into the couch.

"Actually, purple was her favorite color. It's my birthstone. She wanted to give me something that would remind me she's always with me. She died before my seventeenth birthday. It's almost like she knew she wasn't going to be around for long. My dad and Lisa forgot my seventeenth birthday. They didn't even notice I got my driver's license. I almost didn't pass, but I did it for Mom." My heart aches thinking about it. "Anyway, it was her favorite color, so it became mine too."

"Anything purple makes me think of you. It brings more than a smile to my face." His warm eyes say everything.

"I didn't know such a burly guy like yourself could be so sweet and romantic in a sexy kind of way." I try to deny his honesty affects me. *Do not let yourself feel anything, or you'll get in trouble tonight.*

"I didn't know I was a romantic either until I met you." He tickles my foot. I yank it away in response because I can't stand when someone tickles my feet. It's the worst torture ever.

He stifles a laugh. "Sorry. I'll stop. Keep going." He gently pulls my other foot on his lap and massages it.

"When she gave it to me, she told me something I'll never forget. She kneeled in front of me as I sat on my bed. She took my hand in hers and told me how proud she was of me and made me promise I'd follow my dreams to get out of New Jersey and make something of myself. To follow my desire to travel, to push myself outside my comfort zone, to go after what I want without backing down, to never be afraid of anything. She never did it herself, but she wanted me to explore the world before I was to ever settle down and have a family. She saw how smart I was in school and envied the drive I had. She knew I couldn't handle monotony after I graduated high school." I pause for a second to push back the light tears beginning to form. "She gave me the best gift that day, and it wasn't the necklace. She gave me the strength and encouragement to do whatever I wanted."

My voice cracks as a single tear escapes and trickles down my cheek. I never cry in front of people. He wipes it away with his thumb and gently caresses my face. I touch his hand with mine and lean my face into it to enjoy the comfort of his intimate touch. "But those dreams and ambitions disappeared when she died. I deserved it. Now all I have is this necklace. I wear it every day. I don't know when I took it off last. It'd kill me to lose it, because I'd lose her all over again."

His head flinches back. "Wait. What do you mean, you deserved it?"

"Never mind. Ignore what I just said." I spring from the couch, pissed I slipped like that. He follows me.

He captures my hand in his and places it over his heart. "I'm not going to ignore it. Sit back down and tell me. I promise it'll never change how I feel about you, and I won't tell a soul." He pulls on my hand. I follow and sit back down.

I inhale deeply. "It was my fault that day." I cover my face with my hands. "It was all my fault."

He pulls my hands away from my face. "Why would you say something like that? It was an accident. You weren't even in the car. Right?"

I stare at a speck on the wall. "Things happened that morning between my mom and me. I'll regret it for the rest of my life. That's all I'm willing to say." I scoot away from him. "Please don't push me. I've never told anybody what happened." I force back the tears that are just about to win. *Don't cry.* The one tear that fell was enough.

He remains still, and his face only reflects sympathy, not disappointment.

I search for my bag.

"What are you looking for?"

I sniff in the most disgusting way. "Tissues."

He retrieves a box from the side table. I pull one from the box and blow my nose. His hand presses on my leg. "Please talk to me. It's obvious you have been hiding something for years. You need to talk about it."

I shake my head. "No. I'm not saying anything else. This is something I can't talk about. I never have and never will. Not to you. Not to anyone. I'm sorry I even said anything."

He brushes strands of hair away from my face. "Does anyone know how you torture yourself?"

I shake my head.

"You've been suffering by yourself all these years?"

I nod. "Now you know why I went to the batting cages. I needed to find something to get my anger, regret, sadness, and every other emotion out that was draining me. I'd come home with blisters on my hands and pain in my shoulders and arms. Then I took up yoga to try to deal with it in a softer, healthier way."

"I can't believe your friends and family didn't see what you were going through. It makes me mad." His jaw tightens.

"In the beginning, it wasn't easy, but once things calmed down, I slapped the smile on my face and wore it as much as I could. When I needed a moment, I'd let go behind closed doors. I'd lock myself in my bedroom and sit in my closet and cry. I spent a lot of time at my mom's grave, begging her for forgiveness. I deserved to grieve alone. The more I hid my feelings, the easier it got. Then it became my norm. The teardrop you just saw never happens. I don't allow myself to cry in front of people."

"Doesn't anyone notice you don't cry? Didn't you tell me one time that your sister is a therapist? I'm sorry. It doesn't make sense." He shakes his head with annoyance.

"For a long time we lived apart. We spoke mostly on the phone because we were both in different colleges. When we're together, I'm genuinely happy. Once in a while, someone will ask why I don't cry. I just blow it off."

His body stiffens. "When I'm with you, you seem happy. Is it real happiness, or is it an act?" He tips away from me and looks into my eyes uneasily.

I grab his shirt, pull him closer, and say with complete sincerity, "I've *never* been happier than when I'm with you. What you see isn't an act. The only thing I try to hide is my feelings for you, but you make it so hard because you're so damn cute." I nudge him back and let go of his shirt.

His face softens.

"This is difficult for me to explain. I don't want you to think I'm not a happy person or am completely mental. As time passed, I became content with my life. I got used to it. Lisa still had moments, and I was always there for her. I finished college and graduate school. I live my life; it's just not quite the way I imagined."

"Maybe you should talk to your dad and Lisa. Don't you think you'd feel better if you opened up to them? It's not healthy to keep it all inside."

I shove my hands between my legs. "No. I'd never burden them with this. Then they would feel bad. It would be one big, vicious cycle." I close my eyes and take a few breaths. "Please don't tell anyone. This is between you and me. Don't make me regret telling you."

He takes my face in his big but gentle hands. "I swear on my life I will *never* tell a soul. Thank you for telling me this much. Maybe one day, you'll trust me enough to let me in. It helps me understand you much better. And the obsession with your necklace."

He kisses my forehead, then pulls away. I look into his eyes, and my heart bursts open. If I'm not careful, I'm going to fall in love with him one day...if I'm not already.

I close the gap between us, urging him to kiss me. He looks at my lips and dips his head. This is it. It's going to happen. I don't care anymore.

We spring apart when the timer screeches in the kitchen.

Chapter 19

Gerry

My heart races, but it's not because of the timer. This isn't just sexual attraction. I adore every ounce of this woman. She thinks she caused her mom's death but hasn't told anyone. How could she do that and still be sane? I wish she'd tell me what happened. She wants to change her life, but the first thing she needs to do is get it out and forgive herself. I need to find a way for her to feel comfortable enough to open up to me.

"I'll set the table while the spaghetti cooks. Do you want more wine?" she offers.

And just like that, the last half hour is forgotten. Her smile is back on her face, and the mood shifts to something more positive.

I nod while I pour the spaghetti into the pot. "Want some water? There are bottles in the fridge."

She takes a few out and puts them on the table, then refills our wineglasses.

"Here." I hand her plates and silverware. "This'll keep you occupied." For the next few minutes, we work in comfortable silence. I've never had a relationship like this before.

"Sit down. Everything's ready. I hope you like my special meatballs. They'll melt in your mouth," I say over my shoulder.

She claps her hands like a little girl. "I can't wait to try them. There's nothing like good ole spaghetti and meatballs."

I place the pot in the middle of the small table.

"We're missing something." I rummage through the cabinets and pull out two white candles and holders. "I bought these in case of a power outage. Every once in a while, it happens. But now I can use them for something special." I make room on the table and light them.

"As I said, you're a romantic. I like it. I've never had a candlelit dinner before."

"Thank my mom for that. Ever since I could remember, she's always had candles around the house. She loves them. I'm used to it."

"I'm excited to meet your parents at the wedding. They did a great job with you." She wipes the corner of her mouth with her finger while smiling.

"My dad's also a romantic. He treats my mom like a queen, and they still act like they're newlyweds. Perfect role models for me. For anyone."

"My parents were like that too. I know Dad loves my stepmom, Beth, but it's not quite the same. But they're really happy together. Which makes Lisa and me happy."

We eat in silence because we're inhaling the food.

"These are the best meatballs I've ever eaten. Please make them for me again someday," she says.

I like it when she talks about the future like there will be an *us*.

She pats her belly. "I don't think I can fit another one in here." She sips more wine. "According to my numb lips, I think this is my third glass. I lost count after we opened the second bottle, which is almost empty."

She stares at my hand playing with my eyebrow. "Now it's your turn. How did you get the scar above your eyebrow?"

"I was trying to be adventurous. I wanted to impress a girl in high school. My friends and I were good at doing tricks with our bikes. You know the kind where you ride fast up a ramp and are midair and twirl the bike around and then land?"

She nods with a hiccup. "Sorry." She chuckles.

"I wasn't good at it yet, but the girl I liked came over to watch us. I thought I'd be cool and try something dangerous." I cringe, remembering the pain.

"Long story short, I hit my brakes accidentally and flipped over the handlebars onto my face. Everyone laughed until they saw the blood streaming down my face. I hit a rock—had to get five stitches. Instead of the girl being impressed, she laughed and walked away. Talk about a blow to the ego. The embarrassment was even worse than the pain. I still remember how it felt." I press on the scar again.

She drinks the last drop of her wine.

"Be careful. I don't want you getting too drunk."

"Too late. I'm already drunk...or at least extremely tipsy," she says in a high-pitched voice. I shake my head. I'm feeling the wine a little bit myself.

"So what about you? What's the most embarrassing thing that ever happened to you? The day we met with your sunglasses or something else?" I eat the last forkful of spaghetti.

She relaxes back in her chair and stares at something behind me, as if in deep thought.

"Are you okay? You don't have to answer."

Her sleepy eyes glisten in the candlelight. "I could sit here for hours and talk to you. I know in my heart you won't judge me." She rests her chin in her hand. "And no, it isn't because I'm kinda drunk."

I grin. "Now it's *kinda drunk*, huh?" I tease. "Tell me whatever you want."

She focuses on the flickering candle flame. "I was humiliated once. When I was about to graduate college. I went to my first frat party at another school."

My stomach clamps, and I wish I hadn't eaten so many meatballs. I can't believe she's telling me this story as her most embarrassing moment. Now I'm really a dick.

She tells me about that night when I kissed her and walked away. She doesn't go into much detail but says she could hardly kiss the others. "I felt like we connected. I never had such an intense experience kissing someone. Until recently, I've never felt that kind of pull to someone." She looks at me under her lowered lashes.

It's fascinating to hear her experience was just as incredible. I'm relieved she wasn't into the others, but it kills me that I hurt her more than I thought. Even though she's talking about me, jealousy erupts, as if she's talking about someone else. This entire situation is so screwed up. I growl out loud.

She reaches over the table and touches my hand. "Oh, Gerry, I'm sorry. I shouldn't be talking about another guy to you," she rambles. "I'm not sure I'd want to hear about your history with women."

"It doesn't bother me. I just think the guy was stupid, but what makes you think he didn't feel the same? He could've left for a million other reasons."

"Alexa said the same."

I swallow hard. "You told her?" This could be bad.

"Yes. But she and my two friends that were with me are the only people who know. It was my fault. My adventurous side was begging me to have some fun and do something stupid for once. With the outcome, you can probably figure out I never did anything like that again. It still haunts me. I wish I'd never done it, because now I compare that kiss to every single one I have." She avoids eye contact and drinks her glass of water. "Of course, the details of that entire night came flooding back when I heard about the blindfolded taste testing. It makes me cringe to think of that night long ago."

"I think you're too hard on yourself. There are worse things that could happen. You shouldn't regret things anyway. It happened for a reason, and you learned from it." *I know I did.*

"Other than this bike accident, didn't you ever do something that makes your skin crawl every time you think about it? To other people it might not be a big deal, but it is to the person it happened to."

"I'm sorry. When you put it like that, you're right." I drop my napkin and place my silverware on my plate. If I want her to open up to me, then I need to do the same to her. "I did something over a year ago I'll regret for the rest of my life. Just like you said, it makes my stomach turn every time I think about it. Of course, everyone says it was no big deal, just like I said to you."

She puts her water down and gives me her full attention. "Are you going to tell me why you ran away from home?"

"This is hard for me to talk about."

"It's okay. No pressure."

"I've wanted my own cooking show for years. My agent scheduled meetings with a couple of TV networks. It finally got to a point when I thought my dream would come true. One station wrote up a contract that listed everything I wanted. I showed up for the final meeting to sign the papers, and the executive producer broke it to me that they had to pull the show. Some stupid reason about budget and staff. It was all a load of shit." I grip my fists like I'm sitting in front of that producer right now.

My voice becomes sharp. "We fought and raised our voices, but I didn't win. I was fuming." I rub the back of my neck.

"When I called my agent to give her an update, she told me to go home and sweat it off, but I didn't listen. I took the train back to Hamburg and went straight to my restaurant. I should've just gone home. If I had, the worst night of my life would've never happened." *But I wouldn't be here with her right now, either.*

She rests her elbows on the table. "What happened when you got to your restaurant?"

"First, I took out my anger on my kitchen staff by barking orders at them. They weren't fast enough; the food wasn't hot enough... You understand what I mean. I always treat my staff with complete respect, but that night..."

She nods.

"A server came in the kitchen and told me a male guest wanted to speak to me. I forced myself to calm down before I went to him."

"Does this have to do with the little bit you told me before *The Lion King*?"

"Yes. It gets worse." I scratch my chin. "He immediately complained, loudly, that the food looked like it'd been taken out of the garbage and it was cold. He said the restaurant wasn't worthy of a star. I still remember the embarrassed look on his date's face. And instead of reacting appropriately, I freaked. I took out all my anger on him. I told him to leave the restaurant and never come back. But he refused to leave."

"Why wouldn't he leave, if he thought it was so horrible?"

"I don't know, and that just flipped a switch. I took him by the shirt and threw him out of the restaurant. Dishes and glasses fell off the table and shattered all over the floor. He taunted me and then spit in my face." I put my head in my hands like she had earlier. "I punched him in the face."

Tina gasps.

"Yup. I got him outside and punched him right in front the place. All my guests witnessed it through the windows."

"I'm shocked. You're always so laid back and polite. I just can't imagine you like that."

"Usually I am. It takes a lot for me to get so angry. That's when I realized I needed to change something."

"Did someone call the police? Or an ambulance? I hope you didn't hurt him badly."

"A fat lip but nothing broken. He left in a huff, and I thought that was the end of it."

"But it wasn't," she says.

I grit my teeth and shake my head.

"He ripped me apart in several newspapers. I was branded as *the chef with anger issues*. He also lied, saying my restaurant was dirty, there was hair in his food and cockroaches in the bathroom. I'm most diligent when it comes to cleanliness. For someone to insult me and my restaurant was hard for me to take."

"I noticed immediately how clean your restaurant here is. Your staff was polishing items like they were precious diamonds. The bathroom was spotless. I'm sure you're overly clean after what happened. I would be."

"By chance did you notice the sign with the big *A* on the entrance of the Hofbräuhaus?"

She scratches her chin. "I wondered what it meant."

"It's called *restaurant grades*, or an inspection system. Inspectors come at least once a year to check on cleanliness, rodent control, temperature control, and food handling. The letter *A* means it's passed the requirements. It's the highest you can get. So you can bet your ass, my restaurant will always have an *A*. That *A* is more important to me than receiving a Michelin star.

"That's also why I shave my head. Well, my hairline was receding too. But there's no chance of a long hair falling and being found in one of the dishes I prepared." I stroke my head. "I had a full head of hair not too long ago."

She rests her chin on her hands. "I think it's sexy."

"Let me finish my story before you distract me."

She covers her mouth.

"Now remember, I had a Michelin star by then. Publicity like this can ruin a chef's career. I was mortified. All my hard work had disappeared in a second. So before I could lose my Michelin star, I gave it back."

"What happened to the critic?"

I groan. "Word came out he wasn't a critic—he'd been a chef in the past but could never make it to my level. Apparently, he'd done this to other restaurants before mine, too. Obviously he had issues. But it didn't matter to me, because I'd ruined my own reputation.

"I could've handled the situation differently. It would've saved me so much stress, money, and embarrassment. I was losing money every day with the restaurant. My agent canceled all my events. The decision to go to the US came weeks later. I was only planning to hide out for a couple of weeks, but you know how that turned out. And it all led me to you."

We both jump when a police car speeds past my windows, its siren blaring. She moves her arm, knocking her dirty spoon off her plate. It lands on her shirt. "Oh no. I don't want to stain this shirt. Let me rinse it off." She walks quickly to the bathroom.

Good timing. I don't want to turn this night into a downer. Time for a distraction. I take my iPhone off the coffee table. I hit the button to check the time, and I see Barbara tried to call. I turn it to the side and notice it's on mute. There's voicemail, but I'll listen to it later.

I connect my phone to my sound system and pick a song I hope she'll like. The floor is clear of anything we could trip on.

She walks out of the bathroom with her shirt wet at the bottom.

"Do you want one of my shirts?"

She waves her hand as if shooing a fly out of her way. "Nah. It's not bad. Maybe the cold will wake me up a bit." She takes some of the empty plates and puts them on the loaded counter.

"Forget the dishes. I'll do them later. Come here. I want to try something with you." I reach my hand out to her.

She places her soft hand slowly in mine, as if I'm going to pounce. I tug her close to me.

"What are you doing?" she murmurs.

"Dance with me."

She looks up at me like I've lost my mind. "Together? Hand in hand? Chest to chest?"

"Yes. What's the problem?"

"I don't know how to dance like this." She looks around. "And there isn't enough space in this tiny living room." She pulls away.

I don't let go of her hand and pull her back. "Stop making excuses. I'll show you. It's typical in Germany for high school students to learn to dance. Ballroom dancing especially. I hated it."

She shakes her head, but I wrap my arm around her back to keep her in place.

"I'll just make an ass out of myself again."

"But I like your ass." I drop my hand to the top of her backside.

She squints her eyes and pulls my hand up to her waist. "Behave."

"I'm good at leading. Just try it once for me."

"Fine," she relents. "What do I have to do?"

"First, I'm going to teach you how to waltz. It won't be easy in this little space, but let's try anyway."

"Teach away, big guy. Don't complain when your toes hurt tomorrow."

"I don't care. It's worth it." I peck her on the forehead as a natural reflex.

I place her left hand on my shoulder and hold her right hand. I wait for the next song to start. "Now just follow my lead." The next few minutes are a total disaster but hysterical. Tina almost knocks a lamp off the table with her elbow, and I bang into the folding doors to my bedroom.

"It looks like the waltz isn't your favorite. Let's try another dance. It's good for faster songs." I search through my phone to find something else.

She fans her shirt in and out. "I'm sweating like crazy. We had more than enough exercise today."

I stand in front of her and pull her flat against me again. She gasps. The music begins, and I start tossing her around. She giggles the entire time. I spin her so she's almost airborne.

"Please stop. I'm so dizzy," she screeches between laughs. "I'm going to get sick if you don't."

I slow down and let her body slide down mine.

"My sides hurt, and I'm exhausted." She braces herself against me and lays her head on my chest. "I need to sit down." She takes a step back and wipes under her eyes, smearing her makeup.

I pick her up and throw her over my shoulder. She squirms. "What are you doing? Let me down," she demands, even though she's giggling again.

I walk to my bed and gently lay her down.

"Lie here for a little while. I'll do the dishes and then take you home."

She props herself up on her elbows. "You aren't taking me home. I can do it myself."

I shrug my shoulders and walk away. "Whatever you want." She's so stubborn.

The dishes are finished and still not a peep from her. I peek in my bedroom and find her fast asleep. I watch her for a few minutes and wonder how I've found her again. I may have run away from my life in Germany, but this path brought me straight to her.

It's almost eleven. There's no way I'm letting her go home. I pull the blanket over her and tuck her in loosely. I keep the light on but dim it just in case she wakes up and doesn't realize where she is right away.

I take the other pillow off the bed and grab the blanket draped over the couch arm.

It hits me I didn't listen to Barbara's message. It's probably about something stupid and unrelated to the meeting, but I told her I'd listen to her messages. To avoid waking Tina up, I listen to it in the bathroom. My hands shake as I hear her explain why she called. Holy shit! The executive producer has agreed to a meeting the second week of October. He loves my ideas and is ready to discuss everything in detail. She emphasizes how important it is I get my ass to Germany for this meeting. Is this my big chance? Will it really happen this time? If yes, do I want to move back there, or is it a case where I can live there during filming but come back here? What about Tina?

I lean on the sink with my head hanging down. Why now? The thought of being disappointed again makes me sick. I splash water on my face to calm down.

The bathroom door squeaks when I open it.

I stand next to the small couch, knowing I'm not going to rest well on it with my long legs.

Her sleepy voice floats to me from the bedroom. "Come lie with me."

I turn around and walk toward her.

"I promise I won't bite—not until our project is over anyway." She smiles sweetly with her eyes closed.

"Are you sure? I don't want you to be mad when you wake up tomorrow and see my drool on the pillow or I smell like garlic or... Oh. Sorry. That's Alexa's problem."

"Stop playing around and come cuddle with me."

I freeze at the end of the bed to see if she's serious.

"I'm not drunk. Please come lie with me. It's been so long since

I've been held. Friends cuddle, don't they?" she pleads.

Not really.

I turn the light off next to the bed. The thought of lying behind her and holding her already has my hormones in an uproar. I kneel on the bed and secretly place a pillow between us to hide the evidence of the body part that has sprung into action and might poke her in the back. I shift myself to the correct position on my right side and spoon her. She pulls my arm around her waist and laces her fingers through mine. My face nuzzles her silky hair and neck. This is exactly how it should be.

I squeeze her hand and whisper, "Are you feeling okay?"

She nods. "I'm perfect. Today was perfect. You're perfect."

I squeeze her tighter to me. *"Das bin ich nicht."*

It's true. I'm not perfect. After what she told me tonight, I don't deserve to lie here with her. I should've told her the truth. But I'm a coward because I know the chance of losing her has increased even more.

"Go to sleep, *Süße*." She shimmies closer to me. Thank God, the pillow is between us. "Sleep well."

I know I need to tell her, but I'm going to enjoy the time with her until the website is finished. At that time, I'll come clean.

"Gerry?" she mumbles.

"Hmm."

"You're the best friend I've ever had."

I'm going to hell.

Chapter 20

Peggy and I show our badges as we walk into the office building. I tap her elbow with mine. "Thanks for going to lunch with me today."

"I should thank you. Your secret updates remind me of my husband and me." She places her hand over her heart. "So nostalgic."

When we enter our floor, I pull her arm. "Let's stop by Tim's cube. I want to see how he's progressing with the videos of the restaurant table layouts. If anything delays us, it'll be them." I put my finger over my lips. "Let's scare him," I whisper.

She nods.

We tiptoe into his cube and roughly shake his chair. He rockets up from it like firecrackers shot off in his pants.

Peggy and I grab our stomachs while hysterically laughing.

He yanks off his headphones while panting. "You two are going to be the death of me. I thought that's the role of my twin daughters. It's not fair, two against one." He tosses his headphones on the desk and falls back into his chair, his arms hanging to the sides.

"If you're through with your ridiculous scaring tactics, I searched for you both before."

"What's up?" I say.

"Rumor has it," he whispers, "there's discussion of opening a California office. Supposedly, some of the staff from here will have the option to transfer. Granted, it's only a rumor. I heard it by the water cooler."

I look at Peggy and roll my eyes. "Definitely a rumor then."

He shrugs his shoulder. "Whatever. Think what you want." He sips his coffee. "I'm assuming you're here to talk about the videos. Let's talk fast. I've a deadline. Remember?"

When we're finished, I leave his cube wondering if a California office is just a rumor. Maybe it's true, since Thomas mentioned several clients are located there. He never said anything about expanding, though. I slide my pendant from side to side. He wouldn't ask me to relocate anyway—I've only been here a couple of months. But it'd be a dream come true if he did.

The ringing of my phone interrupts me. My fingers touch everything but my phone in my bag. Finally, I find the vibrating object and whip it to my ear.

I don't recognize the number. "Hello."

"Hi. Is this Tina Schmitt?"

"Yes. How can I help you? I don't want to buy anything." Since when do I get telemarketing calls?

"Gerry Maier asked me to call you regarding this Saturday. Is this a good time?"

Why is someone else calling me?

I'm already pissed because Gerry hasn't contacted me directly this week, especially after I spent the night at his apartment. But he did ask me to go out this Saturday. When we woke up on Sunday, he made us an awesome breakfast before he had to go to work. He wanted to take the day off again, which shocked me. But I said no. I wanted nothing more than to spend the day with him again, but I had no fresh clothes.

We had spoken every day before that night. Now, not a peep from him. Maybe I shouldn't have told him some of my secrets. Gerry's the first person I've ever told the full story behind my necklace, and now I regret it.

"Yes, it's fine." My tone sharp.

"He'd like to pick you up at your apartment at five thirty Saturday evening. You'll need to wear a nice dress, and you shouldn't eat beforehand. Will that work for you?" the man inquires politely.

"Yes. But why are you calling me and not him? Is he sick or something? Or doesn't he have the time?" I drill him.

A light chuckle breaks through his professional tone. "He said you'd probably be annoyed. I guarantee he has only good intentions. He promises to tell you why on Saturday."

"Fine," I say through gritted teeth. "Thank you for your call. Can you please tell him he'd better have a good reason, since he hasn't contacted me this entire week?"

"Yes, ma'am. I'll do so. Have a good day."

"Thank you." I hit End hard with my pointer finger.

What the hell? Why would he have someone else call me? Maybe this is when I'll see the real side of Gerry. The man with anger issues. Then I won't like him anymore, and this crazy escapade will be over.

But my life would be so boring and empty without him.

I refused to contact Gerry for the rest of the week. Not even by email regarding work. I had Peggy do it, which I know is unprofessional. But two can play at this game. It was really hard though. I miss him more than I should. Now I'm standing in front of my bedroom mirror staring at myself. I shouldn't care how I look, but I do. On purpose, I look sexier than ever. I'm wearing the dress I originally bought for the wedding—a beautiful sleeveless maroon dress that sweeps across my waistline, accentuating my curves. My shoes were a gift to myself. High silver strappy sandals that promise to make my legs look long and toned. I have curls in my hair, which Alexa insisted on. Now he'll be sorry for not calling me all week.

I startle when the doorbell rings. "Be strong and don't gush as soon as you see him," I say to myself in my magic mirror.

I take my time answering the door. The bell rings again. *Good. Keep him waiting.* "Coming."

I open the door, and my bitchy thoughts vanish. We both stand like statues. No words are spoken, but they don't have to be. He looks like a dream. His hair and scruff look newly trimmed. He wears black pants and shiny black shoes with no laces. The light-gray button-down shirt matches his black-and-gray tie. His eyes glow as they trail down my body and back up again. All my anger has turned into a hungry erotic mess. Why, oh why, am I being tempted like this?

"Hi, Tina. *Du siest sehr schön aus*," he says with a sultry voice. "Simply beautiful."

"Hi there, handsome. It's good to see you...and to hear your voice. I've missed it," I easily confess.

"I've missed you to. That's why I had a friend of mine call you about today. Maybe it was stupid, but I wanted to see how we'd handle not hearing from each other for several days. It seems to have confirmed my assumption."

"And what was that?" I inch forward.

He grazes his fingers gently across my cheek. "That I can't stand a day where I don't hear your voice, don't see even an email or text message from you. This agreement we have is killing me, especially after last weekend. I want tonight to be special."

"I was furious with you. Now that I know why you did it, you're forgiven. It seems to have worked in both directions. Even though I was mad, I've been counting the days until I saw you again. I don't know if we can consider ourselves just friends anymore."

He takes my hand and kisses it. "Since we slept in the same bed, I think we're borderline."

I tap his chest. "We only *slept* in the same bed. Don't embellish the details."

"I believe we spooned all night. That's not borderline?"

I hold up my hand. "Stop, or we'll never leave."

He stands up straight, and the sexual tension eases.

"Where are we going? I'm dying to know."

"It's a surprise." He holds up two fingers. "Two surprises, actually."

I twirl. "It's fun to dress up like this. This is the original dress I bought for the wedding."

His heated stare traces my curves, and the sexual tension comes screaming back. "If the other is sexier than this one, I'm in a lot of trouble. Actually, *you* are."

His jaw tightens, and my mouth goes dry. *I certainly hope so.*

I grab his arm and squeeze it. "I'm so excited. I can't wait."

"For tonight or the wedding?" he grumbles.

"Definitely both, but one more than the other."

We walk out of the station. "I'll hail us a taxi. The first surprise is too far away for you to walk in those sexy heels." His hungry eyes trail down my legs.

He really needs to stop doing that.

A taxi stops short in front of us, and we get in. "Please tell me where we're going," I beg as he closes the door.

"Be patient, *Süße*." He taps my nose then leans over the seat to tell the driver where we need to go.

I relax in the seat. "What does that even mean? Is it German or French? You said it the other night."

"It's German and means something like *sweetie*."

Well isn't that the cutest thing ever. "Let me try to say it. How does it go again?"

He strokes his temple. "Try this. Think of Seuss in Dr. Seuss. Then add an *a* sound to the end. *Süße*."

I try it and even I think it sounds okay.

"Not bad for your first try."

He angles himself toward me. I purposely sit close to the middle so I could sit closer to him. "Is it okay to call you that?" He plays with a lock of my hair.

"Mmhmm." I grin like a little school girl.

"I hope you like where I'm taking you. It's a French restaurant known for its roast chicken."

"Sounds delish. I'm sure it'll be excellent...as long as there are no red currants."

"You're mean. Just for that comment—"

He grabs me and starts tickling behind my knees and my ribs. However, it's not as much as a tickle but a need for him to touch me in other places. I want him to glide his large hands up my sides and down my back while pressing feather-light kisses on my neck. But then I hear the horn of the taxi.

I look up to see the driver observing us. "Are you going to get out and pay or just pet each other all night?"

We quickly sit up. Gerry pays him fast, and we're out of the taxi in seconds. I burst out laughing when I hear the taxi tires skid on the street.

I tug on the arm of his shirt. "I swear—we're trouble when we're together. Behave in the restaurant, young man."

We walk toward a restaurant called Burnett's. "Oh, how lovely. Look at those doors. I love the textured glass," I say.

"Let's go inside. We're a little late for our reservation, but I know the owner. It shouldn't be a problem."

When we enter the restaurant, an older woman greets Gerry in French. He kisses her on both cheeks. His voice is like silk when French drips off his tongue. A part of me wants this night to end before I do anything stupid.

He introduces me to her. I hear behind me, "Gerry." I step aside and then more French swirls in the air. I'm clueless.

"Burnett, this is Tina. She's the one I wanted to surprise with the reservation in the Sky Top Lounge tonight."

He kisses the top of my hand. "*Bonsoir.* You must be someone special to dine up there this evening. I hope you enjoy it. Please follow me. I'll escort you to your table."

Gerry places his hand on my lower back and urges me to proceed in front of him. What in the world is a sky-top lounge?

My head turns in every direction in awe, and I almost trip up the stairs. It's so romantic with its contemporary dark shades of purple and red décor. The walls are covered in mirrors, making the room look even bigger and leaving me a little disoriented. I follow Burnett up the stairs to a glass-enclosed small dining room with only one table set with soft candles burning.

I glance at Gerry, my eyes wide. "We're eating alone up here?"

He nods with a chuckle.

Burnett pulls a chair out for me to sit down. I hang my handbag off the back. Gerry sits as he receives a wine menu. He leans in. "They have a huge wine cellar. Do you want me to order a bottle? Red or White?"

"I'm in the mood for red. But you choose since you're the expert."

Gerry converses with Burnett in French. Burnett nods with a smile, bows, and disappears down the stairs.

"Gerry, I'm blown away by all this," I say with my arms stretched out. "It so beautiful, and the aromas floating through the air smell so delicious."

"It's the roast chicken you smell. I could eat it every day—it's that good."

"This room overlooks the gigantic gourmet kitchen." I stand up and walk over to the glass wall, marveling at what I see. "There must be fifteen chefs down there." I walk back over to the table and sit down. "Did you have a kitchen this size in your restaurant?"

"No. Mine was much smaller. The restaurant was more intimate."

I trace the polished silverware with my finger. "How do you know Burnett?"

"He was one of my mentors while I studied in France. A couple of years ago, he opened this restaurant. He's done a great job with this place."

"I'm sorry to bring this up, but does he know what happened to you last year?"

"Yes. He was very supportive because he understands how difficult it is to deal with critics. Some critics aren't appreciative of his talents. I know my situation was a lot worse, but it comes with the territory. Everybody has different tastes and expectations. Sadly, everyone remembers the few bad reviews instead of the hundreds of excellent ones."

"You think people will only remember you for that one bad incident. Maybe you need to go back to face it. Maybe you'll be pleasantly surprised."

He readjusts himself in his chair. "My agent, Barbara, begs me to go back. She unexpectedly showed up at the restaurant the other night."

Burnett appears with a wine bottle, and my thoughts flow like the red wine in Gerry's glass. I like the different sides of him. The other night, we had classic spaghetti and meatballs, and tonight we're dining in a fancy French restaurant. He's happy in both elements. I think I am too.

I watch him swirl and smell the red wine like a professional. He smiles at Burnett.

He pours each of us a glass, hands us dinner menus, and leaves again. I gasp as my eyes bulge when I see the prices. Is he crazy? But I don't say anything because I don't want to be impolite.

"Something wrong?"

"No, nope." I shake my head. "Just surprised about the incredible menu choices."

We sit quietly while we look over the menus. Gerry then explains how to taste the wine. You need to look at the glass from different angles to see the color, swirl it a special way with your hand on the stem, and then hover your nose over the rim to smell it. You can take a sip, or you can suck air into your mouth, like drinking it with a straw...or something like that. It looks rude but is supposedly acceptable. I'd probably inhale it wrong and choke on it. He shows me, but I stick with appreciative little sips.

"Back to your agent. Why did she show up?"

"She was tired of me ignoring her messages and emails. Long story short, several people are requesting me for big social events."

I put my wineglass down. "What?" My voice screeches with excitement. "That's great."

His face lacks expression.

"Aren't you happy about this? It proves what happened is in the past."

"Maybe, but it's not what I'm looking for." He sets his wine glass to the side. "I told you how I was ready to sign a deal to have my own cooking show. Barbara claims a known German TV network is interested in my ideas around blind tasting. She thinks this is the chance I've been waiting for."

I crinkle my eyebrows. "Um. So what's the problem?"

"What's the problem?" His face stunned. "I told you. I've been in this position several times before, and it's never worked out. Why should this time be any different?"

"Gerry. You have to go back and try one more time. You'll regret it if you don't."

He looks away and loosens his tie.

"Look at me. You need to do this. Don't give up. Face whatever waits for you back there. Maybe you can have some closure. Or maybe it's the big deal you've been waiting for."

What if he does get this show? Does that mean he'd move back to Germany? Where would that leave us? We aren't together, even though my heart tells me I'm his.

I'm pulled from my ping-pong thoughts when Burnett arrives again. He places a small dish in front of me with a tiny portion of food. I have no idea what it is.

"Tina? What would you like to eat? Do you want an appetizer?"

"I'd like the roasted chicken please. As for an appetizer...why don't you surprise me?"

"Did you ever have duck before?" I shake my head. "Well you will tonight." He smirks and closes his menu.

He tells Burnett our choices, and then he tops off our wineglasses. Gerry looks around the room. "I've always wanted to dine in this room, but I never had someone special to bring here, and I'm always working." He gives me a soft smile as he raises his glass. "To us."

We toast and I take a generous sip this time. It glides smoothly down my throat. "This is the most delicious red wine I've ever had. Like satin going down. Be careful—I might drink this entire bottle before we leave, and I'll pass out on your bed again or spill more secrets."

"I liked it when you slept in my bed. My pillow smelled of lavender like your hair when I went to sleep the next night."

Waking up wrapped in his arms was the most incredible experience I've ever had. I felt special, comforted and desired. He always makes me feel like that. It surprises me how much I crave his affection.

"But we still have surprise number two after this, and I need you sober. Let's get some food in your stomach. Try the *amuse-bouche* that was placed in front of you. It was given to you by the chef to complement the wine I chose."

Before he puts his fork in his mouth he asks, "After all of the things we've done together, what has been your favorite? Should we still call this game *just friends*?"

I wait to eat mine. "It's hard to say. We haven't kissed, which means we haven't crossed the line yet." I smirk. "To answer your first question, I've loved everything. But my favorite of all favorites was hanging out at your apartment. We opened up to each other that night. You showed me how to dance. You fed me the most divine meatballs. We were ourselves and didn't worry about the boundaries. Granted, I drank too much and told you a few things I regretted the next day."

"Never regret telling me anything. I love learning everything about you. I told you—there's nothing you could do or say that would change how I feel about you."

"Now you. What was yours?"

"Let me think for a minute." He closes his eyes, and then a smile slowly forms. "I can't say there's one specific thing. Just being with you makes me happy. I've never wanted to be around a woman as much as I do you. I want you with me all the time, whether we're friends or more." He reaches for my hand. "As we spend more time together, we're more relaxed and enjoy each other's company without worrying about business. After last weekend, I'm glad I left Germany, because I'm right where I want to be. And that's with you."

I release a soft sigh. He's lucky there's a table between us. His fiery eyes reflect exactly what I'm thinking. Our silence is broken when the first course is served.

The dinner flies by in a rush. While we wait for our main course, we watch the kitchen through the window. He explains how the kitchen is run and what each chef is responsible for. Depending on the restaurant, the height of a chef hat shows the rank of each chef. The number of pleats can also represent levels of experience or how many different ways the chef can prepare an egg.

I eat dishes I've never heard of. Things like *foie gras*, *magret de carnad*, and *macaron*. It was a magical experience I'll never forget. I'm not sure the second surprise can beat this one.

Chapter 21

Gerry

I love watching the excitement in her eyes. She searches out the window for some clues to help her figure out where the next surprise is. Her eyes grow wide as the taxi stops in front of the Empire State Building. I offer my hand to help her out and can't help but admire her long legs as she stands. *Look away!*

"I can't believe you brought me here. To other people it's only the Empire State Building, but to be here with you means so much more."

"There's still a bit of a line, but it should move fast. I've read the wait isn't so long this time of day. Let's hope it's true."

She looks up and then at me. Her face has a mask of fear, and then she grabs her necklace. "I've only seen it on TV shows and movies. The building looks so much higher. Suddenly I'm afraid of heights. Or maybe it's the wine."

"You're scared?"

"A little. I've never been that high before. What if I freak out?" She looks up again and shivers.

"Haven't you been in a plane before? That's much higher."

"No. I told you I haven't traveled much, which includes not being in a plane," she snaps.

"I'm sorry. I won't ask again." I take her hand from her necklace and hold it in mine. "I'll be there with you. There's no reason to be afraid."

She squeezes my hand in response. The line moves forward in a slow crawl, but I don't mind.

"How did your parents meet?" she asks.

"My dad was an exchange student at Mom's high school during the eleventh grade. She helped him get comfortable with the school, and they became good friends during the six months he was there. They both claim nothing happened between them. After he went back to Germany, they kept in touch by writing letters to each other. My mom and her best friend took a trip to London, and he met them there with his best friend. From the second they reunited, they knew they were meant to be together." I squeeze her hand. "Sometimes you just know."

A smile appears but turns into a frown when we reach the elevators.

I tug her forward. "It's now or never. Can you do it?"

"Yes. With you, I think I can do anything." Her other hand holds on to my arm. "You said the eighty-sixth floor?" Her grip tightens.

I switch hands with her and wrap an arm around her waist. I pull her tightly against my side...where she'll always belong. The elevator doors close.

After what feels like an hour, the elevator chimes, and the doors open. We let everyone else out first. Once we're alone, we take our time walking out onto the deck, inching a bit closer to the edge.

I feel her body relax, so I let go of her waist and stand behind her. The timing couldn't be better. The sunset is amazing. We remain silent and enjoy the view. "Hey, instead of taking a selfie, let's ask someone to take our picture with this view behind us."

She responds with a big smile.

I take my phone back from the stranger, but Tina doesn't look at the picture. She turns away and leans her forehead against the barrier. "It's astonishing how far away I can see. We couldn't have asked for a better night. Wow. What a great view of both the Hudson and East Rivers and Central Park. And look! There's Jersey City and Hoboken. I can't believe I've waited so long to do this."

The sunset fills the sky with soft oranges and reds; a hint of purple spreads behind scattered gray-blue clouds. "It's unbelievable, isn't it?" I whisper in her ear as I cage her in from behind. She leans back into my chest with her head angled to the side. She has no idea what her touch does to me. I wrap my arms around her. This is against the rules, but I don't care anymore. She doesn't seem to mind either, because she squeezes my arms and pulls me closer to her.

"It's so much prettier than I imagined. Thank you so much for bringing me here."

We stand like this for a few minutes, me enjoying the touch of her warm body against mine more than the view.

"There's no one else I'd rather be here with," she says sweetly.

I graze my cheek against hers. "Me neither."

We wait until the sky is black and we can observe the city full of lights. She turns and faces me. "This has been the most romantic night of my life. Thank you for making so many of my wishes come true." Her warm gaze glides to my lips, inviting me to kiss her.

I cup her face in my hands. "I want to kiss your wine-stained lips more than you can imagine, but we promised we'd wait. I don't want you to regret it after."

Her face droops in disappointment.

"You're right. I know you're right, but I don't want to do the *right thing* anymore." She moves closer to me.

I whisper against her cheek, "I don't either. Please be patient. It'll be worth the wait. I promise." I kiss the top of her head, my lips lingering longer than they should.

I step back. "Let's get our last glimpse of the view so I can get you home and not get us in trouble. The next time I see you will be on Friday when everyone meets up for the bachelor and bachelorette parties. The wedding and work will take up too much time for me otherwise. I'm sorry we can only see each other then."

"I don't like it, but I'll be busy too. Someone's website needs to be finished soon, which means late nights at work." She smirks and tugs on my tie.

"Two of my friends are visiting next weekend. Kayla said it's okay that they come out with us. It's also Lisa's birthday."

"I'm not sure I'll be able to go out with the guys. It depends on how busy it is. I'd rather secretly follow your group to make sure everyone behaves. No dancing on the bars, if you know what I mean."

She plants her hands on her sexy hips. "Now do I look like the type, or even Kayla?"

I laugh. "No, but alcohol can make it a lot easier."

"You have nothing to worry about. If I'm going to dance for anyone, it'll be for you in private." She walks ahead and flashes me a smile over her shoulder.

Matt's wedding can't get here fast enough.

Chapter 22

Lisa, Alexa, Larissa, Cori, and I pack ourselves into the bus headed to the city. We find four empty seats together. Alexa offers to stand.

Tonight's the last night I'll see Gerry until the wedding. We're going to his restaurant earlier than Kayla's group to hang out for a little while. I secretly want to watch him in manager mode and see how he interacts with his guests.

Lisa turns to me in her seat. "Does Gerry know we're coming early?"

Alexa chimes in, "No. But Tina wants to check him out when he's on the job. Maybe even spy for a little while before he sees us." She takes her phone out of her clutch.

I must be an open book. "Whatever you say, Alexa."

Alexa motions with her arms to squeeze together. "I want to take a picture before we party. We need before and after pictures of tonight so we can look at them tomorrow to remember what we did." She chuckles.

"You ladies can get wasted, but there's no way I'm getting so plastered I don't remember anything," I say as Lisa nods in agreement.

The bus takes a sharp turn. Alexa's clutch falls on the ground and opens. We all bend over to look at what falls out. Five different color red lip glosses and her wallet.

"Alexa, are you kidding me?" Lisa says as she helps pick them up.

"What could you possibly need five different ones for?"

Larissa and Cori choke back their laughter.

"To mark her territory," I joke.

"You know it!" Alexa exclaims while shoving everything back in and snapping the clutch shut.

Once we're off the bus, we walk the same route I did when I met Gerry for the first time. I tell them my sunglasses story, and we can't stop laughing. Anything for a good laugh, even if I'm the butt of the joke.

"That's going down in the books. I can just see you standing there, thinking you look all hot and businesslike, but meanwhile you look like a pirate. I can't stop laughing." Cori snorts as she holds her stomach.

My laughter turns into nervous cackles. "Here it is. I hope it's okay to show up early. Maybe our tables aren't available yet." I step away from the entrance with second thoughts.

"I highly doubt he'll have a problem. How many times have you gone out together? Why is this any different? We're here, and we aren't leaving," Alexa declares.

I shoot her a look that clearly means to shut the hell up.

"Wait a second," Lisa interjects while her head bobs from Alexa to me. "So there *is* something going on between you two. How many times have you gone out with him?" She crosses her arms. "And why am I the last to know?"

"We've hardly spoken during the last few weeks because we're so busy. I'll talk to you later about it. There's not much to tell." I try to brush it off like it's nothing, but Lisa keeps giving me the evil eye.

Alexa reaches out to open the door, just as a group of loud guys funnels out. We stand to the side. None of them hold the door open for us. Such gentlemen. She tries again, and we're blown away by how busy it is.

"He's probably swamped. Don't get mad if he can't pay much attention to us." *I* shouldn't get mad.

I snoop around for any trace of him as we approach the hostess stand.

"We're part of a party that has reservations tonight for eight o'clock," I tell the young woman.

She looks at the computer screen and types away. "Yes, under the name Matt."

"That's correct. We're all friends of Gerry's."

"Oh, okay. He's in the beer garden. He can show you which tables are reserved for your group. Do you know where the garden is?"

"Yes. Thanks!" I say.

I look over my shoulder. "Come on, ladies. The beer garden is great. It's the perfect place to start the party."

I walk out the open glass doors and see him in an instant. He doesn't see me right away. I stop to watch him. Lisa bumps into my back, which leads the others to bump into Lisa.

"What the hell, Tina? Why'd you stop like that?" Alexa snaps. "We looked like total jackasses."

"I just want to watch him for a few minutes. I've never seen him like this before. You can see by his face he loves it here. He told me he loves this atmosphere, loves speaking with his guests."

"Go. There are people behind us trying to get through," Larissa complains.

We move aside and let them pass.

"Hey. Larissa and I are going to the bathroom to check our hair. We'll be right back," Cori says.

Gerry lifts his head and zones in on me. A smile immediately stretches across his bright face. My stomach twists in delight, and my face becomes warm.

He walks swiftly over to us, almost banging into a server.

He comes up to me first. "Hi, *Süße*," he whispers in my ear without touching me.

I lean away giggling. "That tickles."

He steps back to let someone pass through.

"We hoped to see you in action as the big bad manager," I tease.

Alexa jumps forward. "Hi, Gerry. You remember Tina's sister,

Lisa? We're celebrating her thirtieth birthday tonight too. Maybe we can get some drinks before the gang shows up. She needs to let loose." She shakes Lisa's shoulders.

"Well, you've come to the right place. You aren't the first to show up. My cousin Tyler flew in for Matt's wedding. He's Kayla's brother and my partner. Maybe you've met him before. He's sitting at the reserved tables."

"I think I met him once at a party Matt had. That was a while ago," Lisa comments.

"He lives in Seattle and doesn't visit here often."

Gerry takes my hand and pulls me to him. "You look quite beautiful tonight. Is that for me, or are you hoping to meet some other guys?"

His whisper sends enticing shivers down my back. "Only for you," I purr.

"Just friends, my ass," Lisa chimes. "Stop whispering and show us where your cousin is."

We approach a table with a guy talking on the phone and two beer mugs standing tall in front of him. One full and one half-empty. He finishes his call with an angry face and guzzles the rest of the beer in one mug. Slamming it on the table.

"Watch it with the mug," Gerry warns. Tyler ignores him.

"Hi, Tyler. Remember me? I met you at Matt's once. I'm Lisa, James's wife."

His eyes squint, and then they soften when he recognizes her. "Yes. How are you?" He scratches his head. "Man, that was a while ago."

"I'm great." She pushes Alexa forward. "Tyler, this is James's sister, Alexa."

He looks her up and down like she's a piece of meat. "Alexa," he says, his voice smooth as butter, or was that a slur? He stands up and wipes his hand on his shirt. When he goes to shake her hand, he loses his balance and grips the table to prevent himself from falling over.

"Tyler, I think you've had enough to drink. Pace yourself. It's going to be a long night," Gerry urges.

Tyler grunts in response.

Gerry clears his throat. "This is Tina, Lisa's sister."

Tyler flashes me a fake smile. "Nice to meet you, Tina."

He motions to the table. "Since we're the first to arrive, first round is on the house, beautiful ladies. Right, Ger?"

Gerry shrugs his shoulders. "No problem."

"Cool. Thanks," Alexa says as we take our seats.

"I need to check on the kitchen since we're packed tonight. I'll send a server over to take your drink orders." He winks at me as he struts away.

I watch him walk off, taking a sneak peek of his butt in those black jeans. I notice Larissa and Cori walking toward us. As he passes them, he does a double take. Almost like he knows them. Weird.

"Was that Gerry?" Larissa says as she approaches the table. "He's hot. I'm not much into the hairless thing, but not bad."

Hands off. He's mine.

"Tyler, this is Larissa and Cori," I say.

He responds by wolfing half of the second beer and looking them up and down. "I probably won't remember any of your names tonight, so don't be disappointed, sweethearts."

"Let me drop a tear for all of us sweethearts," Alexa snidely remarks.

His eyes shoot daggers at her.

My first impression is he's an asshole.

"So how do you sweethearts know the infamous Gerry? Did you meet him through Matt and Kayla?" He slurs again.

Yup. Definitely drunk. It's hard to believe he's related to Gerry and Kayla.

"I've been working with Gerry on the new website for this restaurant. Did you know he's having it completely revamped?"

"Nope. He controls the restaurant." He swigs his beer again.

We all look at him blankly.

"Anyway, we found out at the taste testing Matt and Kayla had weeks ago that Gerry is Kayla's cousin. I ate something I was allergic to, and my lips swelled up like a balloon."

Alexa and I crack up. It wasn't funny then, but it's funny now.

"I don't live here, so I never know these things. Where's the damn server? We need some drinks," he barks and smacks the table.

"Chill out," I snap. "It's packed tonight. You don't need to make a scene."

We remain quiet as Alexa tries to get a server's attention.

"So, Tyler, when did you arrive?" Lisa asks.

"This afternoon. A bunch of my frat buddies from Jackson College met me here for a couple of drinks. I haven't seen them in years. They left just before you got here."

My pulse spikes. Jackson College...frat brothers. Images of the game flash in my head. There are a lot of fraternities at that college. It couldn't possibly be the same one. But Cori taps my leg with her foot under the table. I eye her and notice both she and Larissa are staring at me.

Lisa bumps my arm. "Hey, Tina, Cori, and Larissa went to New Jersey Tech. It's not too far from your college. Right?"

He burps loudly, then nods. I'm floored he's related to Gerry.

"Which fraternity?" I say, already regretting I opened my mouth.

"Alpha Phi Delta. Do you know it? I was the president while I was there."

My stomach sours. *This isn't happening.*

"No. I'm not familiar with that one. I didn't hang out at fraternities." I've been good lately, but it's time to yank on my necklace.

"Gerry visited me there a couple of times. He was always shocked about the frat parties. We could tell you some really crazy stories. Did he ever tell you how he came up with the blindfolded taste-test idea?"

Alexa coughs and Larissa elbows me. I'm two seconds away from puking under the table. They know where this is going—like I do.

"I've always wondered how he came up with something so interesting," Lisa says, completely oblivious.

I don't want to hear this. It can't be true, but I'm fooling myself. I know it is. Number One was from Europe and the cousin of the fraternity president.

Gerry.

My face burns like fire, and I want to kick some major ass right now.

"He played some fucking drinking game. An easy drunk girl was blindfolded and had to kiss three or four different guys who were also blindfolded. I thought he was nuts when he told me. Why would he want to kiss a trashy girl who just had her tongue down other guys' throats? Typical frat chick," he tells us with disgust dripping from his tongue.

I gasp.

"You guys don't have drinks yet," Gerry interrupts. "Didn't a server take your orders?"

Tyler gestures to us. "I was just telling them how you came up with the blindfold idea. That stupid game you played before you went off to culinary school. She must've been one experienced kisser to inspire you like that. She was his muse." He wiggles his eyebrows. "Lord knows, he needs a new muse to get him back in the fucking kitchen."

Gerry's face turns a red-purple color. "Shut up, Tyler." He growls.

He knows who I am.

Alexa shoots a look to me and then to Gerry.

He's known all along. He fooled me. This was all a joke. I told him this story the other night, and he didn't say a word.

My breathing increases as I stand up quickly. I'm pretty sure flames shoot out my eyes at Gerry.

Lisa pulls on my arm. "Tina, what's the matter? You look like you want to punch Gerry in the face."

"That's because I fucking do." I swing my leg over the bench to get out. "Why don't you ask Gerry? He knows exactly why." I grab my bag. "I'm leaving."

Chapter 23

Gerry

"What's her problem?" Tyler snaps. He shakes his head. "You chicks are all the same."

"You're drunk and being an asshole, so shut your mouth," I shoot back, my hands pumping at my sides.

"Go after her, Gerry," Alexa demands as Tina barges through the garden toward the exit.

I run behind Tina and grab her elbow in front of the customers.

She turns to me. "Get your hand off me. And this time I mean it," she says, loud enough so everybody hears. Her snake eyes bore a hole through my head. "You don't want anybody to record this and put it on the internet."

I drop her arm instantly, like I touched a hot plate. "Please let me explain."

"Gerry, there's a problem in the—"

I cut off the busboy. "Have Joel deal with it."

I follow quickly behind her as she storms out the door into a crowd of people on the sidewalk, Tyler and the rest trailing behind us.

"Please, Tina. Let's talk about this. I'm sorry I didn't tell you."

"What's there to talk about?" She hesitates. "Oh. Wait. I know. How about how you purposely didn't tell me how you came up with the blindfold idea? There was always a convenient distraction when I asked you. Or that you were one of the guys I kissed at Tyler's frat party years ago and that I poured my heart out to you the other night?

Telling you things I've never told a living soul." She counts on her fingers.

"How long have you known? And don't try to claim it was when I told you last weekend. Tell me! You weren't supposed to know since you weren't allowed to see me."

"I knew it was you the first time we met again. I'd recognize your face anywhere."

"Oh, please. Don't give me your bullshit." She crosses her arms.

"Fine." I roll my shoulders. "Remember how we saw each other from across the living room during the party? We connected. I remember it like it was yesterday. It wasn't the first time I saw you that night. The first time was when you were dancing with your friends. It was like a beam of light shined down on you. I couldn't keep my eyes off you. I watched you for the rest of the night. I memorized every detail of your face. Your long, wavy brown hair and porcelain skin. The beauty mark above your lip. You wore a purple shirt and white pants.

"I saw you and your friends go into a room. Cori and..." I snap my fingers a few times. "Carissa...Alyssa..."

"Cori and Larissa," she snaps.

"Hi, Gerry." Cori waves.

Tina gives her the look of death. She backs away.

I point to her friends. "They came out and were sneaking around, asking guys to play a drinking game with a beautiful girl. I knew it was you. It was the craziest thing I ever heard, but I knew I had to be one of them. I had to know what it'd feel like to kiss you before I left for France the next day to start culinary school. If I had spoken even one word to you, I would've never left."

She aims her chin up. "It doesn't matter. I should've never agreed to do that stupid game." She turns to walk away again.

"You think it didn't affect me?" I call after her. My chest heaving. She halts.

"That one kiss blew me away. It has *never* left my memory. The one kiss that ruined all chances for other women. Is that what you want to hear?" I yell. "I'll say it again. Not one woman has ever come close to how I feel about you. Not one! And the day you walked into this restaurant wasn't a coincidence. It was fate. We're meant to be together."

"Hey, guys," Matt says as he barges through the crowd. "What's going on? Why are you all outside?"

Kayla and James appear from behind him with the rest of their clan. I glance his way and put my hand up to stop him from coming near us. He freezes, and his face drops.

Tina pulls on her hair and groans. "I can't believe this. Matt, you knew about this too?"

Kayla looks between them. She pulls Matt's arm and whispers something.

Tina's head whips back to me. "Who else knows?" She shakes her head. "You know what? It doesn't fucking matter."

"It does matter. Your body against mine was indescribable. I can still remember how you tasted and smelled all those years ago."

Heads from the crowd are shifting from me to Tina like in a tennis match. This is the one time the city is silent.

She gets up in my face. "It wasn't real. It was only because of that fucking blindfold. I'll regret that night for the rest of my life. I trusted you. Thought we had something special. And here I spilled my guts out to you, and...and you *knew*," she shouts. "You knew all along!" Her eyes glisten from tears.

"I can't believe that for one second, Tina. Look how hard it is for us to keep our hands off each other every time we're together. You feel it. I know you do." I move closer to her, my heart pounding out of my chest.

"These past weeks were a lie. Nothing was real. You aren't real. You played me like a fool the entire time. And I fell for it. I thought you were different. You should've told me," she cries out as she wipes away tears.

She never cries.

"You want to know what's real?" I grab her and smash my lips against hers. I transfer all my angst, regret, and passion into this kiss. She tries to push me away, but slowly her soft, plump lips relax into mine. Her hands wrap around my neck, pulling me closer as our kiss grows deeper. The explosive chemistry we had years ago is off the charts now.

I pull away and take her face in my hands. "This is real. I know you feel it. And this is without a blindfold. I don't need a damn blindfold to know how I feel about you," I say as our lips caress each other's again. "You can't deny it." Whistles play from the audience around us.

She shoves me away. "I won't deny it, but that's all you're going to get. From now on our relationship is strictly business. You can forget about everything else. Go find yourself another stupid muse, or should I say *trashy frat chick*." She storms off.

"Please don't go. Not like this." My voice chases her in desperation.

She looks over her right shoulder. "Do you know what the international phrase *fuck off* means? Don't try to contact me unless it's for business." She pushes through the crowd.

Lisa stomps my way, James stuck to her side. "What the hell did you do to her? She never cries, and I've never seen her so angry."

"Show's over, guys," Matt says to the crowd behind Lisa and James. I notice some have their phones out like they are filming us.

Alexa pulls on Lisa's arm and says, "Go to her. We'll catch up with you in a minute."

"Are you sure? I still don't understand what just happened." She glares at me. "Why were you both talking about blindfolds?"

Alexa huffs in annoyance. "We'll explain it to you later. Go find her," she says firmly while pushing her away. "James, go with her." She nudges his shoulder.

Lisa storms off with James following her.

I fold my hands behind my head as adrenaline pumps through my body.

Matt lays his hand on my shoulder. "That was one hell of a show.

You can tell me later what happened."

Kayla looks at us like he spoke German to me.

Alexa steps forward. "I can tell you exactly what happened." She points at Tyler. "Kayla's drunk brother over here blurted out how Gerry came up with the blindfold idea and how it involved a girl. It was obvious he let the cat out of the bag."

"Gerry, you told us it was from a drinking game you played, but you never said it involved a girl," Kayla says.

"Only Matt and Tyler knew the true story."

Kayla looks at Matt in surprise.

"It's nothing major, but I didn't think it was right to talk about the girl, which happened to be Tina. I asked Matt and Tyler to never say anything."

Cori speaks up. "Amazing. After all these years. It's you with less hair and bigger muscles, but I remember the scar you have above your eyebrow."

"We convinced her to play that ridiculous drinking game. Now I totally regret suggesting it in the first place. Who would've known it'd come back to bite her in the ass?" Larissa exclaims.

"She told me all about it and how horrible she felt after," Alexa throws in with venom in her voice. She glares at me and then at Tyler. "Was this a joke to you both? Did you know who she was, Tyler?"

Tyler raises his hands in surrender. "I had no clue. Gerry never said anything to me about meeting up with her again. It was only a coincidence, so back off, blondie!"

"You're such a dick. Does she look like a trashy frat chick to you? I'm sure you were soooo innocent back then as the president of a fraternity. I'm sure you had more than one 'frat chick' and probably more than one at the same time."

She points her finger at me like a knife. "What about you, Gerry? Was this all a game to you?"

I recoil. "Absolutely not." I'm afraid of Alexa right now. "I really care about her. I'd never do anything to hurt her. This has been the hardest couple of weeks for me. I wanted to tell her, but I knew she wouldn't be happy about it. As we all witnessed, she wasn't."

"Well, what do you expect? She's angry, hurt, and embarrassed, and she has every right to be. She trusted you, and you screwed up big time. You'd better think of something really incredible for her to forgive you, or you'll lose her completely. If you haven't already."

She looks at Larissa and Cori. "Let's go."

They scurry away from us.

"You three better tell me what's going on," Kayla commands.

"Gerry!" Joel yells. "I need you in here."

I want to snap my fingers and disappear.

"Kayla, I can't talk right now. I need to work." I motion to Matt. "He'll tell you what this is all about. Don't be mad at him. Be mad at me. I asked him not to say anything. It's not his fault."

"Gerry!"

"I'm coming, Joel. Back off." I need to calm down. This is what got me in trouble last time.

"Everyone, go inside, and I'll show you your tables."

As I trail behind them, all I can think about is Tina's tears.

"Hey, aren't you that chef from Germany who punched that guy?" someone shouts behind me in German.

I freeze. Then, instead of turning around, I walk into the restaurant without responding.

This isn't good.

Chapter 24

I pace back and forth with clenched fists by a streetlight. With my heart pounding, I force them to open and shake my arms a bit, hoping to relax. No matter how explosive that kiss was, I'm humiliated and furious. Why did I trust him? Because I'm a fool, and I'm still being punished.

A crowd treks across the street. I hear Lisa yell, "Tina! Wait!" She and James approach me, obviously concerned.

"Why are you so angry with Gerry? What's with the blindfolds? Does this have to do with the taste testing?" She blasts me with questions.

I cackle in her face. If it could only be so simple. "I don't want to talk about it. Can we please go somewhere I can get drunk?" I look over her shoulder. "Where are the others? Did they decide to stay with Kayla's group?" I don't care if I spend the night alone. I'm getting drunk either way.

"They're talking to the guys. They'll be here in a few minutes," James responds.

I remain silent as taxis drive by. Two girls giggle as they take a selfie in front of a homeless guy on the street. *Bitches!* A group of guys stand by, lighting up their cigarettes. I should ask them for one.

Lisa looks around and says, "Here they come."

I check if Gerry's with them. My anxiety slightly dissolves when he's nowhere to be seen.

Lisa waits for them to arrive. With gritted teeth, she says, "Since Tina's not fessing up, I'm going to ask one more time. What just happened?"

I stand behind them and pretend to slit my throat so they don't say anything. Alexa butts in. "We'll talk about it later. Tina's had enough to deal with for the time being." She looks at everyone and then asks me, "Should we go back to Hoboken?"

"Yes," I blurt without giving anyone else a chance to answer. "I want to get as far away from here as possible." I beg with my eyes to Larissa and Cori. "Is that okay? I know we agreed to show you a good time in the city, but you see how things have shifted."

Without waiting for anyone's response, Larissa puts her arm over my shoulder. "We'll go wherever you want. I think you need a drink or two or maybe even ten. We want to see you let loose. It's our turn to be your mother hens."

James steps forward and hugs me. "It kills me to see you upset. Should I kick his ass for you? I think I could take him." He puts up his fists.

I crack a smile for a millisecond.

"I love you, James. But I don't want you to go to jail." I give him a hug. Lisa's so lucky.

"I'll tell Kayla you're going back to Hoboken. It's going to be okay." He whispers something to Lisa, and she nods.

"Have fun, but be careful, everyone. Lisa, I'll see you tomorrow. Send me a text message when you get back to their apartment." He kisses her and runs off.

My body aches, and my head feels like it's in a vice. I press my hands to my head and painstakingly roll over onto my back. My stomach brews like a volcano. My dried-out contacts feel like glass shards, making it difficult to pry open my eyes. My mouth tastes like garbage.

"How are you feeling?"

I twitch when I hear Lisa's voice. My bed moves as she sits on the edge.

My head pounds with the slightest bit of noise and movement. "Mmmm." I groan.

"You had a rough night. You passed out on your bed before we could get you out of your disgusting clothes. I've never seen you drink so much. We were scared you might throw up in the middle of the night."

Just her saying that makes my stomach churn. "I'm never drinking again." I pull my blanket over my head.

She snorts. "Famous last words."

"Did I do anything stupid?"

She pulls the blanket down in order to see me. "What did you say?"

"Did I do anything stupid?" I really don't want to know. But with the way I'm feeling right now, I'm pretty sure I did.

Her eyebrows shoot up.

"If it's that bad, I'm never leaving this room again." I lay my arm over my eyes.

She pats the bed. "Get up. Everyone's in the kitchen having breakfast. Come and try to eat something. Then I want to talk to you alone."

"Don't go all therapist on me now. I can get drunk when I want to."

"Man, don't be so defensive. The coffee is fresh and hot," she says and leaves the room.

"She'll be out soon. She can't resist her coffee in the morning. I don't care how hungover she is," I hear Lisa say.

I place my hand on my neck to touch my necklace. It's not there. I move both of my hands around my neck to find it, but I can't feel it. "Where's my necklace?" I shout as I drag my hundred-pound legs over the side of the bed in a panic. My head pulsates as if it's being hit like a gong.

"Where's my damn necklace," I yell louder.

Alexa runs in. "What's the matter? What are you yelling about?"

"My necklace. It's gone. I haven't taken it off since Mom died. Where is it?" My voice cracks as my hands start to shake. I stand up and frantically search like an addict looks for her stash. I lift things up and over, toss my pillows and blanket off my bed, knock over a lamp. "Lisa!"

She runs into the room. "What's wrong? Why are you so frantic?"

"Where's my necklace? Did you take it off me last night?" I get on my knees and search under the bed, even though I'm going to throw up any second.

I get up again and walk aimlessly around my room, picking things up and dropping them down.

"Don't you remember what happened last night at the last bar we were at?"

I freeze while massaging my temples. "No."

"You freaked out in the middle of the dance floor because you lost your necklace."

Tears instantly well up in my eyes. "No, no, no." I shake my head back and forth. "You know what my necklace means to me. Mom gave it to me." I break down crying and rush to the garbage can placed next to my bed. I heave until I'm empty. Alexa runs in with a wet towel and takes the garbage with her. The flood gates open, and I don't think I'll ever be able to close them again.

Lisa rushes to my side and wipes my face and mouth off with the towel. I hear the door close. "It can't be lost, Lisa. It's the only thing I have from her. It means everything to me."

"Ssshhh. I know. It's going to be all right." She hugs me and strokes my face. "Please tell me what's going on with you. Especially what happened with Gerry. You scared me last night, just like you are now. You tried to get on the bar and dance."

My head shoots up. Regretting it immediately. "What? No I didn't!" I press hard on my temples again.

She giggles but then pinches her nose. "Now I got your attention. No, you didn't. You came close though. Do you think I'd let you do something like that? You'd never."

I push her away and try to stand up but end up sitting on the bed. She stays on the floor. "I would've done something like that years ago. Before Mom died. Don't you remember what I used to be like? How I used to get in trouble? Remember when I got caught trying to sneak out of the house when I was in eleventh grade? I was grounded for a month. Or the time I came home drunk for the first time? I was fearless. Willing to try anything once. I wanted to explore the world, go to college far away, and be free to do whatever I wanted."

Lisa remains still as a statue.

"Don't you remember all the posters and postcards I hung on my bedroom walls? I wanted to get the fuck out of New Jersey after high school." I run my hands through my tangled hair. "I don't feel drunk anymore because a surge of adrenaline has replaced it.

"You know she gave me that necklace, but you don't know what she said. She made me promise her I'd follow my dreams and not live in monotony."

"Why didn't you?" Lisa challenges, not having a clue in the world.

"Because she *died*," I yell.

Lisa flinches.

"I had to work at the pharmacy that morning, and she died because of me. Me!" I jab my chest with my thumb. "She begged me to call out of work so she wouldn't need to drive to the other side of town. But I refused to do it because I was a stupid, stubborn teenager." I pull on my hair. "When I think about it now, I don't even remember why I wouldn't call out.

"My seventeenth birthday was in a couple of weeks. I wanted to practice driving since I'd be going for my driver's test. We fought about that too. She said it was too dangerous for me to drive on the slippery roads. But I fought back saying I needed the experience in bad weather."

Lisa moves to the edge of my bed, never taking her eyes off me.

"After fighting about it while you were getting ready, Mom gave in and handed me the keys. She was furious with me and I didn't even care.

"When we arrived at the pharmacy, I jumped out of the car and didn't say goodbye to Mom or you." I shake my head as fresh tears form. "I should've said sorry for being such a bitch. I should've said goodbye. I never saw her again and almost lost you." I sob.

"She moved to the driver's seat but never put her seat belt on. If I hadn't driven, maybe she would've put it on when we first left the house. She always wore her seat belt. If I hadn't gone to work at all, Mom would be alive and you wouldn't have been permanently injured. You would've never been in that area of town." I take a deep breath between sobs.

"I blamed myself and knew my life would never be the same. All my dreams blew in the wind like ashes. I deserved it. I vowed to take care of you and Dad as long as I had to." I separate from her and wipe the boogers off my face.

"Dad also blamed himself for letting her take that piece of crap in the snow. But I did everything I could to make sure he knew it wasn't his fault, because I knew it was mine. When Dad met Beth and remarried, my guilt lessened because he learned to forgive himself. But I still had to take care of you. It killed me every day to look at you, knowing you couldn't have children. I vowed to be a mother to you, take care of you, and never live far from you."

I'm bawling again, and she shakes her head in disbelief.

"But I did get pregnant and was blessed with Felicia. You need to let it go."

"It doesn't matter. I didn't deserve to do what I wanted anymore. You and Dad were my responsibility then. I had to take care of you, so I had to forget about what I wanted."

"I didn't know. I'm so sorry." She wraps her arms around me more tightly than before.

"All these years I've been thinking my punishment was to give up on what I wanted and to take care of my family. I became the mother figure. It was the least I could do—I killed her. I don't regret one minute of taking care of you both. I swear," I reassure her as I squeeze her back, even tighter. We're going to pop soon the way we're holding on to each other.

She pulls away from me and takes my face in her hands. "Never once did I or Dad think it was your fault. It took years to convince Dad it wasn't his fault. It kills me to think you've been keeping this inside for all these years yourself. Why didn't you talk to me!" She pulls me into her arms again, sobbing along with me.

"You and Dad had worse problems. I had to stand up and do what was right. That's the least I could do for Mom.

"Now that you have James and Felicia and Dad has Beth, it's my time to break away."

She holds my hand. "But what does this have to do with the necklace?"

"It's the only thing I have that's a part of her. I felt she was always with me. I can't believe it's gone." I cry into Lisa's shoulder. "What am I going to do without it? Without her? Please help me find it!"

She squeezes my hand tightly. "The necklace could be anywhere in the city or in Hoboken. Alexa plans to call the bars we were at, and Gerry's restaurant." She looks at her watch. "It's almost eleven. A couple open between eleven and twelve. We left my number at the last bar, in case someone finds it. But you can't get your hopes up. If we can't find it, I promise you'll be fine without it." She kneels in front of me. "Mom's always with us—with you—regardless of your necklace. I feel her with me every day." She leans up and hugs me again. "You'll get through this. I know you will. You're one of the strongest women I know, next to Alexa, of course."

I giggle. She's right about Alexa.

I wipe the tears from my eyes. "After all these years, I've never been so unhinged. Maybe everything I've bottled up has finally reached its pressure point."

"Please promise me, from now on you'll come to me about anything. You were always there for me with every little tear that fell from my eyes. I want to be that someone for you now. I was so caught up in my own misery, I never paid attention to yours." Her eyes well up with tears again. "Please forgive me for being so selfish and clueless."

I put my head in my hands out of exhaustion. "You weren't selfish, and don't apologize. I was excellent at hiding things from you and Dad and...even myself."

"From now on there'll be no secrets between us. Do you understand?"

I slowly lift my head and nod.

"I love you, Tina. So much."

We embrace again.

I've missed this kind of affection. *Gerry's hugs were the best, but I'll never feel him against me again.*

She pulls away and smirks. "Boy, you stink, and your breath could kill anyone." Lisa waves her hand in front of her nose. "Go shower and brush your teeth."

I crack a smile.

"When you're feeling better, you're going to spill the beans about Gerry."

"I'm not sure—"

"When you're ready to tell me."

I nod and sift through my drawers for sweatpants. "I need to shower before I talk to anyone. Can you please ask Alexa to start calling the bars?"

"Sure. Now run to the bathroom."

Twenty minutes later, I leave the bathroom with steam trailing behind me. Several sets of sad eyes stare at me. My heart breaks a little bit more, knowing they didn't find my necklace.

"Pour yourself a cup of joe, grab a bagel, and come sit with us," Cori says.

I ignore the coffee that's calling me and walk over to them. I stand next to Lisa.

"No one found my necklace."

"Sorry, sis," Lisa says as she squeezes my hand.

My shoulders slump. I push back the never-ending tears that

want to pour out again.

"Maybe it'll turn up the next couple of days," Alexa says.

I doubt it.

I turn toward Cori and Larissa. "You guys have plans today, right?"

"Yeah. Why?" Larissa asks.

I glance at Lisa. "I want to go home with you because I need to do something. What's James's plan?"

"We're separate today. I told him to spend time with Matt. My plan is to take the train, and Dad will pick me up at the station since they have Felicia. Later on, James will come to Dad's."

"Good. When do you need to leave? Soon I hope."

"We should leave here in an hour to get to the train station."

I nod and rethink the coffee and bagel staring at me on the kitchen counter.

"Hey, Dad."

His surprised face turns into a bright smile. He squeezes me tight like only a dad does and lifts me in the air. "What a great surprise. Lisa didn't say you were coming with her. We haven't seen you in weeks. I guess Hoboken's been keeping you busy."

I force myself to be peppy, but I'm not sure it's convincing. "It has. I love it there."

"We had a late night, so we're both exhausted." Lisa deflects his attention. "How is Felicia? Did she have a good night?"

They turn to the parking lot and walk ahead of me while talking about Felicia. I trail behind, thankful the focus is off me.

When we park in the driveway, I ask Dad, "Can I borrow your car? I want to go somewhere for a little while." I climb out of the car and stand next to the driver's door with my hand out. Lisa heads to the front door.

"Sure." His eyebrows connect. "Everything okay? You're not your normal self. I can't remember the last time you were so mellow. I hope your job isn't too much for you."

I skim the ground with my sneaker. "Nah. I'm just going through some stuff. Nothing to worry about though."

He places the keys in my hand. "Be careful, and take your time."

I sit in the car, and he closes the door. I start the car and open the window.

"Beth will be happy to see you."

"Thanks, Dad. I won't be long." He moves away from the car as I back out of the driveway.

Five minutes later, I arrive at the parking lot of Heaven's Gate graveyard. I exhale in defeat and grab a pack of tissues out of my bag. It's been a year since I've visited Mom's grave.

As I approach her gravestone, I scan the area to see if other people are around. I need to be alone with her. No one's in sight.

I kneel and pull some of the last weeds of the year out of the ground. Lisa adds new flowers each season. They are bright and happy, unlike me at this moment.

I stare at Mom's gravestone and brush my fingers over her name. I break down again as I cover my face.

"I'm so sorry, Mom." I've said it and cried so many times before, but today's different. I'm at my worst and feel so alone. "Ever since Lisa and Dad found their happiness, I thought it was my turn. I believed my punishment was over, and I could finally follow the path I've always wanted. I have a great job, and I met a man I thought I was falling in love with. But he betrayed me. Am I still being punished? When will it ever end?

"I lost the necklace you gave me. It's like you've died all over again. I don't know what to do without it or you. You've been with me every minute of every day, and now it's missing. Have I lost you too?" I wipe my tears away with the back of my hand and breathe deeply.

"I'm so lost and empty. I've never felt so alone. Please make it go away. Show me I'm forgiven." I pull chunks of grass out of the ground. "Please tell me what I should do! Please, Mom! I've said I'm sorry a million times. Please help me find the necklace. I beg you." Sobs return as every part of my body convulses.

I freeze when I hear a slight jingle of keys behind me. I wipe my face and turn my head. Dad and Lisa stand there a few feet away. I jump up and run into their arms. We hold each other tight, crying all together.

"It wasn't your fault. It was no one's fault. This is life, and accidents happen," he cries into my ear.

Which makes me cry even more.

"All that time you tried to convince me it wasn't my fault, you blamed yourself? I don't know how you kept it to yourself and why we didn't notice. I'm so ashamed. We should be saying sorry to you. Thank you for everything you've done for us."

We separate from each other. I hand both of them a much-needed tissue. We're a bunch of snotty messes.

"How did you know I was here?"

"Lisa told me what happened, and my gut told me where you went. We both had to come and help you. It's time for us to take care of you. Do you feel any better getting it all out?"

"I think so, because that horrible weight on my chest is gone. Bawling my eyes out seems to have helped. I haven't allowed myself to cry about anything for so long."

"As of now, everything's going to change. You'll no longer blame yourself. Your top priority is you. Whatever you think will make you happy, do it," Lisa says. "When you need help, you ask for it. We're your family, and we want to see you accomplish your dreams. You've punished yourself long enough." She squeezes my hands and says, "It's your time. Do you hear me? Your time. Nobody else's."

"Thank you both. It'll take time, so be patient with me. I can't just flip a switch."

Dad puts his arm around my shoulders. "Do you need more time alone here?"

I look over at her grave. "No. Mom answered me. She sent you both here to find me." *Thanks, Mom. I love you. I'll make you proud.*

"Beth has a pot roast cooking. We can have an early family

dinner. What do you both say?"

My stomach growls. "You know me. I could never resist Beth's famous pot roast. It'll be comforting to be all together."

Lisa wraps her arm around mine. "As long as you still have your typical appetite, I think you're going to be okay."

I actually grin, but it hurts my face.

"Thank you for coming here. I love you both so much."

"We know, more than ever now," Dad says with a loving voice.

Lisa and I sway on the new swing set Dad built for Felicia. It's high tech with two different slides, a small climbing wall, and a little clubhouse on the top. I'm not sure he understands she's only a couple years old. For safety, he built a huge sandpit under it. He'll probably make her wear a helmet when she's out here. Always Mr. Safety.

Lisa stops her swing and twists to face me. "So what's the story with you and Gerry?"

I stop mine but look at the sand. "I made a complete fool out of myself these past weeks in front of him. I opened up to someone for the first time in my life since Mom died. There's something about him that makes me want to tell him everything. He's so damn cute, I could punch him in the face."

"I guess that's a good thing." She laughs. "It's obvious you have strong feelings for him. I'm not sure why you hid your relationship with him from me in the first place."

"Please don't be mad. It had nothing to do with you. It was fun to keep him for myself. It's hard to explain."

"Try."

"It's partly because we work together. The attraction between Gerry and me is impossible to ignore. We knew it the second we met. We agreed to remain friends until the project is over. So technically, we've done nothing wrong. We just hung out together a lot. There's something fun about having a secret and not having outside influences from other people. But it doesn't matter anymore."

"Didn't Alexa notice something? Nothing gets past her."

"Of course. I had to tell her. He brought me home one night, and she was there. Then we ran into him at Matt's bakery. She left us so we could spend the afternoon together. Who cares. It's over and done with." I lean my head against the swing chain. "I can't face him after last night. Especially after what Tyler said. He made me feel like a slut."

"It was just a game, Tina."

I twist my swing to face her. "I guess the girls told you everything."

"I'm annoyed you wouldn't tell me something like that. It's not a big deal."

I look up to the sky. "Why do I have to defend myself to everyone? It was a big deal to me! When he left, it was like I was being punished for trying to be the old me. And now...he humiliated me both times."

"Oh, come on. You heard why he left. Yeah, he could have stayed and finished the game but he didn't. It just wasn't your time yet. Everything happens for a reason. He seems like a nice guy, and he sounded sincere to me. I don't think he meant to hurt you. I just don't understand why you'd feel so bad about yourself. Other college students have done much worse. You're too hard on yourself for so many things that happened years ago.

"I saw how he kissed you. Was it as good as it looked? I think Kayla's friends were quite jealous. It made me want to grab James and find a dark corner somewhere. It was intense. Good for you."

I slouch, but my insides become warm just thinking about it. "It was better than anything I've ever experienced, including the drinking game. It's unbelievable it was him. We had several moments when we almost kissed, but something always interrupted us. The anticipation was overwhelming. My body was on fire all the time when he was around. I could stare at him all day."

Lisa shivers. "It's all so complicated and weird. What's with you and me and our men? Meet them a long time ago, and then they magically appear in our lives again. And Gerry is connected to Matt.

What are the odds?"

"Gerry and I clicked from the very beginning. He's so laid back and gentle with a great sense of humor. You can tell he has an American parent because he gets my jokes." I giggle. "Well, most of them anyway." I twist my swing around several times.

"He's genuinely a nice guy, but I'm so pissed at him."

"Yes, he should've told you...but is there something else?"

"Well, the drinking game inspired him with the blindfold taste testing. Was he just using me in hopes to find the courage to start cooking again? I'm scared it was all a game."

"Why don't you ask him? Don't you want to know the full truth? Maybe it's not as bad as you think. My guess is your heart knows he wasn't trying to hurt you."

"I don't want people to think I'm trashy like Tyler said."

"And what would that make Gerry? He played the game too. Why is he the innocent one? So stop it right now. You're too paranoid. It's time you get over it and move on!"

I untwist my swing as fast as I can, just like I did when I was a little girl.

Steam from my coffee dampens my nose. I slept in my old bedroom last night. It gave me a protective comfort after all that's happened. My heart doesn't hang in my chest anymore. I'm shattered I lost the necklace, but I'm still hopeful it will show up.

I hear the front door of the house open then close. "Tina?" Lisa calls.

"Yeah. In the kitchen. What's up?"

She walks into the kitchen with a giant smile on her face. "Where's your phone? I guess I could ask Beth to use her computer."

"They left a note that they went out for breakfast." I point to my phone on the other side of the kitchen counter. "Why do you need my phone? Where's yours?"

"I couldn't find it, and then when I did, it was dead. Unlock your phone for me. I want to show you something." I take it and punch in the numbers as I yawn. I slept more than I have in weeks, but I'm still utterly exhausted. "Here." I slouch over the counter and continue to drink my coffee.

"You and Gerry seem to be the stars of social media with nearly a quarter of a million clicks."

My coffee suddenly doesn't taste so good. I snatch my phone out of her hand. "What are you talking about?"

"Just watch."

Chapter 25

Gerry

I hide in my office because I don't want to deal with customers or staff. Joel is in control today and knows to pretend I'm not here. I have a stack of papers to go through.

Through the grapevine, I heard Tina was a mess Friday night. I didn't expect her to return to the restaurant. Her group never even met up with Kayla's clan. Tyler was a total asshole. I never described Tina in that way. I regret ever telling him, but it can't be changed.

It's all my fault. I should've told her right from the beginning. I don't think she wants anything to do with me. Someone called on Saturday claiming Tina lost her necklace somewhere. I remember how she said she'd feel if she ever lost it. I've looked everywhere for it but haven't found it. I wish I could help her, but she'd push me away.

I guess the phone call from Barbara came at the right time. She was able to schedule a meeting with the VOX executive producer in a few weeks in Freiburg, back home. VOX is even paying for my plane ticket. Running away seems to be my profession now.

My phone rings. Kayla. *Again.* She has become a total mental case. Matt must be pulling his hair out. Everything had better go smoothly in the kitchen on Saturday, or I'll never live it down. I'm a little rusty for the size of their party, but I know me. It'll come back as soon as I step into the kitchen.

"Hey, Kayla." I regret answering this call when I hear her voice. "Yes, I'm ready for Saturday." I squeeze my eyes shut out of annoyance. "I've double-checked, if not triple-checked, and confirmed everything on my task list. For the thousandth time, please don't worry. I've catered bigger parties than yours. I'll call you right away if I have any questions. Try to calm your nerves."

I listen to her ramble, but I don't understand everything. "No, I'm not too depressed over Tina and the video to cater the reception." I'm about to say goodbye. "Wait a second. Did you just say video? What video?" My heart rate shoots through the roof.

She explains as I type my password into my computer. "Where is it?" I grit my teeth. "You know I don't have any social media accounts. I closed them all out when I left Germany. Email me the link, and don't tell me not to worry. You know how I hate attracting any kind of attention in the news. That's why I came to the US." I wait impatiently for her email. "Social media is news, fake or not." I remember some people filming us. And then there was that guy asking if I was the German chef. But I thought I was in the clear because I haven't heard anything.

I fidget in my chair. "Did you send it? I didn't get it yet."

I hear a ping and see Kayla's name. "Okay. I got it." My hand shakes as I hover the arrow over the Play button. The title of the video is *Angry Hidden Chef Seems to Have a Soft Side*. Is that bad or good? "Give me a second. I'm nervous to watch it." I click Play and gulp. "I'll talk to you later, Kayla." I hang up before she can say another word. I lean my head on the desk. My phone rings again, but I don't answer it, because I know it's Kayla.

I'm a wreck about Tina, but I need to deal with it after the wedding. She hasn't called or emailed me about work or the video. Maybe she hasn't seen it, which I highly doubt. Matt and I haven't spoken since I saw it either. I've been avoiding his and everyone else's calls.

I made an excuse I'm too busy this week to deal with anything other than the wedding. I made Joel the contact for the website.

Tina's team did a great job. The website looks better than I expected. It's up and running, and we've already had reservations made through it. The only thing I did was sign off the last payment to Modern Web.

Someone taps on my door. "Come in."

Joel peeks his head in.

"What's up?"

He walks up to me. "Open your hand."

I do as I'm told. He places Tina's necklace in my hand. I can't believe it. My head jerks up. "No way. Where did you find it?"

"I found it outside in the beer garden. The sun reflected off it a certain way that grabbed my attention. It was between some of the cracked cobblestones. Unfortunately, the chain is broken, but the pendant is still on it. Should I call to let her know we found it?"

I shake my head. "No. I'll take care of it. By any chance, do you know a good jeweler around here who can fix this fast?"

He smiles. "I sure do. My sister's a jeweler, and her store's in the city."

"Can we call her right now? I need a huge favor." He pulls out his phone and taps the screen.

Maybe I have a chance after all.

Chapter 26

Tina

Different forms are sprawled all over my desk. My usual organizational skills have been on strike since last Friday. Thomas needs the one used to approve Gerry's website yesterday. I'd have to say, even though I feel miserable, the website looks awesome. I'm so proud of my team and myself. We're going for happy hour tonight to celebrate. I'm not sure if I'll drink alcohol, since I still feel it in my system from Friday. That was bad.

My hand lies on my collarbone, aching to touch my necklace, but I've accepted it's gone. I've been hoping I'd get a call saying someone found it. But nada. Someone probably saw it on the street and took off with it.

My emotions are all over the place. Opening up to my family has helped me move forward in a positive way. I'm inching closer to putting it all behind me now. Crying has never been easier for me. Lisa says it's healthy and cleansing. Whatever—she's the therapist. Alexa is contemplating buying stock from the companies that make tissues.

The video on the internet throws another layer into this mess. No one will tell me if Gerry has seen it, and I won't contact him to find out either.

When I arrived at work on Monday, I pretended nothing had happened over the weekend. That everything was hunky dory. I received an email first thing that morning from Gerry's assistant manager, stating he'd be filling in for Gerry until the website was finished. Talk about a knife in the stomach. Still, every time the phone rings, my hands shake, thinking it's Gerry."

I cried to Peggy in a café at lunch and showed her the video. Needless to say, she was shocked. "Stay professional," she said. "Don't let it affect work. The video shouldn't make you so upset."

She's been the best since this whole thing started with Gerry and hasn't mentioned his name once this week.

"Tina?"

I look up from my desk and see only Thomas's eyes, staring at me over my cube wall. It's impossible not to laugh.

"Can I talk to you for a second in my office?"

"Sure. I'll be there in a minute. Do I need to bring anything?"

"Nope. Just yourself." He walks away whistling. At least he's in a good mood.

I hope he has another project for me. Any distraction is a good distraction right now. I wouldn't even care if it was to create a website on hemorrhoid relief.

I do another quick search for the form I've been looking for. D'oh! Here it is right in front of my face. *Focus, Tina!*

I knock on the doorframe. Thomas lifts his head up, chomping on a wad of gum.

"So what's up? Should I be scared?" I chuckle. I'm glad I can talk to him like this. Over the past weeks, we've bonded, as if he were my uncle.

"Close the door and sit down. This won't take long." He rocks back and forth in his chair as I take a seat. "You've been off this week. I thought you'd be more excited about finalizing your first website. You and your team did a fantastic job. My confidence level in your abilities has risen tremendously."

I perk up. "Thank you. Did you see how great the restaurant video came out? The one used for reserving tables? Tim did an awesome job. I received an email saying they've gotten their first reservations already, and it worked without any glitches."

"Even with this great news, you've been walking around with a fake smile plastered on your face since Monday."

I push my hair behind my ears. "Sorry. I'm just going through some personal issues. But I've never let it affect my work."

"I know. That's one of the reasons I asked you to come in here. Because you and your team did such an excellent job, I'm giving each of you a bonus. You'll receive one thousand dollars, and the other two will get five hundred dollars each."

My eyes bug out of my head. "Wow. Are you serious?" I lean forward in the chair.

"No, I just wanted to see your reaction. Of course I'm serious." He laughs.

"Thank you for giving me the chance to manage this project. You've made my day and will make Peggy and Tim ecstatic too. You should come for a drink with us. We're going for happy hour to celebrate," I babble out of excitement.

"Why don't you go to Gerry's restaurant since it's his website?"

My mood shifts again as he watches me in a peculiar way.

I play it cool. "We want to stay local since we need to work tomorrow. Did you forget it's only Thursday?" I pinch my lips to the side.

He shakes his head and laughs. "I just thought you might want to spend time with Gerry since the project's finally over." He eyes me again. He knows something.

My throat begins to close.

I twirl a lone strand of hair. "Why would I want to spend time with Gerry?" I say nonchalantly.

"Come on, Tina. I saw you two at Burnett's a couple of weeks ago. I was there with my wife for our wedding anniversary. I thought it'd be better I didn't let you know I was there."

I stand up with my stomach in my mouth. "It's not what you think. We kept everything professional this entire time. We like each other, but I refused to get romantically involved. We weren't on a date." I defend us, but I know I'm fooling myself.

"Relax, Tina. I believe you." He points to the chair. "Sit back down."

I fall back onto the chair. "It's so complicated. Remember when I had that allergic reaction at that taste testing?"

He nods as he blows a bubble. "Gerry was the chef, and I had no idea. I also found out he's connected to my sister's husband's best friend. Then he confesses I met him a long time ago, but he didn't tell me until last Friday. It's all so intertwined and complicated." That was a mouthful.

He rocks in his chair. "No shit."

"I *promise* nothing happened."

He holds his hand up. "I said I believe you. It's quite moral of you to not get involved. But did something else happen?"

I look down at my folded hands. "We had a disagreement and haven't spoken since. His assistant manager has been our contact this week because Gerry's preparing and catering the wedding I'm going to on Saturday." *Or it's because of the video.*

"Man. That does sounds complicated. I think you definitely need a drink. It makes me thank God I'm married." He stands up from his chair, walks around the desk, and sits on the edge. "Is it something you can talk to him about at the wedding, so you aren't so off kilter when you come in on Monday?"

I shrug my shoulders. "There's nothing to discuss. I probably won't even see him because he'll be busy in the kitchen. It's unlikely we'll see each other after the wedding." It saddens me to think that's completely possible even after all that has happened. My heart and mind have no idea what they want.

He taps on his desk with one hand. "Well, I guess you have it all figured out then."

Not really, but I'm not going to tell him that. He already knows too much.

I relax in my chair. "Since this project is finished, will I get another one?"

"There are a bunch of projects being reviewed right now. I have no idea if we'll get them. I know at least two are close to being approved.

I take it back. Please nothing about hemorrhoids.

"One is to revamp a tourist website on California. The other is an online dating service."

Phew! No hemorrhoids involved.

"I'd love the California one." At least I'd be able to travel vicariously through a website. I wish I had the nerve to ask about the rumor of a California office opening up.

"We should know soon, but in the meantime, finish up the loose ends of Gerry's website. Once you're finished, I'll add you to a couple of teams to assist them. Something tells me they'll learn a thing or two from you."

"You're just full of compliments. I'll be walking out of this office on cloud nine. I think a couple of drinks are in full order. Please come with us." I flash a happy, honest smile.

"There's that smile." He pierces his lips. "You know what? I think I'll come along for one drink after all."

"Great. I'm sure the others will be happy, especially after I tell them about their bonuses." I reach for the office door in a better mood. "I'll see you later then."

"Tina, I know this is none of my business, so I'll only say it once. But what I saw at Burnett's wasn't just a friendly dinner. It was much more than that. I saw it the instant you both entered the restaurant. Any stranger would notice." He throws a paper ball into the garbage can. "That video shows it too," he calmly says as he looks for something on his shelf as if he hadn't said it.

I freeze in his doorway. "Um. Okay." I walk away feeling like somebody just turned the light on.

Chapter 27

Tina

Alexa and I search for our table as we take in the grand reception hall. Everything is pure white with lovely elegance. The chandeliers sparkle as if polished for hours just for this wedding. White twinkle lights hang everywhere. The tables are decorated with exquisite white rose centerpieces, white tablecloths, white china. White candles provide a soft glow, filling the room with romance. White, white, white.

Kayla seems to have an obsession with white like I do purple. The bridesmaid's dresses are even white, but Matt has a black tuxedo. A white tux is so eighties. They even had us throw white rose petals after the ceremony. The only color I see is the red heart drawn over the *i* in my name on the place cards.

Our table is next to the dance floor. We're the first ones to arrive. Lisa gets to sit with James and the bridal party.

"I still can't get over how emotional Matt was while saying his vows. There's nothing more beautiful or sexy to see a man so in love with a woman."

I pull my head back in surprise and look under the table.

Alexa looks with me. "What are you looking for?"

"I'm looking for a woman named Alexa Kramer. Do you know where she is?"

Alexa looks at me like I'm mental, which I kinda am these days.

"Did I hear you correctly? Since when do you talk like a greeting card? Are you going soft on me?"

She pretends to look at her fingernails. "Maybe. Maybe not. I see Matt and Kayla, Lisa and James. And now you and Gerry. I just don't think it'll ever happen to me."

What did she say? "Two things to point out. First, maybe you're too picky or you're looking in the wrong places. You've quite the handful of guys to choose from. Second, don't include Gerry and me in your couples list. We were never in love and haven't spoken since our fight."

She leans her chin on her hand. "Do ya think I'm too picky?"

Out of thin air, a tall handsome man appears next to us. "Would the lady in red like another drink?" he says with a sultry voice, his eyes already undressing her.

She flashes her sexy smile. "I'd love another champagne."

Our sentimental moment left as fast as it came. Typical Alexa.

She leans to me and whispers, "You do love Gerry." Then she lifts up her hand for the man to take it.

My stomach turns.

"Go and get another drink and let me be." I shoo her away.

Maybe I was close to loving Gerry, but not anymore. As the days came and went this week, my anger simmered down. He should've told me, and I hope he wasn't using me. It's hard to believe he cares for me.

Until I watch the video.

Lisa says she feels lost when she doesn't have her wedding ring on. That's how I feel without my necklace today. Alexa tried to get me to wear one of her necklaces, but I refuse to wear another one. Instead I borrowed a pair of swanky earrings. I'm trying to convince myself I'm strong and can live without it.

Alexa returned to the table, gushing over that man. Speeches came and went. James's speech was as entertaining as ever. Since they'd grown up together, he told funny stories of their shared childhood. He had the entire crowd laughing and then crying when he became serious.

Dinner dishes were just cleared. The roulade tasted amazing, which I'm not surprised about. I wonder if Gerry's thinking of me. Has he looked for me tonight, even though I'm trying not to look for him? I won't allow my eyes to wander around the room.

I sit alone, drumming my fingers while everyone else mingles or dances. "Hi, Tina." I turn my head to see who rudely interrupted my thoughts about Gerry. I sigh. *Great.*

My muscles tense. "Tyler."

He sits on the side of the adjacent chair to face me. I give him a quick glance. The top buttons to his shirt are wide open, and his tie is hanging loosely around his neck. His hair is drenched with sweat.

"What do you want, Tyler? Need another drink?" I point my thumb to the bar. "The bar's over there."

He laughs. "I want to apologize for last Friday. I was a drunken asshole."

I roll my eyes. "Whatever. I don't want an apology." I grimace. "I need to go to the bathroom." I turn to stand up.

He grabs my wrist lightly. "I don't care if you like me or not. However, I care about Gerry. That entire day was shitty for me. I was a dick to everyone, and I don't know why I said what I did. He never *once* said anything bad about you all those years ago. He told me if he even spoke one word to you that night he would've never have made it to culinary school in France. And he *had* to go. You need to understand that."

I pull my wrist away and rub it.

"After Gerry ripped me a new asshole last Friday night, he explained to me what's happened the past few weeks. He spent time with you because he wanted to, not because he used you. I think the video is proof enough, don't ya think?"

Deep down, I know he's telling the truth. With every minute that passes, I don't even know why I'm so angry at Gerry anymore. Sometimes I'm madder at myself for being too sensitive.

I turn, but freeze when he says, "Don't walk away when you've met again after all these years. That has to mean something to you.

You've both been given a second chance when the timing was finally right."

His words point out what I've refused to admit. I force myself to walk with my head held high. I don't get far when I hear an older woman's voice say, "Who were you talking to, Tyler? Was that Tina?"

Tyler calls, "Tina. Wait." I remain facing away from them.

"Let me introduce you to Gerry's parents."

My heart rate speeds up. I spin slowly and plaster on my award-winning fake smile that has worked for so many years. I ease toward them.

"This is the infamous Tina." Tyler motions to me.

"Hi, Tina. I'm Andreas, and my tiny wife over here is Éclair. Oh, I'm sorry. I mean Claire." He embraces her and tickles her side.

"That joke's so outdated, Uncle Andreas." Tyler laughs.

I cover my mouth to stifle mine.

Claire walks forward and shakes my hand. "It's nice to meet you. Gerry mentioned he was spending time with you. You must be very special, because I haven't heard him talk about a woman in ages. His job takes up so much of his time. But that's what happens in the restaurant business. It's good to hear he's finally come out of hiding."

"It's nice to meet you both. How long are you visiting?"

"We're staying here for a couple more days, and then we're driving through New England to enjoy the autumn foliage. We've always wanted to do it. Once we heard the wedding would be in October, we jumped at the chance and booked rooms at bed and breakfasts."

"I'd love to do that. I'm itching to travel myself."

Andreas looks over my shoulder and nods. Claire stares at something or someone too. I slowly turn around but only see guests mingling. Nothing out of the ordinary.

Claire suddenly says, "Tina, we have to excuse ourselves. We just saw a friend of ours we need to say hello to. I hope we can talk more later. Enjoy the reception."

"No problem. It was nice to meet you." They walk in the opposite direction from where they were looking. Weird.

After using the bathroom, I walk back into the reception room just as the cake is being rolled out onto the dance floor. I'm shocked by how massive it is. I'm too far away to see the minor details, but it's a three-tiered cake with white roses. I head to my table to get a closer look. The roses look real. If they are edible, Matt has serious talent.

Lisa and James are huddled together with Alexa at our table. Lisa waves me over with a giant smile on her face. Alexa also grins ear to ear. Time to cut them off from the alcohol. But who cares. I'm not the mother hen anymore, and we have rooms here. As I approach my chair, I'm stunned to find my plate covered with a shiny silver dome. The other plates are empty.

I eye Lisa and Alexa with suspicion and point to my plate. "What's this?"

Lisa shrugs her shoulders.

Alexa remarks, "I have no idea. It was here when I came back to the table."

Alexa points to the other guests sitting with us. "Did any one of you see who brought this?"

A woman responds, "A server asked which seat was Tina's and placed it on her plate. I asked him what it was, but he ignored me and walked away." She stares at the dome with curiosity like everyone else.

"Stop hiding behind that chair and sit down."

I do as Lisa says and stare at my distorted face in the silver dome. It makes my nose look huge.

"Don't leave us hanging. Take the cover off. We want to see what's inside," Alexa insists while bobbing in her chair.

I lift it slowly so only I can see what's there first. I drop the cover back down and melt into my chair. I cover my quivering mouth with my shaking hands.

"What's wrong? What is it? Can I look?" Lisa asks.

I can only nod because I'm speechless.

She lifts it, and her breath hitches. "No. I can't believe it. Your necklace."

It lies delicately on the plate with a small sprig of lavender placed in the middle of the chain. Above the necklace is a small photo album of the selfies and pictures Gerry and I took. The top photo is from the Empire State Building. I've not seen it before, and it's beautiful. His smile is breathtaking. My lips continue to quiver as my eyes tear. I pick up the necklace and stand up to search for Gerry. My heart flutters when I hear the song "Apologize" from One Republic in the background.

I stumble when I see him standing about twenty feet away, delectable as ever in his tailored black suit, one hand in his pants pocket. He looks like a model in *GQ*. I'm suddenly hungry, and it's not for food. We lock eyes, and he flashes me the crooked smile I love. I've missed every ounce of him.

I shake my head in disbelief, trying not to break down. Lisa told me last weekend I'm an ugly crier. That my face squishes together like the alien in the movie *Predator*. But I don't care. I can't hold back anymore. I run to him and leap into his arms. We don't speak with words, only our lips. To me the room is empty. His soft lips devour mine as my body melts into his. He was right all along.

This is real.

We're real.

And we don't have to resist *us* anymore.

Chapter 28

Gerry

Her satiny lips. Her decadent tongue. I could dance with them all night. "I'm so sorry," I whisper against her lips. "I'm so sorry. I never meant to hurt you." I bury my face into her hair, inhaling her lavender-scented shampoo.

"I know. I believe you."

Hearing her words makes me kiss her deeper.

"The guy over at table ten making out with the best man's sister-in-law is Gerry."

We both pull away out of breath as we hear laughter surround us.

"And the lovely lady in purple is Tina."

She buries her head into my chest and giggles.

I watch Matt to hear what else he's going to say to embarrass us.

"Because I married Kayla, Gerry's now my official cousin, whether he likes it or not." Always the comedian. "He's been a great friend to me since we were in culinary school together in France. If it weren't for him, I would never have met my gorgeous wife. Gerry is the awesome chef who prepared the delicious food tonight. Can we give him a round of applause, everybody?" Matt and Kayla clap as the rest of the guests join in.

I shake my head as the crowd claps and cheers. Tina squeezes me, and I can't resist pulling her even tighter against me. She's not leaving my side for the rest of the night, or my life if I have my way in the future. There's nothing holding us back anymore. I want her alone so I can show her how much she belongs to me now.

The clapping dies down.

"Now it's time for Kayla and me to cut this exquisite cake. Made by me, of course."

The guests start clinking their glasses with silverware.

"You want me to kiss her?"

They yell, "Yes."

He dips her back and kisses her for the crowd and then swings her back up.

Now that the focus is back on them, I pull Tina's chin up. "You look stunning in this very sexy dress. Other guys better not try to dance with you."

Her glowing eyes soften. "Since I walked into your restaurant, I've always been yours." She cups my cheek with her hand. "Thank you so much for my necklace. I thought I lost it and you forever. This week has been total hell without you both. Now I have you both back."

Lisa and James approach us. With her hands clasped over her chest, Lisa says, "Gerry. I can't believe you found it. She's been miserable without it...and..." Lisa hesitates when Tina gives her a dirty look. "Which isn't relevant anymore."

"Where did you find it?" Tina asks.

"Joel told me he received a phone call regarding a missing necklace. I noticed it was your name and phone number. I was on a mission from then on to find it. Days passed, and I was still empty handed. Then Joel came to me with it in his hand. It was half buried in the cobblestone in the beer garden. I saw it was broken and dirty, so I had a jeweler fix and clean it."

Tina holds up the necklace to inspect it. "It's so shiny. Look at how the amethysts sparkle. It looks brand new."

"I had a stronger clasp put on it, just in case you get mad at me again."

Tina pokes me in the side.

"Do you want me to help you put it on?"

She puts it in my hand and turns around. She lifts her shiny long hair, exposing her neck. After I close the clasp, I brush my fingertips down her open back. This dress is going to kill me. I'm not sure it'll be in one piece at the end of the night. I want to take her to my room now, but I need to stay for a while. I straighten my tie and put my arm around Tina's waist when she twists back around. Her fingers massage the pendant.

James shakes my hand. "Great job with dinner. I think it was even better than the taste testing. Your skills are impressive. All I'm good for is grilled cheese sandwiches."

Lisa nuzzles into him. "But they're the best." She kisses his neck as "A Thousand Years" from Christina Perri begins. "Let's dance." Lisa drags James seductively to the dance floor.

I take Tina's face in my hands. "I want to be alone with you, but I need to socialize a little bit since I just finished with the kitchen. We have a lot to talk about, but let's do it later. Is that all right?"

She smiles as I tickle her lips with mine once more.

She plays with the buttons on my shirt. "I don't think we'll be talking much later on."

I growl. "You drive me nuts. Dance with me." I pull her arm.

She resists. "But I was so horrible at your apartment."

"Didn't I say I'm a good lead? We have more space on the dance floor. Dance with me, please. I won't spin you around like last time. That's for later in my room." I waggle my eyebrows.

"Then let's go now." She pulls me away from the dance floor.

I pretend to give in but wrap my arms around her waist and carry her to the dance floor.

"Put me down, Gerry, or I'm not letting you spin me later." She squeals.

We glide along the dance floor. Blocking everyone from our thoughts. Our bodies glued together. "This is one of my favorite songs. Listen to the words," she whispers.

I listen, and my heart connects with hers as we stare at each other. "Kiss me again," she says. "I don't care if anyone sees us. For weeks I've pushed my feelings aside. Now I want you to know what you mean to me. The kiss in the video wasn't enough."

We sway slower and slower as our kiss mimics the rhythm of the song.

Someone smacks me on the shoulder.

"You two at it again? This is a family affair," Matt jokes as he slowly walks away. He then turns around. "Gerry, didn't you say you have a room here?"

Tina looks up at me. Matt winks and strolls off the dance floor. I guess that was Matt's way of saying it's okay to leave.

I steal one more kiss and lead her off the dance floor away from her table.

"Where are we going?"

"Let me introduce you to my parents before we go for a spin in my room."

She pats me on the ass. "You're bad." Her lips touch my ear as she whispers, "But I secretly love it."

My heart bangs out of my chest like a cartoon character. Surely everyone can see it.

"I already met them. Your mom's name is Éclair." She giggles.

I stop abruptly. "Are you kidding? My dad used that joke again? He's been using it since I was little."

"Be nice to your dad. He's sweet. Your mom too. I don't know how you became so big and bulky when your mom's so bitsy like Lisa. Your dad's tall, but nothing like you."

"If you meet my uncles in Europe, you'll understand. My dad's the runt of the family."

My eyes scan the guests around us and then the doors. "Since you met my parents, I want to get us out of here without anyone seeing us. I want you to myself without interruptions."

She looks around too.

I peck her neck. "Do you have a handbag with you?" I pull her toward her table.

"Yes." She snatches it off the chair and waves to Lisa and Alexa in the distance. Lisa lifts her chin with a smile of approval. Alexa gives us a thumbs-up.

"Let's get out of here." Tina grabs my hand.

Chapter 29

We reach the elevator in record time. He hits the Up button. "I'm on the tenth floor. Do you have a room here?" he asks while loosening his tie.

"Yes, I'm sharing one with Alexa. It's on the tenth floor too," I answer as I fiddle with my necklace. A sense of relief gushes through me now that I have both the necklace and Gerry back.

We're inside in seconds, and I push the button to close the doors as fast as possible. It's like pushing through tar. When they finally close, we're instantly pawing each other and kissing. He pins me against the wall and nips my neck. "Remember when we were in the elevator at your office? I wanted to do this then. From the second I saw you again, my hands ached to touch every part of your body." He trickles his hands down my chest, gently squeezing my breasts.

"Gerry," I whisper, my voice dripping with desire.

"I like when you say my name like that." He sucks on my lower lip.

The elevator doors open, and we separate instantly. Granted, anyone would know what we were doing by how hard we're panting and how I readjusted my dress. We step out.

He wraps his arm around my waist. "Do you need anything from your room?"

I shake my head.

"Good answer."

With shaking hands, he swipes his card to open his door. He urges me in, then pins me against the wall as the door closes. He pulls his lips from mine. "Are you okay with this? I don't want to push you if you're not ready."

"You're not the only one who has been waiting for this." I pull on his tie one hand at a time until we're face to face. "Please shut up so we can continue what we started."

I remove his tie as fast as I can and toss it to the floor. My hands glide up his chest, under his jacket, and slide it off his arms. If I was strong enough, I'd rip his shirt off. One by one I undo each button of his shirt until it's wide open. His eyes never leaving mine, he takes his shirt off and drops it. My fingers and lips trace his bare, perfectly sculpted, hairless chest.

I turn around and sway my hair over my shoulder, revealing my back.

He traces his fingertips across one shoulder as one strap falls down my arm. "I can't believe I can finally touch you," he whispers against my skin.

Bolts of heat rush through my veins as he grazes on my shoulder like he hasn't eaten for days.

"Unzip it," I urge.

He pulls the zipper slowly down, trailing its path with soft kisses, nips, and licks. It slides off and pools at my feet. I brace myself on the wall as I tremble. He places his hands over mine as he leans against me. Goose bumps dance on my skin feeling his warm, hard body against mine. I arch my back and grind against him. "Now my bra."

He removes his hands from mine and reaches to the front to unclasp it as he kisses my neck again. Slowly he pulls it away with his fingers tracing over my nipples. All I'm wearing is a pastel purple silk thong and high heels.

"Turn around. I want to see you. I *need* to see every part of you," he says with a sultry voice.

Sparks enflame my skin as his golden eyes trace every curve of my body. I know he wants to touch me, and it turns me on even more because he doesn't. I brush my breasts against him. "What are you waiting for?"

His jaw clenches. "For the rest of your clothes to come off."

"I like this game. Is this how German men seduce their women?" I murmur as my last shoe falls to the ground.

"No, this is how it's done when a man wants to enjoy every second gazing at the most beautiful woman he's ever seen. And watch how his gaze lights her on fire."

He inches closer and bends over. "You have the sexiest legs I've ever seen. Long, golden, with a silky touch."

His hands trace up my legs as he brushes his lips over my breasts, making my heart split open. He picks me up to wrap my legs around his waist, kissing me deeper than ever before.

He gently lays me on the bed and kneels over me.

"Take the rest off," I command.

He lifts one eyebrow. "Bossy. I like it. What else do you want me to do," he says as he reveals his naked body.

"For you to *finally* touch me like we've both wanted for weeks...with the lights *always* on. I want to watch everything we do."

He searches through his bag on the nightstand and takes out a huge box of condoms. "I came prepared."

"Wishful thinking, huh? Did you raid Costco?" I trace my hands down my curves as he moves closer.

The nerves in my body explode as he trails kisses from my stomach to my neck. He pins my arms above my head and spreads my legs.

"I'm the luckiest man in the world." His body throbs against mine as our lips finally connect again. We moan in unison. "I can't hold back anymore."

I arch my back. "Then don't. We've waited long enough."

What is it about him that makes me want to turn into an animal? The pull between us is so intense right now, but I need to slow it down. The feel of his hot, glistening body against me and the salty taste of his skin relieves some of the cravings. I rub up against him and take his mouth roughly with mine.

"I love your plump lips. They are a sweet temptation every time I see them." He moans into my mouth. He cups my face, pulling me closer as he devours mine. "Now I can kiss and touch you whenever I want."

"Even though I don't want to, we should slow down. It'll be over before we get really started. This is our first time, and I want to enjoy every second." I push him gently off me and kneel on the bed.

He follows, then takes my hand and shows me exactly where he wants me to touch him. "I want you to touch me, taste me. Show me what it's like to be desired by a woman like you." He moves in a slow gliding motion.

I inhale deeply as he caresses me at the same time. "If this is what it's like the first time with you, I can't wait for all the next times."

Chapter 30

Gerry

"What time do you think it is?" I ask while kissing her stomach and squeezing her like she's held captive.

"I don't care. I want to stay like this forever." She traces her fingers over my head and giggles.

I look up at her. "What's so funny?"

"It's amazing how little hair you have compared to those years ago. I remember it being so thick and wavy. Granted, I saw you for less than a minute across the room. But it was enough to have a special place in my memory."

I prop my chin on her belly. "Is there anything else you remember?"

She lightly scratches my back. "You tasted faintly of licorice. As I told you already, that's my favorite candy. So of course when you had a bag of licorice at our first meeting at Modern Web, I thought of that kiss."

I smile while I trace my finger around her belly button.

"Your crooked smile, but then I second-guessed whether it was a cocky smirk. I should've recognized you just from your smile. But again, your lack of hair threw me off."

"I thought you were beautiful then, but when you were in front of me again, I was in a daze. I thought I was dreaming. You age well, like a fine wine or cheese." I roll onto my side, facing her.

She leans up on her elbows. "Hey, matey, don't ever compare me to cheese. Cheese smells.”

“Fine, how about a banana? I want to peel off your clothes, layer by sexy layer.” I trail my fingers down her side and watch the goose bumps form on her skin.

“I’m already naked.” She can’t stop giggling. “You’re such a goofball. I love how much we laugh together.”

She rolls over to face me. “I like your banana, especially when it’s ripe.”

I pull her closer so we’re almost nose to nose. “I could see that from the past hours. You must’ve been starving.”

“I’m still hungry for you.” She sucks on my bottom lip. “Last week was shitty without you. I meant what I said when I stayed at your apartment. You’re my best friend. Is that weird to say after only knowing you for a couple of months?”

“No. It’s the same for me. I’ve never felt this way, never been able to be so open with any woman. Maybe it helped to not get sexually involved right away.”

“I told my dad and Lisa everything about my guilt. It helped. I know you don’t know everything, but I promise I’ll tell you, just not now. In the end, I’m so glad I told them. I’m ready to move on now.”

“You tell me when you’re ready.” His eyes turn serious. “I’m sorry I didn’t tell you who I was.”

I place my hand on his heart. “Why didn’t you?”

“Too many reasons. Some which are obvious. It would’ve been messy if you didn’t handle it so nicely. Which you proved correct. Believe me when I say I was going to tell you.”

“You know what? Let’s not rehash it. It’s all out there now. The video convinced me you were telling the truth. I can’t believe our kiss got so much attention. Thankfully, it only showed when we kissed. It was pretty steamy.”

“I wasn’t told for days there was a video out there on the internet. My family and friends were afraid to tell me. I was relieved it was something positive this time, not making me look like a monster again.”

"Let's not talk about it anymore and start fresh." She snuggles into me and traces my chest with her soft fingers. "I love that you have no hair on your chest."

"I guess it makes sense since I'm losing the hair on my head."

"Well, I find you sexy as hell with peach fuzz."

She props herself on her elbow. Her flawless breasts so close and so enticing.

"Sorry—there's one more thing I want to ask. Did I really inspire you to come up with the blindfold idea?"

"The entire experience helped me. But if I wasn't so attracted to you then, I would've never played that game. Maybe I wouldn't be here with you right now. Please don't ever regret that night again."

"You're my favorite regret." She kisses me softly.

"That's better than worst regret, so I'll take it."

"After that game, I've never looked at a blindfold the same again."

"The cooking show I've always wanted would be with blindfolds. It'd be a little bit like *The Taste*, but the chefs are blindfolded and need to guess what they're eating with only one spoonful. Presentation of the food wouldn't be a focus. Only how it tastes and smells. There's still a lot of details that need to be ironed out."

"Did you hear anything from your agent?"

I don't answer right away and pull her on top of me. "I have a meeting scheduled with the network I told you about to discuss details about the show."

She leans up on her hands and tempts me with her breasts again. My eyes lock on them, not on her face.

"Wow! You must be so excited."

I force myself to look at her face. *Really?* What if I really get the show? Will she still be happy if I need to move back?

"I'm not excited, because I know it won't work out. I've been through this so many times. I'm doing it just to get the feel of how I'm perceived back home." I place my hands on her hips. "I need to go to Germany soon... Why don't you come with me?"

Her eyes widen. "Go to Germany with you? You're crazy. I need to work."

"You just finished this project. You've always wanted to travel and get a stamp in your passport. Here's your chance, and you'll be with me. I can show you where I'm from."

"You're serious." She exhales loudly. "But it's not that easy."

"It'd only be for a week. It's the best time to go because it's harvest season when the grapes are picked in the vineyards. My parents said it's still unseasonably warm and the best golden October is predicted."

She rests her chin on my chest. "Even though I want to go, I'm not sure."

"You finally have the chance to travel. Please think about it. My parents have a furnished apartment attached to their house. They'll return from their trip a couple of days after we'd arrive. We can skinny-dip in the pool and have the entire house to ourselves."

"I don't know." She hems and haws. "You make it sound so exciting though. I never thought my first big trip would be to Germany."

"I promise you it doesn't look like World War II."

Her mouth drops open.

"I know that's what you're thinking. That's what most people do when they haven't been there before. We can spend a day in France or Switzerland. Will that tempt you even more?"

"Well, I'm still thinking about the skinny-dipping." She leans closer to my mouth.

"The pool's heated, and the garden's secluded. My mom made sure of that." I caress her backside and pull her against me, igniting the fire between us again.

"I'll think about it. Text me the dates, and I'll see if I have the nerve to ask Thomas for vacation time. I'm not sure how he'll react."

"Your team deserves it. It looks better than I imagined. Did he give you another project?"

"He says new projects are being discussed but haven't been approved yet. One is for a touristy thing for California, which I'd love to do.”

She taps my chest. “I forgot to tell you. He saw us at Burnett’s, and the video.”

My body stiffens.

“Your face is probably what mine looked like. Don’t worry. I told him we were never involved. Even though we kissed on the video.”

“Did he believe you?

“I think so. He spoke as if it wasn’t a secret we had feelings for each other. He could see it just by how we acted at the restaurant.”

“He’s a smart man.” I kiss her neck. “Definitely ask him then. I think he’ll say yes.”

We kiss for a while, to the point her face is raw from my scruff growing in.

“I’m going to look like a clown tomorrow. Or today, depending on the time,” she says.

“Don’t worry. People will be jealous because they’ll know what we were doing all night.”

She props herself up on a pillow and covers herself with a blanket.

“Uh oh. You have a serious face. What’s up?”

“Now that we’re together, where do we go from here? You work nonstop, and I live in Hoboken. Do you want to be in a relationship?”

I push her hair away from her face. “Are you really asking me that question? Can’t you see how I feel about you? Can’t you feel it? Especially the last hours. Should I remind you?” I trail my finger down her most sensitive spots under the blanket.

“It’s very obvious how we feel about each other. I haven’t had a relationship in so long. If you can even call them relationships. I don’t know how to do this.”

“Let’s act just the way we always have and add a lot of sex to it. Sound good?”

She nips my shoulder and purposely trails her hand down to the body part that’s ready for her again. “You won’t hear me complaining.”

Chapter 31

Gerry

I like her sleeping on my shoulder. Even the drool spot on my shirt. "Tina," I whisper while shaking her gently. "We'll be landing soon. You need to wake up." I nudge her again.

She sits up straight and blinks several times. "How long did I sleep? My neck feels so stiff." She leans her head side to side and stretches her arms over her head.

"A good couple of hours. We hit some rough turbulence. I'm surprised you didn't wake up."

The captain comes on the intercom, stating we'll be landing in fifteen minutes.

"I'm sure the motion sickness medicine and two glasses of champagne are to blame." She rummages through her bag and pulls out a small bottle of eye drops and some gum. She drips one drop in each eye. "Ah. Much better." She blinks several times.

"I'm glad you were able to sleep. The drive from Frankfurt to my parents' house will take about two and a half hours. You can sleep in the car if you need to."

"Hell no. I'm staying awake as much as possible. I want you to show me everything." She pops a piece of gum in her mouth then offers me one. I take it because I can't stand the way my mouth tastes after being on a long flight.

I open the window shade next to her. "Since this is your first landing, watch as we go down."

Her hand squeezes mine every time there's a sudden drop or the plane leans to one side to turn. I explain that it's totally normal. She twists her body to look out the window at every angle. Once we land, she turns to me with that gorgeous smile of hers. I realize I'll do anything to make her smile like that every day.

The seat belt signs go off. We take our carry-on luggage and wait to get out. I glance back at her. "Ready to get your first stamp in your passport?"

"I sure am."

What feels like hours later, we finally find my parents' car in one of the car parks. When I made my plans to come for my meeting, my parents and I made an agreement that they'd leave their car here for me to drive home. When they arrive, they'll take the train from Frankfurt to the local station in their town.

"Nice BMW, and a stick shift no less," she says as she traces her fingers over the dashboard. "My little Ford Fiesta was a piece of tin compared to this. I sold it when I moved to Hoboken. The parking there is horrible and so expensive. Alexa has a parking spot that came with the apartment. But she pays for it in addition to the monthly rent."

I drive toward the exit. She begins to laugh. "*Ausfahrt*. What does that mean?" She continues to laugh.

"I know. It sounds like *fart*." I've heard it a million times. "It means exit."

"I'll have to tell Lisa and Alexa that one. Do we get to drive on the *Autobahn*, or whatever that one road is called?"

Now I laugh.

"What's so funny?"

"*Autobahn* means highway. It's not a particular street. And yes, we're taking the highway."

"Good to know." She grabs my right arm. "Does this mean we get to drive really fast?"

I shake my head because her excitement cracks me up. "Yes. But it's dangerous. We have the whole day ahead of us, so we don't need to drive so fast. I can tell you're going to be a riot this week."

"You'll probably be sick of me by the end of this trip."

I stop the car before the exit and check that there's no one behind us. I place my hand at the back of her neck and pull her over to my side. "I promise you—I'll *never* get sick of you." I kiss her long and hard. We separate slowly. "Believe me now?"

She nods. Her hand goes to her necklace but she notices me glance at it. She pulls it away and shoves both of her hands between her legs.

I smirk and put the car into first gear. "Now sit back and enjoy the ride."

Chapter 32

Tina

Holy crap, he's driving fast, and other cars still pass us. "Okay. I get the point. Foot off the gas." He slows the car down and drives to the far-right lane.

"Now I can say I've experienced the *Autobahn*." My pulse slows down, and the death grip I have on my seat belt loosens.

"Alexa would love it here with the way she drives. But Lisa would have a cardiac arrest because she's afraid of driving in any car. Do you drive that fast on a normal day? I can't imagine the accidents."

"I'm guilty to have driven as fast as one hundred sixty kilometers per hour. That's about one hundred miles per hour."

"That's sick. Don't ever go that fast when I'm in the car with you."

He takes my left hand and kisses my fingertips. "*Keine Sorgen, Süße.*"

I give him the look I'm sure he has come to understand when he speaks German or French to me. "Sorry. My German cap is back on. We're in my country now. It means *no worries.*"

"Speaking of worries. Since you haven't been back here since you moved, how are your nerves holding up? Are you still worried about how people will treat you?"

He readjusts himself in his seat. "I'm fine right now, but I don't know about later. Since we've gotten together, it's not as much of a focus."

I massage the back of his neck.

"I look forward to introducing you to my family. Mom has planned a barbecue when they come back in a couple of days."

"Do you like to barbeque? My dad hates to cook but loves to barbeque."

"I love to grill. You'll have fun. Most of my cousins speak good English. One cousin is married to a woman from England. They have five-year-old twins. A boy and a girl. What's the term in English?"

"Fraternal twins."

"Right." He points out his window. "Over there is the Black Forest. There's great skiing in this area, not too far from where we're going. It takes about an hour to get there. You said you used to ski. It's too bad it's not wintertime. I could've taken you."

"I haven't skied in years. I'm not sure I'd be any good anymore."

"Now we're approaching the exit where you'll see vineyard after vineyard. I'll drive the backroads so you can see them better. Once we get to my parents' house, we can unpack and shower." He grabs my hand and kisses the top. "Together."

"I like our plans already." Is my seat heated? Because I feel a bit warm. I don't think I'll be tired anytime soon.

"Then we can go to some of the wineries for wine tasting. A lot of them have something called a *Straußi*. The winery has a small restaurant where people can drink their wine and eat typical cuisine from this area, like *Flammkuchen* or *Wiener Schnitzel*."

"Yummy. Sausages from Germany."

He bursts out laughing. "You think sausages because I said wiener?" He laughs even louder.

"Yeah, or maybe hotdogs. Am I wrong?"

"It's breaded veal cutlets that are fried. Then you squeeze lemon juice over them. The dish is originally from Austria."

Now I feel like he's making fun of me. Without responding, I turn the music up and stay quiet. The song I turn up isn't even in English. I cross my arms and rest my head on the seat. From the corner of my eye, I see Gerry turn his head back and forth from me and to the road.

He turns the music down. "What's the matter?"

"Just remember—I've never been outside the US. I'm sure I'll say and do stupid things. Be patient with me."

"I'm sorry. I thought it was funny." He puts his hand out for me to hold. "This is something I dealt with all the time when I visited the US, or even when I moved there. Just like me using the word *handy*. You laughed at me. Now you're in my territory."

"I don't want you to think I'm stupid."

"Tina." He huffs. "I wish I could stop this car right now and kiss you senseless. This is another country. Of course you're going to do funny things. But I don't care because you are, by far, the smartest, funniest, and most fascinating woman I've ever met. This is our vacation, and we're here to have fun."

"If you put it that way, handsome, laugh away." I reach over and kiss him on the cheek. "Let's talk about wine tasting here. I'm not a fan of Riesling. It's too sweet."

"Riesling seem to have that reputation, but it's not always true. It's possible you won't like any of the wine here. The white wine isn't made in wooden barrels, so it doesn't have the oaky taste. When you're used to California wine, you might not appreciate wines from here."

"I'll try some, and if I don't like it, I'll drink beer. Having fun and acting a little crazy is my priority—and skinny-dipping before we go to bed would make this day complete."

"That's what I'm looking forward to most. Well, and the shower." His hand roams up my leg, high enough for my hormones to scream *don't stop.*

"Behave and hands on the steering wheel." He doesn't move his hand, so I grab it and place it on the steering wheel. "I promise, you'll be smiling later."

He presses on the gas pedal.

Chapter 33

Gerry

She points out the window with enthusiasm. "It's just like in my magazines. Little towns here and there with a big old church towering in the middle."

I love how excited she is, and we've only been in Germany for a couple of hours.

"Oh, and look at the different colors of vines. They're in perfect patches along the rolling hills. Why is there a patch of red in the middle of the others?" She babbles.

"It's just a different type of grape. We can take a walk through the vineyards by my parents' house. Then you'll see the differences between the varieties. I don't think they're all picked yet."

She turns to me with a giddy grin. "I just can't believe I'm here. The surroundings are breathtaking. The Black Forest doesn't look real when it's this close. Just like a postcard."

"My mom was right about a great golden October this year. There are more yellow and orange leaves than red in Germany. You can already see it. The colors will probably be at their peak in a week or two. The one *Straußi* we'll go to has an incredible view of the forest. An excellent spot for taking pictures."

She hangs her head out the window, her hair blowing in the wind. "Look at the colorful patch of fresh flowers. Are they for anyone to pick?"

"Yes. You'll see several along the streets."

"They're for free?"

"No. There is a money box on the edge of the field where you put the money."

"Come on. You think people really pay? Someone can easily steal the money box or the flowers."

"Yes, people do pay. Honor system."

She nods and relaxes in her seat.

"This area is known for tourists, so the towns put a lot of money into making everything look nice. You see what taxes pay for."

We drive through a town that's five minutes away from my own. She points at things and asks questions.

"In this area there are a lot of hotels or bed and breakfasts." I point at one. "This one is a quaint hotel. If I remember correctly, the building is nearly four hundred years old. The restaurant has a Michelin star."

"Vibrant flowers are everywhere. I love how the large stream flows through the middle of this town."

"It's called a *Bach*. Not all of them are large like this one. We had a drought years ago, and the stream was almost dry. It smelled, and the fishes were dying."

"Fish."

He shakes his head. "Fish and deer are the two I always get wrong. I say fishes and deers."

"Anyway, what were you saying?"

"It doesn't matter. It was very hot, and most houses and businesses don't have air conditioning. If they do, it's a special system. You don't freeze like in the US. Most offices and hotels have windows that open. It's a different culture here."

"I'd love it since I told you I hate AC. I'd be happy with a ceiling fan."

I turn right onto one of my favorite roads. "This is the main street that takes us directly to my hometown. If you look ahead, you'll see my favorite view of the Black Forest. I love how the street is lined with trees. In the spring, they have white flowers and now, orange-red leaves. There are a lot of cherry, apple, and plum orchards here."

"Do you ever get homesick?"

I downshift and put on my left blinker. "Sometimes. Mostly during the holidays. Christmas is my favorite holiday here. Lots of festive lights and Christmas markets in every town. Mom loves that time of year, so she decorates the house above and beyond. My parents hold an annual Christmas party. They really make it special. I won't be able to spend Christmas here this year."

"Why? Because of work?"

I pull into the driveway and park the car. I take her face into my hands. "No. Because I want to spend Christmas in New York City with you."

Chapter 34

Tina

I fall backward on the bed. "This was the best day ever. My brain is on overdrive. I wish I'd brought a journal. Maybe I can buy one tomorrow."

Gerry leans over me with his hands at the sides of my head. "I can't believe we're still awake after the amount of wine we drank and the time change. We should be dead at this point."

"It helped we took a nap before we went out. If we stay on the bed like this, I'll pass out though. Let's go for a swim. It'll wake us up for a little while longer and make it a perfect end to a perfect day."

He kisses my cheek and backs away from the bed.

"Where did you put my sneakers? I need to see how wet they still are. I can't believe I stepped into that tiny canal. I'm so glad a shoe store was open."

He takes the sneakers out of a plastic bag. "Come on. It was funny how you sounded like a duck quacking every time you took a step."

"Maybe to you but not to other people. They probably thought I was farting."

He chuckles. "I'll take care of them. I learned something when I was younger that will help them dry faster."

"I'm going to rest for a minute and reminisce about today." I stay on my back.

"Don't fall asleep. I want to see you in that bikini you packed in your suitcase. Granted, it won't be on you for long. I'll be right back."

"Give me one more kiss." He pecks me on the lips. "You have the softest lips. They're lethal," I tease as he leaves the room.

I fold my arms behind my head. The Black Forest, vineyards, and orchards are all extraordinary in their own way. I can't imagine being surrounded by this beauty every day. Or the wine. That could get dangerous. The forest must look like a dream when there's a dusting of snow in the winter.

It's peaceful. No crazy, loud traffic except for the motorcycles that pass. I didn't see any malls or stores on every corner. It's nice for vacation, but I'm not sure I could handle it on a day-to-day basis. I'd save a lot of money though.

We walked through some vineyards so Gerry could point out the differences between the grape varieties. The colors ranged from electric purple to a pale yellow. I found out red wine is red from the skin of the dark grapes, not the juice. Most white wine bottles have twisty caps, not corks. I'd always thought only cheap, bad wine had twisty caps. He told me it's because they don't age white wine like red wine. The white wine meant to age for a longer time will have a cork. I've learned so much in less than one day.

The house creaks wherever Gerry walks. I love this house. There are tall wooden beams throughout. A massive fireplace stands in the middle of the open-space living and dining room area. It reminds me of Swiss chalets I frequently see when I look through my travel magazines. The apartment section of the house is decorated the same and is very cozy.

I force myself off the bed to dig my bikini out of my luggage. We were too lazy to unpack when we first arrived. I roam to the bathroom. The pool had better be heated.

I've hardly worn my suit this year. I twist and turn in front of the sink mirror. Not too shabby. I brush my teeth and wash my face. No need for my makeup to run down my face when I'm in the pool. A thought hits me. What if he wears a banana hammock? He has a great body, but am I ready for something like that? I know cultures differ, but come on now.

I jump when he knocks on the door. "Did you fall asleep in there?"

Let's get this over with. I open the door with a smile. He stands in front of me with a fluffy white robe hanging over his arm in front of him. "Want to see my new Speedo? We're in Germany now," he says proudly.

No he doesn't! I swallow hard. "Yeah, um, sure."

He hands me the robe to reveal his black swim shorts. "Just kidding." He snickers. "I know how you women hate Speedos. The look on your face was priceless."

I take the robe from him with relief dripping from my smile. "You mean banana hammock," I correct him.

"Don't worry. I don't like Speedos either. Especially after swimming for so many years."

"You have a great body, but I don't know. A banana hammock could break us." I wink at him.

"Let's go before I rip that tiny purple bikini off of you before we even leave the room. You'll need the robe when we get out of the pool."

"I haven't gone swimming at night since I was little."

Minutes later we hang off the edge of the lit, heated pool.

"The water is just the right temperature. I feel like I'm in a hotel in your parents' fancy backyard. It's so secluded with the high bushes and trees. I don't see any other houses," I say as I push off the edge and swim to the other side.

He swims behind me.

"Where are you going? Are you trying to get away from me?"

"Maybe." I look back at him over my shoulder.

I turn around and put my arms around his neck. He wraps my legs around his waist and then hugs me tightly. He wades us through the pool wrapped around each other in silence.

He kisses my nose. "You're quiet. What are you thinking about?"

"You showed me such amazing things today. I'm already in love with your country."

He lets me go, then turns around so his back is facing me. "Jump on my back. I'll take you for a ride around the pool."

"The food was so fresh and delicious. I'm surprised you don't get drinks with ice. I guess it's a good thing because you get more to drink."

"But you never get refills like you do in some places in the US."

"You were Mr. Popular today. I hope your picture of how people perceive you has changed. It seems the entire town knows you, and the people were genuinely happy to see you. I didn't understand what they said, but their big hugs and smiles told me everything. Do you think you can move on now?"

He stands up slowly to let me slide off and then dives under the water. Did I piss him off? I wait for him to come up for air by the stairs. His body emerges like a big bear, and then he sits on a step.

"Are you okay?" I say as I swim toward him.

"*Ja.*"

I smile. "Finally a German word I know. Yes."

He claps the water next to him for me to sit down with him.

"When we were out, I didn't really think about what happened a year ago. My focus was on us having fun. Slowly it's sinking in my reputation isn't as bad as I believed, or maybe I don't care anymore."

"I think you care, but you have other things going on that distract you from it. Maybe you focused on it too much, which made it worse. A lot of time has passed too."

I submerge myself under the water because the air is cold.

He follows me and pulls me to him.

"It still amazes me how my life has changed since I met you. I'd never in a million years guess that two months later, I'd be in Germany with the sexiest man alive, in a pool." I grind against him and nip at his shoulder.

He nuzzles my neck. "Get used to me being around, because I'm not going anywhere. I want to show you everything. Explore things together we've never done before. You make me excited about things I never dreamed of."

I try to wiggle out of his grip when he tickles my ribs.

"I have a confession." He wraps his arms around me again. "Before I met you, I thought I knew what would make me happy. But I realized how wrong I was." He squeezes me against his body. "You, Tina, are and will always be my happiness."

My heart just grew two sizes. When he says sweet things with his cute accent, I fall in love with him a little bit more. It scares me it's even possible to fall so fast and hard. But he makes it easy. I don't know if he can see what he means to me, but I'm going to make him feel it.

I hug him tightly and ask, "Are you sure no one can see us? Even with the pool light on?"

He nods, and something clicks between us. Our mouths and tongues connect at the same time. He presses me against the edge while still straddling him. One of his hands unties the bikini straps around my neck. He pulls away to watch it fall down and reveal my breasts. The next tie is undone, and he lays the top on the pavement.

I hang off the edge and arch my back. He devours me without hesitation. His hot mouth scorches every part of my revealed wet skin. His strong hands pull my bikini bottom off. He wraps my legs around him even tighter as he grinds into me.

"I'm not the only one who's going to be naked in here," I pant.

Within seconds, his suit is off and tossed somewhere. Our bodies connect. I think I see steam rising off the water from our body heat.

"I don't think I've ever been more turned on by a woman. My desire for you grows every second of every day," he moans.

The water splashes around us, making waves crash off the sides. "I wish I could take you right here, but...no condom."

"No matter how much I want to fulfill this fantasy, we do need to be careful," I say as I touch him. I love it when his eyes become heavy because of the pleasure I'm giving him. "Do you want me to stop," I ask in sync with the motion of my hand.

"Yes, or it'll be over before we're back in the house."

Chapter 35

Gerry

As soon as she steps out of the pool, I scoop her up, and within seconds we're back in the bedroom.

We both kneel on the bed, soaking wet, teasing every sensitive spot until our bodies quake. Her silky tongue on my skin sends flames through my body. She touches me in ways no other woman ever has before. Is this what it feels like to be completely in love with someone? When I want to consume and embrace every ounce of her, but it'll never ever be enough? To give her pleasure physically and emotionally, more than I receive? To put her happiness before my own? This is one moment I'll never forget, because it's clear I want to spend the rest of my life with her.

"Gerry," she says passionately. "This is almost too intense. Please."

She watches as I slide it on. It's the most erotic thing I've ever experienced. I sit back on my knees, resting on my legs. "Come here," I say with a rough voice. I stay in position as she moves closer. I lift her up and lower her onto me slowly. We don't move at first to enjoy the tight, warm connection between us.

She holds on to my shoulders as I gently move her up and down. Our bodies scream for more as we increase in speed. I lose all control when the most incredible warm pulses rip through my body. She captures my mouth with hers as we unravel together into a dreamlike state I hope we never wake up from.

Chapter 36

Tina

Gerry and I walk out of the main train station parking garage with his mom, Claire.

He grabs my hand. "My meeting shouldn't be more than two hours."

I love that he's affectionate and likes to hold hands even in front of his family.

"Where do you want to meet up?" he asks Claire.

"How about the Münsterplatz market? I'm going to take her to my favorite ice cream place. Since it's her first time here, she needs to see the market. We can buy the fresh food we need for the barbecue tonight. I want to show her the flower vendors." She turns to me. "They're my favorite. I could spend hours there."

"Sounds good. I'll call you when I'm done. Have fun." He gives me a soft kiss goodbye.

I grab his shirt. "Good luck. If it's meant to be, you'll get it. Show them who's boss."

He pats me on the butt and walks in the opposite direction of us.

Why am I encouraging him to get this show? I don't want him to leave New York City. But I'd never ask him to give up this chance just for me. Especially since we've only been together for a few weeks. Ridiculous!

Claire and I walk down the busy street in silence. I lay my sweater over my shoulders. "It's a bit cooler today."

"I think the little heatwave is over, and fall has finally arrived. Time to close the pool."

I blush when she mentions the pool. Before we went to sleep after our swim the other night, I made Gerry get our bathing suits from outside before we forgot they were out there. I didn't want his parents to know what we were doing.

She points up in the sky. "See that steeple pointing out over those buildings? That's the Münster in the middle of the marketplace. It's a beautiful cathedral. Maybe before we leave, we can take you to a beer garden nearby that has a spectacular view of Freiburg. It's a little touristy."

"Well, I am a tourist, so we have to go." We both chuckle.

"Is there somewhere I can buy a little cuckoo clock for Lisa? She thinks it'd be fun for Felicia. Maybe I can find something for Dad and Beth too."

"There's a store right near the market. I can show you after we have ice cream. If you see any other stores that look interesting, let me know. We have time."

"I didn't bring a big suitcase, so I need to watch how much I buy. But I'm definitely loading up on chocolate and licorice to take home. I'll make sure Gerry does too."

She tugs on my sweater to go to the left. I'm awed at the size of the cathedral towering in the middle of the bustling market. "This is the Münsterplatz," she says with pride.

I stand still and absorb my surroundings. It hits me again that I'm in Germany. In Europe. The crystal blue sky adds to the wonderful scene before me. "Wait, Claire. Let me take a picture. Then we can take a selfie together if you'd like."

"Sure, I'd love to. You also need one with the cathedral behind you."

After spending the past couple of days with Gerry's parents after they arrived home, I can see Gerry is more like his mom. She's warm, loving, and spunky. I didn't spend much time with his parents after the wedding, but when she saw me again, she embraced me like I've been a part of their family for years. I already want to call her Mom.

After taking several pictures, we filter through the thick crowd. She points to a café with several tables outside. "Here's my favorite ice cream place. There's an empty table in the sun."

I follow her and listen to the range of languages being spoken. "I'm amazed how many people speak English here. Everywhere we turn, I hear it. Well, it's the only one I clearly recognize."

"You'll hear a lot of English in this area because of the number of tourists and students. There's a big university here in Freiburg. Your generation and younger speak it very well. They start English classes during the fifth grade. In other parts of the country, they start in first grade."

"Wow. I didn't start Spanish until the seventh grade. I think it has changed since I was in high school. Kids might start earlier now."

We pull seats away from an empty table, making a horrible scraping noise against the cobblestone. The poor people sitting around us. We take our seats and look through the picture menu. "See, just like I said yesterday—ice cream is a form of art here. What would you like? Let's get the biggest ones possible. I'm always hungry for ice cream. Andreas doesn't eat as much as I do."

"I think you just found your match. Bring on the ice cream."

I point to a picture and try to pronounce what it's called. "*Schokobecher.*"

She laughs. "You sound just like I did when I first learned German. You want a chocolate sundae."

She teaches me how to pronounce it correctly. It takes a few times.

"Not bad, but still with a heavy American accent," she points out. "I never lost mine. It was hard when I first moved here. I took classes, but it wasn't easy to submerge myself. I'd speak German, but when my American, or maybe I should say *foreign* accent, was obvious, people tended to switch to English.

"One time I asked for cheddar cheese in German, and the worker responded in English. Was it because I asked for cheddar? I'm not from Ireland. It was frustrating because I wanted to learn. To top it off, the people from this area have a thick dialect. Even though I can speak German, it's still hard to understand some people that are from this area. It's the same in the US. We're from New Jersey, but when we hear someone from maybe Louisiana, it could be a problem for us."

A server takes our order and leaves us to bask in the sunshine. I relax in my chair and aim my face to the sun.

"What was it like when you first moved here? Was it major culture shock, other than the language?"

"Yes," she grumbles. "I have some good stories from my first couple of years here." She taps on her chin in deep thought.

"Here's one. It was the first time I cooked Thanksgiving dinner. I wanted to celebrate with my in-laws. The one thing they didn't know was I was two months pregnant with Gerry. I went to buy a turkey, but the stores didn't have turkeys prepared like in America. I was hormonal, so it angered me. Andreas asked a good butcher for a fresh turkey." She hangs her head in annoyance but with a smirk on her face. "We pick up the darn turkey, and it looked like they just gutted it and plucked the feathers. It didn't look anything like I had ever prepared before. I was surprised the head wasn't still on it."

I burst out laughing.

"Laugh away. I laugh at it now, but boy, was I angry then.

"When we got home, it was difficult to fit the turkey in the roasting pan. And the ovens are much smaller here than in America. I didn't even think about it when Andreas ordered it from the butcher. On top of that, I had mild morning sickness. I wasn't a happy camper, and I was exhausted. Turkey was not my best friend during the months that followed."

The server places our sundaes in front of us. I blink my eyes several times because it's enormous. "How many scoops of ice cream are in my dish?" I count them. "Five?" I say in shock. "I'm glad I'm starving." I take a quick picture of our masterpieces.

We dig in with smiles on our faces. I sigh because this is the best ice cream I've ever had. So creamy and rich in chocolate. Screw frozen yogurt in a paper cup.

"Back to the turkey. Was the meal ruined?"

She shrugs. "Not really. It turned out okay. Everyone said the food was delicious, but I didn't know if they were telling the truth or not. Lesson learned. Gerry takes care of the turkey when he's home. I'm sure he won't be home for Thanksgiving since he's visiting now."

"Tell me some more stories. More that'll make me laugh."

She eats one more spoonful of strawberry ice cream. "Andreas traveled a lot for his job back then. One day I decided to pick him up at the train station to surprise him. At that time, I had just learned how to drive a stick shift. I parked our Volvo station wagon and went upstairs to wait at the track for him. When we walked back to the car, we couldn't find it. I was on the verge of tears. I was swearing like hell, thinking the car was stolen or I'd forgotten where I parked it."

I feel nervous for her, as if I was standing there when it happened. "Don't tell me it was stolen?"

"No. It gets better." She huffs. "I forgot to put on the emergency brake. The station wagon rolled out of the parking spot and went straight into the empty one directly across from it. Because the car rolled backwards, it hit the wall and shattered the back window."

I choke on my ice cream and cover my mouth. "No."

"Oh yes. I'm a crier when I'm angry. So, of course, I cried. I was furious with myself. Here I was, all excited to surprise my husband, and that's what I get in return. The police had to come, and the German version of Triple A."

"Could you imagine if a car was in the parking spot? It would've been in the middle of the car lane," I comment.

She gestures with her hand. "That's what was weird. The parking deck was full, but it just happened that the one across was empty."

"How did Andreas handle it?"

She sighs and relaxes in her seat. "He's such a patient man. Gerry has that trait from him. He basically said, 'Shit happens.'"

"Whenever I had driven the car I'd panic when I had to stop at a stop sign on a hill. I'd break into a sweat when I needed to press the gas pedal and release the clutch. The car would stall or I'd grind the gears and it'd make a high-pitched screeching sound. Once I had to get a neighbor to help me up a hill. Mortifying." She shakes her head. "Every car we bought for me after that was an automatic. Years back, it was rare to drive an automatic here. Now you see them all the time."

She sits up and leans her elbows on the table. "Now I look back and laugh. I've learned things I most likely never would've learned in America. Every culture is different, and you learn to adjust. Don't get me wrong—it takes a while. I had my moments of hysteria. I was annoyed there was no mall around the corner. When I first moved here, the stores were only open until one p.m. on Saturdays and closed on Sundays. Over ten years ago, the stores changed their hours to stay open until eight or even ten. But they're still closed on Sundays. It's not bad though, because it means you're forced to relax on Sundays. I've come to really appreciate it. I take a lot of naps."

She eats another spoonful of her melting ice cream. I swat away an annoying fruit fly who has been trying to land in my ice cream. Smiling at me, Claire motions I have something on my nose. I giggle as I wipe it off.

She continues with her stories. "I couldn't believe how many people didn't have clothes dryers and still don't. Washing machines were the size of my pinky. They're bigger now, but nothing like the US. Some Germans complain Americans like everything extra-large. I guess that's true in a way.

"There are so many things I can mention, but in the long run, I'm very happy here. We always thought his job would move us back to the States, but it never did. He always found a job in Basel, Switzerland, so we never had the chance. Basel is only about a forty-five minute drive from here. We decided to stay in Germany because the cost of living is much cheaper."

"Do you think Gerry will move back?" Why do I ask questions I don't want to know the answer to?

"Hi, Claire." An older woman comes from behind me.

Claire's face lights up. "Hey, Stephanie. How are you?" She stands up to give her friend a hug. "Let me introduce you to Gerry's American girlfriend, Tina. They're staying here for the week."

She shakes my hand with a friendly smile. "Nice to meet you." Her eyes squint. "Oh, I recognize you. You're the girl in the video. You're even prettier in person," she says with a grin. "Good for you. He's a great man with a wonderful family."

She looks back at Claire. "You must be so happy he's here for a visit. It's been a while since he's been back. Right?"

I look away feeling embarrassed. Even people in Europe have seen the video.

While they talk for a few minutes, I sit back in my chair and tune them out. I'm sitting in a photo in one of my magazines. Pictures of colorful European cities where people are doing exactly what I'm doing right now. How did I get so lucky? I touch my necklace and have an epiphany. My punishment is finally over, and I can do whatever I want. Gerry's the blessing I've been waiting for.

Claire's friend waves to a man waiting for her in the distance. "Sorry. I need to go. I just wanted to stop and say hello. Hopefully, I'll see you soon at the next meeting." She disappears into the crowd just as the clock on the church chimes. Music to my ears.

Claire sits back down and scoots her chair closer to the table. "She's one of the members of an English-speaking women's group I belong to. It's a great way to meet other English-speaking women from all over the world. Including Germans.

"Now, where were we?" she asks, then scrapes the last remnants of her ice cream soup.

"I asked if you think Gerry will move back here." I set my spoon in the dish so I can digest a little bit. I'm ready to burst.

"I'll be honest. Gerry has always loved America. Sometimes I felt he was more American than German. In my gut, I knew he'd move there one day. I'm not happy why he moved there, but he's an adult. Andreas and I visit my family once or twice a year. We'll visit him then also. Now that he's met you, I don't think he'll move back to

Germany." She winks at me.

"What about this cooking show? Wouldn't he move back here if it worked out?" I stir the last scoop of ice cream in my dish to make it soft...the best way to eat it.

"That's for you both to discuss. It's been his dream, but he's always been let down at the last minute. Just like him, I don't get my hopes up anymore."

"I can't expect him to stay in New York if this is what he's always wanted. We've just started dating." Could I handle a long-distance relationship? Again, too early to think about.

She agrees. "Worry about it if the situation arises. Enjoy your vacation here. Tonight you'll be thrown into the pit of our family and friends. They'll be surprised he has a girlfriend. An American, no less. German men love American women. At least in this family, they do." Her laugh lines become more evident with her big smile.

"I've never seen Gerry cook for a lot of people. He made me dinner once. I look forward to seeing him behind a barbeque."

"I promise we'll all be stuffed. You'll hear French, German, and English mixed together. By the end of the night, you'll be screaming for your bed, or at least for silence."

She grabs my hand resting on the table. "You're biting your lip. Are you nervous?"

Instead of playing with my necklace when I'm nervous, I've started biting my lip. Not a good option either.

"A little. These past days have been overwhelming. It's been years since I've been introduced to someone's family. I want to make a good impression."

"Don't worry." She squeezes my hand. "Everyone's going to love you. I already do."

I smile uneasily.

I'm afraid I'll love them too.

Chapter 37

Gerry

My body needs a massage to relieve the tension in my shoulders. As expected, the meeting didn't go as well as I'd hoped. There's still a chance it could work out, but I'm not holding my breath. For some reason, I'm not as disappointed as I thought I'd be. Is it because I'm used to being let down? Or is it because I'm not the same man since last time? If this doesn't work out, it's not meant to be. Strangely, I'm okay with that.

If I do get it, how would the relationship between me and Tina work? Maybe I could live a couple of months here just to film the show and then go back to New York. But she deserves better than that. She seems so supportive about the show, and she's aware I'll need to come back here. Why, if it means we'll be apart?

Tina's a part of me now. To me, we're a package deal. I have no idea if she feels the same. Well, that's not true. In my heart, I know she does.

As I approach the market, I see Tina and Mom. No need to call them. They're standing in front of a tourist shop with tons of cuckoo clocks. Hands full with bags. I guess they either had fun shopping, or I took too long. Tina looks into the display window and points at something. I sneak up behind her and wrap my arms around her waist. She jumps and squeals at the same time.

She wraps her arms around me. "Hey there, handsome. How did it go?" She sweetly pecks my lips.

I look at both of them. "I have no idea. One second I think it went well, and then I doubt myself. The producer and I couldn't agree on a couple of things, which could kill the deal. Let's see what happens. Time to stop thinking about it. We're still on vacation."

Tina squeezes me tight. "I'm so proud of you."

"Thanks." I take her bags from her. "Did you find a clock for Lisa?"

"Yes, and I bought something for Dad and Beth. I'll show them to you when we get back to the house."

"Did you see the flower section of the market?"

"Yeah. You can get every kind of flower there. Types I've never seen before. Especially purple ones. The entire city of Freiburg is spectacular. I avoided walking near the little canals. No need for soaked sneakers again. Claire and I are stuffed from all the ice cream we ate."

"Mom, you finally met someone who likes ice cream just as much as you do."

Mom glances at Tina with a smile. "It's about time. It's like pulling teeth to get Gerry or his dad to go for ice cream with me."

I drape my arm over Tina's shoulder. "Let's walk around the market and buy some food for tonight. Dad's in charge of buying the meat. I need to get back soon so I can prepare some marinades that need to sit for a while."

Mom steps to the side, away from the crowd. We follow her. "Gerry, let's take her to Kastaniengarten first. She needs to see the view overlooking Freiburg and we can have one quick beer." She nudges my elbow. "Then we can go shopping at the market."

I can't say no when two beautiful women stand there with big smiles on their faces. "All right. One beer. I think I deserve one after this meeting."

I pull on Tina's waist and tuck her under my arm.

She turns to Mom and says, "Did Gerry tell you about my allergy to currants?"

"Hey!" I tickle her side and whisper into her ear, "Just for that, you're getting punished later."

She yanks on a belt loop on my pants. "Is that a promise?"

"Is what a promise?" Mom interrupts as she looks over her shoulder.

"Nothing important." I squeeze Tina's ass when Mom's not looking. "Always causing trouble," I whisper again and nip her earlobe.

Chapter 38

Gerry

I grab my black leather jacket off a hanger. "I have a couple of surprises for you today, since we fly home tomorrow. We wouldn't have been able to do them if the weather wasn't nice this afternoon."

She looks up at me like I'm a giant next to her. "You spoil me. Give me a hint."

"*Luft.*"

"Gerry." She swats my arm playfully. "English, please. It's exhausting after hearing different languages nonstop this week."

"Sorry. I know it's not easy to be around people who you don't understand. But when we get to our secret destination, I'll tell you what I said." I peck her on the lips.

"Let's go to the garage," I say as I take a set of keys off the table next to the front door. "I need to get something for today. I bought it when I received my Michelin star. When I moved to the US, I had it stored here. I didn't want to sell it, even though I never had time to use it."

When the garage door rises, she peeks in, and her face lights up. "No way."

"Way." I glide my arm toward it. "Say hello to our transportation for the day."

She points at it. "We're driving a motorcycle...riding that today?" She bounces from foot to foot. "You never mentioned you had a motorcycle."

She drags her fingers along the soft black leather seat. "It's so clean and sparkly."

"My dad cleaned and polished it for us while we were out yesterday." I push the motorcycle out of the garage.

"I know you told me you wished you could ride one. We got interrupted or something, so I didn't have the chance to tell you I had one." I go back in the garage and fetch two helmets off a shelf. "Sorry. I don't have a purple helmet."

"Ha-ha. Black is fine."

I place it on her head and secure it. "Damn, you look hot as a biker chick."

She crinkles her nose and looks down at her jacket. "With a denim jacket instead of a leather one, I don't think so."

I put my jacket on and secure my helmet.

"Now look who's the hot one in all black." She fans herself.

Once we're ready, I show her how to get on the motorcycle and explain how to ride as a passenger.

I wrap her arms around my waist. "Do you understand how to sit and what to do when we go around curves?"

She nods her head. "I'm focusing more on my arms being wrapped around your tight waist."

"No holding on to anything lower than this, or we'll end up in the hospital. Anything below can wait for tonight. So behave."

Mom comes out of the house just as I'm ready to start it. "Let me take a picture of you two. Give me your *handy*."

Tina giggles.

Time ticks by. "That's enough, Mom. Twenty should do the trick."

She hands me my phone. "I need to take so many because you can never take a serious picture." She nods toward Tina. "He's always been the clown of the family."

"You should see how many selfies we took during the last month. Most of them were deleted because Mr. Cool Rider over here couldn't act normal," Tina adds.

"Now get out of here. Have fun. I know I would if I were going.

Be careful." She waves and walks back into the house.

"She knows where we're going?" Tina says.

"Yes. She helped me plan it."

"I'm so excited. Let's go," she says as she squeezes me tightly.

We take the scenic route, called the Wine Street in English, which connects the vineyards and the Black Forest. Several tractors pulling massive barrels of freshly picked grapes slow down traffic. It's hard to pass them on this curvy road. I don't mind taking it slow though. Having Tina's arms wrapped around me is more than I could've asked for. Right now, I don't care about anything other than us. I dread flying back tomorrow because I know reality will kick in. Will we be able to handle it?

She tugs the side of my jacket and then points in the distance. There's a rainbow-colored hot-air balloon rising over the trees. I pull over and turn off the engine. We remove our helmets after we get off the bike.

Her long locks pool wildly over her shoulders. "I'm sweaty from the helmet. I can't imagine what my hair looks like."

She points again with enthusiasm. "Look. Look. There's two more rising from the trees. They're so close. Let me take some pictures."

"You're obsessed. You must've taken at least two hundred pictures this week."

"Probably more than that. I need to take advantage, since I won't be back here anytime soon."

I get back on the motorcycle. "Want to go check them out? I think we'll pass where they're taking off from."

Her helmet's on with lightning speed. She swings her leg over the back like a pro. "Let's go. Fast." She squeezes my stomach so hard, it's like she's giving me the Heimlich maneuver.

I grin ear to ear. If she's already freaking out, I can't wait to see her face when she sees what I have planned.

Chapter 39

Every day this week, I've thought this trip couldn't get any better. But we always end up doing something else that blows my mind. I've never seen a hot-air balloon so close before. We gradually drive into a valley clear of trees.

Several hot-air balloons are still on the ground in the distance to the right. He turns off the road in that direction. As we move closer, I think he's just going to drive right by. But then he turns and drives to the balloons. He stops and motions for me to get off.

"Do you want to go closer and watch?"

I smile in delight. "Really? Of course I want to."

He takes my hand and walks us closer to the balloons, and then a little closer. I watch people attaching the balloons to the baskets. We stop to watch one take off not too far from where we're standing.

A man walks up to Gerry and they shake hands. "Hey, Henrik," Gerry says in English. "I'm glad the weather worked out for us today. This is Tina."

He shakes my hand. "So you're the lucky passenger today?"

I think I'm going to pass out.

My head swivels to Gerry and then back to Henrik. "Did he...did you just say what I think you said? Are we riding in one?"

Before either can even answer, I jump on Gerry and kiss his cheek. I almost knock him over. "This is awesome. I can't believe you did this." I let go but wish I could hang on to him forever.

I squeeze Gerry's hand. "You're coming with me, right? There's no way in hell I can go up there alone."

"You aren't going without me. Believe it or not—I've never done this before either. I planned to a couple of times, but the weather always ended up bad. We're lucky."

"The balloon is ready to go. Follow me," Henrik says.

I wrap my arm around Gerry's waist while following Henrik. "I can't believe you did this. Do we really have to go home tomorrow?" I pout.

"I don't want to think about it, but we both have jobs to get back to. Let's not worry about tomorrow and just enjoy today."

I'm afraid to think about how our relationship could change with one sentence from Gerry. That he got the show.

The balloons are enormous when you're right next to them. Henrik opens the basket door. Gerry lets me in first. It's like I'm Dorothy in the Wizard of Oz.

Other balloons have more people in the baskets.

I search around to see if other people are walking toward our balloon. "How many more people are we waiting for?"

"None," Gerry responds with a smirk.

My heart and brain can only take some much in one day. "We have this balloon ride to ourselves?"

Henrik and Gerry laugh at the same time.

"I'm sorry." I cackle then take a deep breath. "This is an exciting moment for me. I can't help it." My heart beats in my ears. "I'm like a kid in a candy store."

Gerry wraps me in his arms and whispers, "I want to make you smile like this every day. It's worth all the money in the world."

He's too good to be true. I'm happier than I've ever been.

I get the fright of my life when a loud swoosh of fire is ignited by a massive blow torch.

"Ready to go?"

Gerry gives Henrik a thumbs-up.

Henrik explains how the balloon is controlled by the hot air created by the flames. The balloon has to stay hot to stay afloat.

We ascend higher and higher. I have a death grip on Gerry and refuse to look down. "How safe is this? What if something goes wrong? Are there parachutes?" An excessive amount of adrenaline pumps through me.

He points to the torch. "There's double of everything. If something breaks, there's a backup."

That helps me relax a tiny bit. Well, not really.

"Why is there no wind?" Gerry asks Henrik.

"The balloon travels as fast as the wind. That's why we don't feel it."

I move to the other side with tiny steps, afraid I'll shake the basket. I'm in awe of the view. The French Vosges mountains are so clear, I feel like I could reach out and touch them. It looks like the sun has dusted the trees with vibrant gold and orange sparkles. Rolling hills of vineyards hide between patches of forest.

Every few minutes, Henrik blasts the torch to keep hot air in the balloon or to make us climb higher. My stomach churns from fear and excitement.

"Don't worry. We're at our peak. Just look around and enjoy the ride."

Gerry wraps his arms around me from behind. "Having fun?" He nuzzles into my neck.

I turn around in his arms and place my hands on his chest.

"I'm so glad this worked out for us today. Do I get brownie points again?"

"You have no idea what this day means to me. Or this whole week. I can't thank you enough. For the first time in years, I feel alive and completely at peace with myself. There's so much I want to say, but only certain words come to mind. I've never said them before."

Just say it.

We stand in silence with only the whistle of air passing by us. Our eyes on each other, not the scenery. Forgetting Henrik is on the other side of the basket.

"I—" My voice cracks, and my eyes tear.

"Say it, Tina," Gerry pleads softly while his thumb strokes my cheek. "Please let me hear you say it."

I close my eyes to gather the courage I need. They flutter open and stare into his golden eyes of fire. "I love you. More than I ever thought I could love a person. I never dreamed my life would change so beautifully the minute I met you. It's not because of all the surprises these past weeks. It's because of you as a person. In a short amount of time, you have become a permanent part of my life. Part of my heart. You're gentle, kind, selfless, passionate, beyond sexy. You make me laugh more than anyone else. No one has ever cared for me the way you do. I've never been in love before, but I'm so glad when the time was finally right, I fell in love with you."

He tickles me with his soft lips against mine. "There's nothing better than to hear those words come out of this sexy mouth of yours. Every time I've seen you, those three words wanted to flow out of my mouth, but I held back. I was afraid to scare you. But now I can." He pulls me in his arms and whispers, "*Ich liebe dich auch*. I promise I'll love you forever. Not one day will ever pass when you'll have to question my love for you."

We watch the view with me tucked under his arm. Henrik points out landmarks, but I don't care. I'm in love with Gerry and he with me, and I finally believe I deserve it. I'm not only flying high. I'm flying high in heaven with the man of my dreams.

Chapter 40

Tina

My magic mirror didn't make me feel like the prettiest girl in the world when I left for the office this morning. My lower face is inflamed from Gerry's scruff. We had a last minute make-out session after we arrived back at my apartment from the airport. The time adjustment coming back from Europe is easier than going.

I turn my face right to left as I stare at myself in the ladies' room mirror. At least I have no marks on my neck. Peggy laughed when she saw me, knowing exactly why I look like this. I want to hide somewhere. I walk back to my cube with my hand casually over my mouth.

My coworkers pounced on me as soon as I arrived, asking me how my trip was. But most importantly telling me more rumors are going around about opening a California office. They say Thomas has been bustling around the past days. Strangely, Thomas sent me a calendar request for a lunch meeting today.

"Ready?" Thomas says.

Speak of the devil.

"Yep. Just waiting for you. Do you even have time? You've been so busy this morning."

"Everything's good. Let's go. I only have forty-five minutes because I have a meeting scheduled."

A few minutes later we sit in a café I've never been to before. I order a turkey sandwich the size of a football. Leftovers for tonight.

"What happened to your face? Sunburn gone wrong?" He chuckles.

Now my face stings even more from blushing.

"I tried a new facial lotion. I guess I'm allergic to that too. Not my best couple of months when it comes to trying new things."

"How was your trip?

I beam.

"By the look on your face, I guess it was great." He smirks with mustard on his mouth.

The next few minutes go by with him asking me questions about my trip and how I liked it there.

"I told you how beautiful Germany is," he says with mustard now in his beard.

He's a great manager but such a disgusting eater.

He relaxes back in his chair, his arms resting on his belly. "Let's talk about something else. There seem to be rumors going around that an office is being opened in California and some employees from this office will be given the chance to transfer there."

"I've been told something of the sort, but my source said it was heard by the water cooler. You know what that means. It's like playing the game Telephone."

His eyes dart around the café as if we're being spied on. "Keep this confidential."

Holy shit. Is he going to ask me? I swallow hard and nod. My palms are sweating. They never sweat. At least I don't think they do. That would be gross.

"The rumor is true. Management has asked me to name five people who are the most innovative and, most of all, willing to relocate."

My neck is so extended I feel like E.T. I need to hold on to the edge of the table.

"I'd like to nominate you as one of the five. Would you be interested in relocating?"

I can't believe it! I think I'm going to wet myself.

"You may be new compared to the others, but I've seen some incredible ideas come from you, and you've dealt well with complicated challenges and requests." He looks at the clock on his phone. "Is this something you'd seriously consider?"

This is a no-brainer. "Absolutely," I blurt out. "I've always wanted to live in California."

Gerry.

"I'm glad to hear that. You were the first person I wrote on the list."

I press my hands on my twitching legs to stop them. I'm going to twitch out of this café if they don't.

"You're the last one to be asked. A series of interviews have taken place with the other candidates. A couple of people from upper management would like to talk to you tomorrow morning. Human resources will tell you more about what it will entail. The negative of this entire situation is upper management wants the new office up and running relatively fast."

Gerry.

"Again, this is strictly confidential. No talking about it by the water cooler," he adds. "Congratulations on being one of the nominees." He extends his hand to shake mine.

"Thanks, Thomas. I'm honored you have so much confidence in me. I won't let you down."

"My pleasure. Again, don't tell anyone." He looks at his phone again. "I have to get to my meeting."

He walks away, but I remain seated, not ready to go. I'm overjoyed about this, but so much has happened in such a short amount of time. My appetite is gone. I push my sandwich away from me. I just said I'm willing to relocate. What about me and Gerry? We just got together. Do I need to tell him? I probably should, but only if upper management picks me.

I slouch in my chair while thoughts whirl in my head. What if I'm offered the job and he the show? How would that work? Why stir things up if it most likely won't happen? But what if it does? What about my family? I'm sure they won't be happy. The whirl quickly becomes a tornado.

How will I keep a secret of this magnitude when I'm so excited? Just when I thought my life was where I want it to be, this makes me question *everything*.

Chapter 41

Gerry

We've been back for over a week, and I haven't seen Tina since I dropped her off at her apartment when we came back. I've been working nonstop, and Tina's swamped at work, to the point there are days when we don't even talk. When we do, she sounds distant sometimes. Vacation was very different from our real lives. We were stuck to each other's hips the entire time, and now we hardly see each other.

Barbara hasn't heard anything from VOX. We were told we'd hear something last week. As the days go by, I care less and less. I question if I really want the show anymore. After the week with Tina in Germany, my wants and needs have shifted to her. Her happiness is more important to me.

My phone rings. I see Joel's name on the screen. I groan. All I wanted was to have a couple of hours to myself this Saturday morning before the restaurant opens.

"What's up, Joel? The restaurant better be on fire. I told you I was coming in late this morning."

"Sorry to bother you, but Mike fell last night and broke his arm. He can't work for the next six weeks. Who's going to manage the kitchen during that time?"

I bow my head and close my eyes. "What about Carl or Jackson?"

"Seriously Gerry? They don't know how to run the kitchen," he says with annoyance.

I press the bridge of my nose. "I'll do it."

"You'll find somebody? On such short notice?"

"No. I mean I'll manage the kitchen."

"Wait. What? Really? His voice perks up. "You're willing to cook here? That'd be awesome for the restaurant. You know it's busier now since the word's out you're a famous chef."

"Yes, I'm serious. It's my restaurant and my kitchen. Let's discuss it when I get there. I'll try to be there within the hour. Bye."

I lean on the kitchen counter and think about what I just agreed to do. I'm now the head chef of Hofbräuhaus. Something clicked during the week in Germany. No one brought up what happened to me last year. Everyone was truly happy to see me and treated me just like they had before the incident. I enjoyed cooking for my family and felt more relaxed than I have in a long time. A lot of it had to do with Tina being by my side.

I push off the counter when the doorbell rings.

I open the door and Tina stands there beaming. I don't give her time to say anything because I pull her immediately into my arms. We kiss with a force and speed I've never experienced with her before. Our hands are all over each other. She sucks on my lower lip to the point it's deliciously painful. I gently pull her hair to expose her neck. I lick and bite the skin then nibble on her ear.

I kick the door shut without letting her go.

As our lips meet again, she fumbles with my belt buckle. I bend over and pick her up. In seconds I stand her on the side of the bed. Our jeans drop to the floor, then our shirts fly in the air. We lay on the bed, grinding and moaning in sync. I'm in a fog, forgetting everything. We don't speak, but I know her body's ready for me.

She nips my neck, and with every thrust, I moan "I love you" until we both cry out as she shatters around me and I quickly follow.

We're slick with sweat and out of breath. When we're able to breathe again, we turn to each other and say hi at the same time with grins on our faces.

"How are you?" I say.

"Even better now. That's the best greeting I've ever gotten." She giggles.

"It was such a surprise to see you on the doorstep, I couldn't help myself. This week without you felt like a year."

She skims my face and sighs. "I know."

I kiss her forehead. "Give me a second to clean up. Don't go anywhere, *Süße*." I head for the bathroom and come back a few minutes later to find her getting dressed.

"Going so soon?" I joke.

"I don't want to, but someone needs to go to work in a little while." She tosses my black jeans to me.

As I pull them on, I ask, "So what made you come here this morning? You should've called. I might not have been here."

"Then I would've hunted you down at the restaurant."

"Hunted me down for what? You didn't just come here to use my body?"

"You'd love that, wouldn't you?" she laughs as she throws a pillow at me.

"You told me when you were going to work today. I've missed you so much. I can't stand that we haven't seen each other. And I have something important to talk to you about."

"It must be great whatever it is, because you're glowing from head to toe. Or is it from our little work-out session a few minutes ago?" I toss the pillow back on the bed.

"Definitely both."

When we're fully dressed, she pulls me into the living room. She sits on one of the armrests of the couch. "Come sit next to me."

The air shifts as if blowing out a candle.

"Other than Alexa, you're the first one I'm telling this, for obvious reasons. Actually you should've been the first," she says with a pained face.

I get goose bumps.

"Why are you fiddling with your necklace and biting your lip? What's going on?"

"I'll start from the beginning. Weeks before the wedding, there were rumors going around Modern Web might open a new office. I didn't pay much attention to it. However, the day we got back from vacation, Thomas took me to lunch. He clarified it wasn't a rumor." Her mouth turns into a smile. "In a few weeks, Modern Web is opening a new site in Long Beach, California."

She moves onto the couch closer to me with an even bigger smile. "And guess what? I was asked to go." She squeals and then hugs me. "Can you believe it? My head has been spinning. I can't believe this is happening."

I pull away from her. "You've known this since we've been back and haven't told me?" I say with a mixture of shock and anger.

She puts her hand on my knee. "Yes. I was out of my mind excited, but I needed to speak to human resources and some upper management first. I didn't want to say anything to you because there was a chance it'd fall through."

I see red because I'm so pissed off.

She stops talking. "Gerry, are you okay? Your face is like marble."

I stand up. "I've been up front about the cooking show from the beginning. I don't understand why you wouldn't tell me."

"Please don't be mad. You know I've always dreamed of living in California. This is my big chance." She stands up with her arms open to the sides. "So much has happened during the last couple months. I can't keep up." She wiggles her hands. "I'm just so overwhelmed with every kind of emotion. I don't know what to do with myself."

Was our trip a dream? "You already told them yes, didn't you?" I want to be happy for her, but I'd rather punch the fucking brick wall behind me.

She sighs. "I haven't said anything yet. I wanted to talk to you and my family first."

"Talk to us about what? It sounds like you've already made up your mind," I snap.

She folds her arms. "Why can't you be happy for me? I've been supportive about the cooking show. Why is this any different?"

"You want to know why it's different?" My voice is harsh. "After I met you, my world shifted. The second I had the meeting in Freiburg, I was questioning if I really wanted it anymore. As days have gone by without a word from my agent, it's been a relief. You have become my priority, not the show. Did our trip mean nothing to you?"

My phone rings on the kitchen counter. I walk over to put distance between us. It's Joel again. It can wait. I swipe *decline*.

I turn back to her. "If you accept the offer, when will you leave? In a couple of months?"

She hesitates. "In two weeks."

It feels like she just slapped me in the face. I shake my head. "Two weeks?" I burst out. "Are you kidding me? Why so quickly?"

I deserve this. I walked away from her years ago to follow my dream. Now it's her turn to walk away from me.

She comes closer and goes to touch my arm but pulls back. "They have a huge load of work and need help right away. If I accept, they'll give me an exact date. I'd live in temporary housing until I find my own apartment."

I turn away and place both hands on the counter.

She wraps her arms around my waist from behind and rests her cheek on my back. "What do you want me to do? Tell me what you want," she whispers. Vibrations from her voice, sting my back.

I have no desire to be touched right now, so I remove her arms from my waist.

"You know what I want, but it doesn't matter. This isn't about me. You've got an opportunity of a lifetime. It's what you've always wanted. I'm not going to take that away from you. You and only you can make the decision. Don't worry about what others think you should do."

Chapter 42

I look him straight in the eyes. "You want me to go?" I ask with disappointment.

His eyes turn cold. "Don't twist my words. That isn't what I said."

"Then explain to me what you said. Because that sure as hell sounded like it." I seethe.

"Fine. I want to be selfish and tell you to stay here with me. Here in New York City. Where I can taste your skin and smell your lavender hair every day. Where I can add more of your quirky words to my Tina dictionary. Where I can see your stack of travel and tech magazines on the table. Where we can take a million ridiculous selfies of our adventures. Where I can massage your feet when you've had a long day. Where I can cook for you every day until you get sick of my food. Where I can watch you play with your necklace endlessly. Where I can give you everything in purple. Most of all, where I can love you without restraint."

Tears pool in my eyes. "What would you say if I told you to stay if you got the show? The one thing you've always dreamed about. Would you say no and stay?"

His eyes pierce mine, and his answer comes immediately. "I'd give up everything for you. Especially after I told you I love you."

A tear breaks through and slowly flows down my cheek.

"But you know what the difference is?" he says. "I didn't hesitate with my answer. You've already had a chance to say no to your boss for days, but you haven't. That means you want to go."

I want to say something, but nothing comes out, because he's right.

"But it's not about me. This is all about you. I can't and won't tell you what to do. Especially after we've been dating for only a month. Even though you told me you love me. But forget about that little detail."

His phone rings again.

"Please don't answer it," I plead.

He answers it anyway.

"What the hell, Joel?" He looks at his watch. "I'll be there in ten minutes!" He tosses his phone on the counter.

I take my bag off the floor and twist the door knob. "You need to go to work."

He presses his big hand against the door to prevent me from opening it. "You knew from the beginning I have a hectic schedule, and now even more since I just agreed, right before you got here, to run the kitchen."

My eyes shoot open. "You did? I can't believe it. That's great."

I go to hug him, but he flicks his hand. "I don't want to talk about, and I really don't care," he retorts.

I deflate with sadness. "It's amazing. Last week was a fantasy, and now we're back to reality." I press my lips together tightly. "I don't like how this feels between us right now." I shake my head. "I'm so confused. I don't know what I want."

He opens the door for me. "Yes, you do," he says flatly.

I bow my head and walk out the door. I turn to him to say something, but he stays in the doorway with his arms crossed and his legs planted wide. There's a scowl on his face I've never seen before.

"I'll give you time to figure things out. I'll be working even more hours since I'll be in the kitchen."

"Then why does it even matter if I'm gone? You'll be married to your job anyway. I'd only be in *your* way," I respond with a nasty tone I never knew I had.

He turns around and slams the door.

My heart splits into two. I turn at the corner of the building and burst into tears. What did I just do?

After a few minutes, an elderly woman comes up to me. "Honey, are you okay? Do you need help?"

I wipe tears from under my eyes. "No, thanks. Just a bad morning. I'll be fine."

"Everyone needs a good cry sometimes. You'll get through it." She rubs my arm and continues on.

I stand tall. She's right. With or without Gerry, I need to do what's best for me. It's all about me now. Screw everyone else. California. The place I've always wanted to go to. Is it still what I want?

I dial Lisa's number, and she answers on the second ring. "Lisa, it's me. I need to talk to you. Will you be home today? Can James pick me up at the train station?"

She asks me what's wrong and everything else under the sun. "I'm okay. There's some things going on I need to talk to you all about. Can you call Dad and see if he and Beth can be there too?"

She asks me the most ridiculous question.

"No, I'm not pregnant. I'll call you when I know which train I'm taking."

I repeat *it's all about me* a million times as I head to the train station.

Lisa's head distends off her neck as she leans over the kitchen counter and places the baby monitor in the middle of us. "You're not really considering moving there? You'll be on the other side of the US. Alone."

James pulls her to his side.

"Sorry. This is the last thing I thought you'd tell us. We thought you were running off with Gerry to Las Vegas to get married." Lisa plops down on one of the kitchen stools. "What about Gerry? Did you tell him?"

I look to the ceiling, blinking to hold back the tears. They come anyway. "I really hurt him today. He was pretty angry when I told him about the offer."

Beth hands me a tissue.

"What did he say?" James asks.

"He's says I know I want to move to California. Hesitating to say no to my boss means I want to take the offer."

"Did you ask if he would go with you if you said yes?" Lisa says.

I crinkle my eyebrows. "No way. But he didn't offer either."

"Well, you've only been together for a short while. I guess it's understandable," she points out.

I raise one eyebrow. "And you thought we were getting married or I was pregnant? Which is more bizarre?"

Lisa presses her lips together, and Beth chuckles.

"Do you love Gerry?" Dad asks.

"More than anything."

"Do you think you can live without him?"

"I don't want to think about it, period. Why do I have to give up one for the other? Everything is so fucked up." I look at Dad and Beth and cover my mouth. "Sorry." I still feel like I shouldn't swear in front of them.

"Germany was a dream, but now reality has kicked in. We said we loved each other. But did he say it because we were in dreamland? I said it because I truly love him."

Beth puts her arm around my shoulder and squeezes me. It feels nice.

"He runs a restaurant, so you can't expect him to drop everything and move across the country with you in two weeks," James adds, and Dad nods in agreement.

Men!

"Did he ever hear from his agent about the show? What would he do if he got it? He was open with you from the beginning. Didn't you ever discuss what would happen if he got it?" Lisa asks.

I wipe the tears and makeup from under my eyes. "He told me

today he hasn't heard anything. I've wondered what would happen, but he sounded so convinced he wouldn't get it most of the time. Every once in a while, it would creep into my head, but I just ignored it."

Everyone leans in a little closer.

"He supposedly has questioned everything lately because of us. He surprised me by saying he'd give up everything for me."

"But are you willing to do the same?" Dad asks.

I don't respond.

Lisa smacks her cheeks like Kevin in the movie *Home Alone.* "If you say yes, you'd move in two weeks." Her eyes droop with sadness.

"I've always wanted to live in California. It's crazy to think about it because I've never even been there. And it might be a horrible experience—but at least I have to try. If I say no, I'll always wonder."

"Then there's your answer. If you stayed for Gerry, it'd always be at the back of your mind. There's no time for what ifs or regrets," Beth says.

"Again, Tina, this is your time. You need to do what's best for you and nobody else. Experience it and figure out who you really are." Lisa squeezes my hand, then puts the tissue box in front of me next to the flashing baby monitor making noises.

"Thank you, Dr. Lisa Kramer."

"Give yourself and Gerry a couple of days to cool off. I think the silence will do you some good."

"Aunt Bina," Felicia squeals as she runs into the kitchen.

I sweep her up in my arms and kiss her chipmunk cheeks.

"Did you just get up from a nap, you little stinker?"

She nods.

"When do you need to give your boss an answer?" Dad asks.

"Tuesday," I say as I put Felicia down. She runs off to the dogs sitting by the sliding glass door.

We stand there in silence except for Felicia, who's talking gibberish to the dogs like they're her best friends.

"If you had to give an answer right now, what would it be?" Lisa asks with her big blue eyes watering already.

I hand a tissue to her because I know she'll need it just as much as I will.

Chapter 43

Gerry

It's Monday afternoon, and I don't have the energy to do anything else right now, but I have to go back into the kitchen in fifteen minutes. Lack of sleep since Tina left my apartment on Saturday has left me numb and on autopilot. Joel and some of the other staff keep asking me what's wrong. I never tell them. I haven't heard from Tina, and I don't have the will to call her. The space has given me the time to think.

No matter how much I hate to admit it, she needs to go. She has finally broken away from her family obligations. It's time for her to think about herself. She has the chance to fulfill her dreams. An opportunity like this doesn't come around often. I can't take that from her. She has to say yes, even though it will break us apart. If she stayed because of me, I'd feel guilty for the rest of my life. And she'd be filled with regret. Again.

My eyes are heavy. I set the timer on my phone to go off in ten minutes. I relax in my chair and close my eyes, but I'm interrupted by the ring of my phone. I ignore it, but what if it's Tina? I give in after the third ring. It's Matt. I haven't spoken to him since the wedding.

"Hey, Matt. When did you get back? How was your honeymoon?"

The next minutes fly by as he tells me everything. He has no idea Tina went to Germany with me. At least I don't think so.

"Isn't the bakery open today?"

"We decided to close the bakery on Mondays. We need a break

during the week. It's the slowest day anyway."

"I need to talk to you as soon as possible. It's really important." I tell him about the cook and how I'm running the kitchen now. "I don't have much time, but if you come around eight tonight, I'll make sure I'm covered. Bring Kayla if you can. I need a woman's opinion."

He agrees, and we say goodbye. It's going to be another long day.

"Enough about us. Are you going to tell us why you haven't shaved and why you look like you haven't slept in days?"

I touch my head and feel around. My hair is too long, but I hadn't noticed.

"I thought you'd be in a good mood—Mom told me Tina went with you to Germany." Kayla taps the tabletop. "Too much sex making you tired?" She chuckles.

I huff. "Yeah, she did go to Germany with me," I respond with a sullen voice.

"Why do you sound so sad? What's the matter?"

I tell them about Germany and the meeting with VOX.

Kayla clasps her hands together with enthusiasm. "That's great. I'm so excited for you two. Watching you in front of the restaurant and at our reception proved how much you love her."

I finish the rest of my water. "It's not that easy. Things changed almost immediately after we came back home," I say as a lone chestnut falls from the tree and lands on the table.

Kayla reaches over to pick it up.

"What could've possibly happened in such a short amount of time?" Matt questions.

"She surprised me with the news she's been asked to relocate to Long Beach, California. She's known since we got back from Germany but just told me a couple of days ago. And get this—she'd have to go in less than two weeks."

Kayla's face drops.

"Did she say yes?" Matt asks.

I shrug. "I don't know. We've haven't spoken since she told me." I pause and take a deep breath. "She knows what she wants to do, and it isn't to stay here with me."

"What about the cooking show?" Kayla questions. "Doesn't that complicate things too? You'd have to leave too."

I laugh nervously. "Want to know how much I love her? If I was offered the show, I'd give it up in a second if she wanted me to stay. I'd give up everything for her."

Kayla gives me sympathetic face.

"Oh, and don't worry about my show. I never heard back, and it's been nearly two weeks. They said I'd hear something right away. My agent has tried to contact them, but there's been no response."

I explain how Tina always wanted to live in California and what she's dealt with in her past. "I've come to the conclusion she needs to do this for herself and by herself. She always takes care of everyone around her. This is her time to be selfish and to think only about herself."

"What about a long-distance relationship? A lot of people do it," Matt suggests.

I shake my head. "I thought about it. I love her more than anything, but I have to let her go without her worrying about me over here. No matter what she says to me, I can't let her stay. I don't know why I feel so strongly about this. I'm following my gut."

Kayla rests her chin on Matt's shoulder. "I'm sorry, Gerry. This totally sucks. I wish there was something we could do for you."

"Wait a second." Matt sits up straight. "If Barbara calls you today and says you got the show, what would you do?"

"Of course I would take it if…"

Kayla's eyes spring open. "Gerry…" she says while shaking her head, motioning for me to shut up. Matt's head shoots to the left and he does a double take.

I turn my head in the direction they're looking and jump up instantly. "Tina. What're you doing here?" My stomach churns, and I turn red.

"Is this why you want me to move to California? Just in case you get your stupid show?"

Chapter 44

Tina

He looks around him to see if anyone is watching us. "Tina, can we go to my office and talk? I don't want to make a scene."

This reminds me of the night I found out who he was.

I agree out of respect for myself, not for him. He tries to touch my lower back, but I shimmy out of reach.

He closes the office door behind us. He walks behind his desk, separating us.

I don't give him time to speak. "You want me to leave so you can go to Germany for that show. Then you won't feel guilty when you leave me behind."

He throws his hands up. "Tina, please calm down. You didn't hear the full story. If you would listen and not jump to conclusions, I'd tell you I still haven't gotten a call about the show, just like I told you a couple of days ago. Matt asked me what I'd do if you left and I was told I got the show. If you leave, I have nothing to keep me here. I have my restaurant, yes, but my life won't be the same here if you aren't in it anymore."

He looks like a lost puppy dog. My hard shell softens, and I walk over to him.

"I love you." I wrap my arms around his neck.

He squeezes me tight and buries his head in my neck.

Something comes over me, and I blurt out, "Come with me. We can make a life there together."

He stiffens and takes a step back. His jaw clenches.

"*Nein.*"

He takes my hand in his and crushes it against his heart. "This is something I believe in my heart you have to do alone. You always worry about everyone else but yourself. Just like your dad and Lisa said weeks ago, it's your time now. I'd only be in the way."

I squeeze his hands. "Then I'll say no and stay here with you."

"*Nein.* Absolutely not."

I flinch in response to his directness.

"Why?" I say with tears in my eyes. "You said you love me. How could you let me go so easily?"

He lays his hands on my shoulders. "Because you know you want to go alone, but you won't admit it. I do love you. I love you more than anything. But I've been lucky to do the things I've dreamed about. This is your chance. It came later than you thought, but it's a sign. You need to go. You have to leave me."

I take a step back. "So this is it then? I leave, and we're through?"

He looks at the floor and doesn't respond. Silence means everything.

I shake my head. "Who are you? The person standing in front of me now is not the man I fell in love with. You made me believe in us and that we were the real thing. I trusted you with my life. I don't care we've only been together for a little while."

He moves forward but stops. "No matter what I say, you *don't* want to hear me. I'm pushing you away *because* I love you."

"You are so full of shit. This isn't how love works. People who are in love try to work it out. And you're obviously not one of them."

I know he loves me, but I want him to push me away so I don't feel bad for leaving. Why am I doing this?

I spin around to leave.

"Tina. Don't leave like this."

I look back at him and notice tears in his eyes.

"You know what's *real* now, Gerry? I'm leaving, and you'll never see or hear from me again." *You don't mean it.*

I walk out and don't look back. Matt and Kayla stand several feet away from Gerry's door.

I keep my head down and walk right past them.

"Tina," Kayla calls out behind me.

I ignore her.

A loud crash comes from his office. My instinct is to stop, but I force myself out the door, knowing I've seen him for the last time. Once I cross the street, my heart shatters into a million pieces, and the dams in my eyes break free once again.

So this is what a broken heart feels like.

Chapter 45

Gerry

My phone lies in several pieces on the floor in front of the door. I spill the pens out of the glass beer mug on my desk. I'm about to whip it at a wall, when Matt and Kayla burst in. The broken pieces of the phone scrape across the floor.

"Gerry! Stop! Are you crazy?" He grabs hold of my arm right before I let go of the mug.

"Oh, Gerry." Kayla closes the door. "You're crying."

I touch my eyes, and I feel tears on my fingers.

I point to the door with aggression while breathing heavier than a horse in a race. "I just let the love of my life walk out that fucking door, and I didn't try to stop her. Instead I pushed her away. My heart aches in a way I never thought possible. She left thinking I don't love her." I punch the palm of my hand with my fist. "I tried to explain I had to do it for her. Now I need to convince myself I did the right thing." I fall onto my desk chair and wipe the tears from my cheeks.

Kayla approaches me with caution.

I lift my hand up to stop her. "You don't want to come near me."

She puts her arms around me anyway.

"I don't agree with what you just did, but you have the biggest heart. It proves you love her because you put her needs before yours. You're willing to hurt so she can follow her dreams. I know this isn't easy for you to see her walk away, because you've got a heart of gold and never hurt anyone."

"The only way she'll leave is if she's angry and thinks we're through."

Someone knocks on the door.

"Yeah?" I snap.

A server pops in. He looks down at my shattered phone on the ground and raises his eyebrows. "Um. Sorry to interrupt. Gerry, they need help in the kitchen. A large group of fifteen just came in."

"I'll be out in a minute."

He closes the office door behind him.

I turn in my chair toward Kayla and Matt. "Sorry you both saw all this go down, but I'm glad you're here."

"We need to leave so you can get back to work." She kisses me on the cheek. "But please rethink what you just did. Ask yourself if you can live without her."

"I know I can't live without her. But I have to."

Her shoulders slump. Matt takes her hand to pull her to the door.

I breathe deeply to force myself to calm down. My eyes focus on the computer screen saver. It's a picture of me and Tina in the hot-air balloon. The best moment of my life.

Chapter 46

My suitcase is the size of an emergency raft. At least I'll have something to cling to if my plane goes down. *Good attitude.*

"If you've forgotten something, call me, and I'll send it. Granted, you can just buy what you need in Long Beach." Lisa babbles out of nervousness.

Lisa, James, Felicia, Alexa, Dad, and Beth came to wish me off. Gerry and I haven't spoken since I left his office. James tried to talk to Matt about it, but he refuses to talk. Gerry probably told him not to.

I thought as each day passed without Gerry, things would get easier. I've been trying to convince myself I made the right decision, but sadly, I think I was wrong. I miss him even more. I still can't believe we're over before we really began. No matter how angry I am at both of us, I can't stop thinking about all we went through in the weeks leading up to Thomas offering me the job. I thought Gerry was the one. But if he is, then why am I leaving? Or why isn't he coming with me? Was I that ignorant to think we were the real thing?

I hand over my check-in luggage to the attendant behind the counter. She hands me my boarding pass and wishes me a good flight.

Tears threaten again because it's now time to walk away from my family. My eyes meet Lisa's, and hers are full too. I pull her in my arms as we blubber together.

"Promise me you'll come visit as soon as you can," I beg.

She pulls away and nods while wiping her tears with a crumpled tissue. "We have Skype and Facetime too."

I step over to James. I kiss him on the cheek and look directly into his eyes. "Take care of your family. My family. I'm counting on you."

"Love you, sis. You've got nothing to worry about."

I nod and snatch Felicia from Lisa's arms.

"Be good for your mommy and daddy, my little pooper."

"Lub you, Aunt Bina."

I laugh and cry at the way she talks. I'll miss her so much.

I put her down, and Alexa pulls me into a bear hug. "I hate that you're leaving, but I'm so damn proud of how courageous you are. Think of this as the best thing you could ever do for yourself." She kisses my cheek and immediately wipes it off with a tissue. "Sorry. Red lipstick."

Dad and Beth are next. I hug them at the same time. We cry together. I'm tired of crying.

"I love you both. Again, please come visit. It's about time you traveled a little more."

I move away, but Dad captures me with his arms again. He whispers, "It's your time, Tina. I'm so proud of you. Start over and do what makes you happy. You've endured so much. I'm confident everything will work out for the best."

I cry into his shoulder. "I hope so. I love you, Dad." I tug Beth toward me. "I love you too, Beth."

I take a step back and roll my shoulders.

"Okay, everyone. I need to leave, or I'll make a fool of us by sobbing too loudly."

All I hear are sniffs and blowing of noses, including mine. I take hold of my hand luggage and blow everyone a kiss.

"Go." Lisa shoves me. I nod with a pensive smile and turn away.

I walk toward security with my head held high and tears streaming down my face. My mind wanders while I trudge along the security line.

"Miss. Step forward please," says one of the stocky security personnel. No sirens go off, so I guess I'm free to go to my gate. I glance one more time to where my family was standing. They're gone. I turn my head to move along, but I do a double take. My heart's in my throat. I could've sworn I saw Gerry's golden eyes staring at me from behind the glass. But there's no one there now. I step to the side and brace myself against a wall. Breathing deeply, I massage my pendant to the point I almost cut the skin on my finger.

How am I going to do this without Gerry? I hate him so much, but I'd drop everything if he showed up here right now and begged me to stay. I search for him again, but there's no sign of his peach fuzz. My heart shatters into a million pieces for the thousandth time. I'm surprised there's anything left to break.

Chapter 47

Gerry

It kills me to watch her walk through security. It's real now. She's leaving. But I see the sadness and unease in her eyes. My heart ached when I watched her say goodbye to her family. She constantly played with her necklace. I miss her quirks already.

Not just her quirks—I will forever miss everything about her.

Matt found out what her flight information was and which airport she was leaving from. I had to see her one more time before she left. Every minute of every day has been spent forcing myself to stop thinking about her, but my heart wins every time.

She's through security now and packs her items in her bag. As she moves away, she glances in my direction. Our eyes connect for a millisecond, but I duck out of sight. I don't want her to see me.

I had to have a last glimpse of her before she creates a new life for herself. The one without me in it. Do I have the strength to do the same?

No.

I'm covered in food and grease and smell like it too, but I plunge backward onto my bed anyway. I'll wash my sheets tomorrow...when I find time. I've been working fifteen-hour days for the last three weeks with a day off here and there. All I do is work. Matt asks me to go out sometimes, but I usually tell him I have to work. I thought it would help me forget her.

I never knew what a broken heart felt like. It's like someone's pressed a block of cement into my chest and walked away. My body feels heavy, like I'm dragging my arms along the ground like an ape. I'm working myself to exhaustion to forget her, but it's not working. I cook *Wiener Schnitzel* for a customer; I think of Tina. I see my stash of licorice; I taste her. I smell lavender somewhere; I smell her. She's all around me, but not physically. When will the craving for her end?

Barbara's called me twice today, but I ignored her calls. She keeps checking up on me, and it's grating on my nerves. She left some messages, so I guess I should see what she wants now. I pull my phone out of my pocket and listen to voicemail with my eyes closed. I hear Barbara's high-pitched voice telling me to call her back as soon as possible, regardless of the time. I only hear that voice when she's excited about something.

I look at the time. One in the morning, which is seven in Germany. She's always up at the crack of dawn. I dial her number.

"Gerry!" she squeals in delight.

I pull the phone away from my ear.

"It's about time you called me back."

"Sorry. I'm busy running my restaurant, if you don't remember."

"The executive from VOX called me! He apologized for the long delay. VOX has agreed to everything you want!"

Fuck the show. I don't even want it anymore.

"He wants to call you this week, sooner than later, to discuss the contract and timelines, and so on. He should've sent you and your lawyer an email with the contract to review. Did you check your email today?"

"No. I haven't had the time."

"Isn't this great? It's time for a big comeback. Just when we finally gave up and assumed VOX backed out, I get a phone call. This is what you need to get out of the funk you're in."

I roll off the bed and walk over to my desk like a zombie.

"Gerry? Are you there?"

"Yes. I'm opening my email. This is a lot to take in right now, so be patient," I say as I check my inbox.

"I received it, but I'll read it when we get off the phone."

"No problem. I'm assuming early in the morning your time is the best time for you to speak to him. I'll see what I can do. Make sure you're available and you talk to your lawyer!"

"Thanks for sticking with me again, Barbara. I know I'm worse than I was after the food critic incident."

"A broken heart is never easy to get over."

I huff. *Especially when it's self-inflicted.*

"Cheer up—things are about to change for you. I'm so excited for you!"

"You drive me nuts half the time, but you can always make me laugh. I think you're more excited than I am." I chuckle for the first time since Tina left.

"Well, someone has to be excited about this until you snap out of your depression. I'll talk to you soon."

My apartment is silent as I stare at the open email. I can't believe what I'm reading. It's exactly what I asked for. I'll be the producer and director. Skimming through it further, I freeze. Start date is right after the holidays. The holidays I thought I was going to spend with Tina this year.

The farther away I am, the better. I'll make it work.

Chapter 48

Gerry

How much makeup do I need to wear for this? I didn't think I was that ugly. We're just about to shoot the first show, but I'm not excited. I hate it here. I've become a great actor. Hiding my emotions gets easier every day. I thought the distance and time was the solution to forgetting her. Wrong again.

Matt assures me she's doing well in Long Beach and has made friends. I didn't ask if any of them are guys. I'm surrounded by a lot of women every day in the studio, but I've no interest in anyone else. No one will ever replace her.

Then why am I here? I'm miserable in Germany. This show is what I thought I wanted, but it's proving me wrong. It's amazing how my dreams have changed as I've gotten older, from the different paths I've taken. Nothing seems to matter without her.

She was the best thing that ever happened to me. I felt I could fight the world with her by my side. Now I don't care about anything. There are days when I wonder why I'm even here. I should be in California with her, where I belong. Hip to hip, no matter where we end up. I can be a chef anywhere.

"Gerry, ready to go? We did several test runs, and they went brilliantly."

Whatever.

"Here's your blindfold. Please put it on securely, like we've practiced."

I should just take this blindfold and throw it at the moderator and tell her to shove it up her ass. My entire being tells me to walk out and get on the first plane to California. I can't do this anymore. Tina's a part of me, and I need her with me. I don't care where we are.

"Three, two, one. Blindfold on."

I hate blindfolds now. I hear the click of the spoon on the plate. *Walk out. Go to her and beg her to take you back.* Every second I waste will bury me even deeper.

"Gerry. The first spoon has been placed in front of you. Please take your time and enjoy your surprise."

Surprise? What does she mean? That wasn't the wording we used during the rehearsals or tests. I don't give a shit.

My hand connects with the spoon. Per the rules, I should smell it.

I don't react right away, so the moderator clears her throat. "Don't you have an appetite?" she says as the audience laughs.

I fake a smile and smell it. Huh? I shove the spoon in my mouth, knowing something's up. I cough instantly and spit it back out. I drop the spoon onto the table. Is this some sick joke? The first course is licorice?

Tina.

The air leaves my lungs. I rip off the blindfold and see the most remarkable woman smiling at me. Her eyes shimmer. I leap over the counter and squeeze her in my arms.

"You're here. I can't believe it." I kiss her senseless in front of all the camera crew and audience.

I pull away. "The cameras aren't running, are they?" I say to the lead camera man. He shakes his head.

I kiss her again. Our teeth hit this time. "Why? How are you here? What about your job?" My lips are on hers again.

She puts space between us while laughing and wiping the tears from her eyes. "I'll tell you if you stop kissing me."

"I'll stop, but I'm never leaving your side again."

Now she's kissing me. The audience in the background claps.

She pulls away for some air. "Your mom and Barbara helped me."

I chuckle. "That doesn't surprise me."

"Long Beach wasn't what I expected. I'm not the same as I was when I was a teenager. Maybe I didn't try hard enough to settle there, but my heart wasn't in it. My dreams have changed, but I didn't know it until I landed in California.

"I tried to call you but heard you'd moved back here. It ripped out the little piece of my heart that was left. I broke down and called Matt. He told me everything. No one has ever risked their own happiness for the sake of mine. I know I needed to do it alone, but I had to give you up to do that. I'm so sorry I hurt you. I broke us. It was all my fault, not yours. Everyone says it's my time and I should do what I want. So I asked myself what I truly want, and look—I ended up here. Being here with you is what I want."

I cup her cheeks with my hands. "I've never stopped loving you. I wanted you to be happy. I ended up back here to escape in hopes this show would help me survive without you."

She places her hands on my chest. "Did it?"

"No. Right before they put that spoon in front of me, I was telling myself to leave and go to you. Just like you, my dreams are different now. They became nothing without you in them."

"And what are they now?" Her eyes dip to my lips.

"You're the dream I never knew I had. You make everything sweeter, funnier, and more exciting. I want to sneak you off to all the places you want to go and experience them with you...as your husband."

She covers her mouth with her shaking hand.

"I promise we'll never be apart again. You're stuck with me for the rest of your life. Marry me. Please."

"Yes, yes, yes." She jumps into my arms. "I don't care where we are as long as we're together. And we don't have to give up our professions. We can do them anywhere in the world. Where you go, I go. What do you say?"

"Anywhere in the world sounds good to me...future Mrs. Maier."

Acknowledgments

Where do I even begin? This is my second book, and I have learned so much since I released my first book of the Collide series, *Lives Collide*.

I want to thank my husband and kids with big hugs and kisses. They have been so supportive and proud of me. The excitement that radiates off them pushes me to keep writing and to stay sane. I love you more than words can express.

I didn't use beta readers with *Lives Collide*. After it was released, I read how important they were, so I made sure I used them this time. To my beta readers, your honest feedback was priceless and helped me make my story stronger. Trish Walker, Silke Law, Jennifer Kreider, and Vicki Motz, thank you, thank you, thank you.

And of course, to my editor, Dori Harrell from Breakout Editing, and proofreader, Rachel Overton from Wordscapes. I loved working with you both again and have learned even more from this experience. I appreciate how patient and detail oriented you were. Your constant enthusiasm for my books pushes me away from self-doubt. Thank you!

I love the book cover design process. Thank you, Sarah Hansen from Okay Creations, for designing another unique cover for my Collide series. You always seem to know what I want before I do. I'm already looking forward to designing the third and final book cover to this series. Ideas for that book are already spinning in my head.

Thank you, Rik Hall from Wild Seas Formatting. You've been so easy to work with. Even with stressful timelines, I could always count on you. Thank you for making the formatting process as easy as possible.

Many thanks to Cathie Larocca for helping me with the ins and outs of Hoboken and public transportation routes to New York City.

I had the pleasure to interview a German chef, Matthais Dahlinger, regarding the entire process of receiving a star and also giving it back. It was extremely fun and informative. I would also like to thank Annette Senn for introducing me to him. She is the *Leiterin Stabsstelle Breisach-Touristik*. She's a great friend and helped me gather touristic information within the wine region where I live in Germany.

I have met several wonderful people within the book community. They range from authors, bloggers, editors, and readers. Saying thank you doesn't describe how much I appreciate every compliment, word of advice, laughter, and encouragement. Thanks for taking a chance on a new indie author. You're the best.

If you are curious if Alexa finds her match, check out the final book in the Collide series, Souls Collide. Please follow me on my website and social media for updates on future books and events.

www.kristinabeck.com
www.facebook.com/krissybeck73
www.twitter.com/krissybeck96
www.instagram.com/krissybeck96
www.goodreads.com/kristina_beck
www.amazon.com/author/kristinabeck
www.bookbub.com/authors/kristina-beck

Other books by Kristina Beck

Collide Series
Lives Collide
Souls Collide

About the Author

A Jersey Girl herself, Kristina was born and raised in New Jersey, USA, for thirty years. She later moved to Germany and has lived there for over fourteen years with her German husband and three children. She is an avid reader of different genres, but romance always takes precedence. She loves coffee, dark chocolate, power naps, and '80s movies. Her hobbies include writing, reading, fitness, and forever trying to improve her German-language skills.

www.ingramcontent.com/pod-product-compliance
Lightning Source LLC
LaVergne TN
LVHW041456170726
843492LV00005B/1252